The
Mark

MATT
BROLLY

THOMAS & MERCER

Text copyright © 2021 by Matt Brolly
All rights reserved.

Published by Thomas & Mercer, Seattle

www.apub.com

Amazon, the Amazon logo, and Thomas & Mercer are trademarks of Amazon.com, Inc., or its affiliates.

ISBN-13: 9781542031400
ISBN-10: 1542031400

Cover design by Tom Sanderson

Printed in the United States of America

For Matt Wulff

Chapter One

The disorientation was nothing new for Sam Carrigan. His multiple addictions meant the borderline between consciousness and oblivion was usually a fine one. Being present wasn't an issue he usually had to face but it was something he had to consider now.

He was running.

He'd been lost before, had woken up in back streets and doorways countless times. That he couldn't remember reaching the beach wasn't a surprise either. In these warmer months, the shelter of the sand dunes to the south of Weston's main beach acted as a beacon and, at any other time, the distant sound of the mud-tinted sea would be a comfort. But this time the temperate breeze heralded another, unwanted, sound.

The laughter from behind wasn't pleasant. He was attuned enough to understand the difference between kindness and the menacing noise reaching his ears. They had been chasing him for at least twenty minutes. Although 'chasing' wasn't quite correct – he wasn't being chased, he was being stalked. Played with like a cat toying with a petrified mouse. Or like a sheep, being corralled by a border collie.

Yes, that's what it felt like. The laughter was only metres away, but every time Sam turned all he could see were shadows of the dunes, the long stretch of the beach, and in the distance the blinking lights of civilisation.

He felt as if he were running in circles and the laughter suggested that was exactly what they wanted.

The panic was like drowning. His lungs felt overinflated, as if they could implode the brittle frame of his ribcage at any second. Blood raged in his ears, his mouth hung open, catching the salt-tainted air as his body twisted in short, sharp movements and he ran from his invisible foe.

In the end, the blow to the back of Sam's head came as a relief. The pent-up air was expelled from his lungs as he collapsed on the powdery sand that shifted on to his dry tongue as if it were about to fill his body.

The laughter ceased. For a blessed moment, Sam thought that maybe this was the end; that his pursuers had had their fun and would now leave him alone.

Then he caught the faint whiff of stale sweat and the feel of clammy skin on his exposed calf muscle. The next thing he knew, he was being dragged backwards up the dune. He tried to speak, to plead, but his mouth was full of sand. It ripped at his face, catching in his eyes, as the laughter returned.

'You've been a bad boy, Mr Carrigan,' said one of the voices: male, the accent hard to place. Sam had no idea what he'd done and he wasn't going to be given the option to argue his case.

'This is going to hurt a little bit,' said the man, as another smell filled the air.

Sam was face down in the sand but sensed the change of temperature, the hint of sulphur in the air as one of his assailants knelt on his back. Once again, his lungs were fit to burst and he didn't put up a struggle as his right arm was yanked from under him, the sweat-drenched cloth of his shirt ripped away, exposing the flesh of his forearm.

'Not much to work with,' said the man, flipping him on to his front. 'Thought you'd like to see this.'

The two assailants were both wearing masks. Sam squirmed as the man held his arm, his fingers completely encircling Sam's forearm, his grip so strong Sam feared he would snap the bone in two. But that wasn't at the forefront of his mind. What caught Sam's attention was the blue flame coming from the blowtorch held by the second assailant.

Sam's eyes were filled with sand, but something. primeval made him begin to struggle. His other senses had taken over and he bucked and shook, accessing never previously used sources of strength to try to shake off his captors. His skin prickled with sweat, and the smell of heated metal drifted towards him before the man clamped down on his arm and a pain he had never known before engulfed every sense in his body.

Sam didn't fall unconscious immediately. He felt paralysed as the weight of the man was lifted from his body, the smell of burning metal replaced by the stench of burning flesh.

Chapter Two

At times like these, the decision to move in with her parents felt like a blessed decision for DI Louise Blackwell. She had the upper floor of the house in Sand Bay to herself, as well as a private entrance, but this morning she had decided to unlock the door to the adjoining staircase. She wanted to see her niece, Emily, before heading to work. Opening the door, however, it wasn't Emily who greeted her but the new family puppy, Molly, who jumped up and managed to scratch Louise's leg by way of greeting.

'Hello to you, too,' said Louise.

Louise loved the dog but was thankful it lived downstairs with her parents and Emily. She'd read that Labrador puppies could be a handful, but it had soon become apparent that was an understatement. The dog needed constant attention, and more than once she'd been woken in the middle of the night by the sound of her father opening the garden door to let the puppy loose.

'Mum not up yet?' said Louise, grabbing a piece of toast from the centre of the kitchen table before kissing Emily on the forehead.

Her dad shook his head, and it took all of Louise's willpower not to check the recycling for evidence of last night's crimes. As a family, they'd endured so much over the last few years. They were still coming to terms with the brutal murder of Emily's father and Louise's brother, Paul. Her mother was usually an early riser and there were only two possible reasons for her to be in bed now: she was ill, or hung-over.

'I'll wake her up in a minute,' said her father, exchanging a knowing look with Louise.

She sighed, deciding now wasn't the right time for a discussion about her mother's drinking. It always reminded her of Paul's descent into alcoholism, and that was something she didn't want to face. 'What do you guys have planned for today?'

'Beach,' said Emily, bits of toast falling from her mouth.

'I'm very envious,' said Louise, kissing Emily once more and leaving before it became too hard to drag herself away.

Another positive of the move from her old bungalow in Worle was that the new journey into work took in a drive next to the sea. Working out of the purpose-built offices in Worle, sometimes it was easy to forget she was living on the coast. The drives to and from work gave her a connection to the town. The water was in this morning, the surface glass-like as it shifted beneath the early August sunshine.

As she headed away from the seafront, Louise was once again envious of the freedom her parents and Emily would enjoy that day. The feeling intensified as she remembered her day's itinerary, which included an inter-departmental meeting with the station's new uniformed inspector, Dan Baker.

She took Locking Road towards Worle, preferring the route through the town rather than the bypass. She enjoyed the tranquillity of the route, the way the area felt almost untouched since her childhood years, when she'd visited the town on summer day trips full of excitement and promise, sitting in the back of the car with her brother, willing the miles away until they were by the beach, and everything Weston had to offer.

The sight of a black Skoda Kodiaq in her rear-view mirror interrupted her reminiscing. It was four cars behind, the nondescript car grabbing her attention as she'd seen the same vehicle two days earlier. Louise didn't have a photographic memory but she was always alert, and when she'd last seen this particular car it had followed her for two and half miles before making a detour.

Chances were it was a coincidence, but something about the steady way it followed, the car far enough back that Louise couldn't catch the driver's face, hinted that the driver knew what they were doing. Louise hated the idea she was succumbing to paranoia, but ever since her last major investigation she'd grown concerned she'd been put under surveillance by the so-called Ghost Squad – the constabulary's internal Anti-Corruption team.

During the course of that case, involving two missing children in Cheddar Gorge, Louise had managed to integrate herself in the investigation into her brother's murder. She'd been warned to stay clear and, even though her interference had led to a positive result, she still faced the prospect of a misconduct meeting. Her boss, DCI Robertson, had told her it was simply procedure; a formality she didn't need to worry about. She trusted Robertson, so wouldn't usually have given it a second thought, if it hadn't been for DCI Tim Finch, lead detective of MIT – Major Investigation Team – at headquarters in Portishead.

Her and Finch's mutual animosity went back a number of years, to the time she was working at MIT. Together they'd been working on the serial killer, Max Walton, after which case their relationship deteriorated. The thought of Walton made her eyes water as she remembered the overpowering smell of decay she'd encountered at Walton's farm one night. Ever since, Finch had been trying to find a way to get her out of the force. He wouldn't hesitate to liaise with the Anti-Corruption team, if it meant he would get his way.

Louise slowed down and was about to pull over when a call came in from the station and she was forced to make a U-turn. Her pursuer was quick to react, making a sharp left turn at Baytree Park so Louise was able to see only the rear of the vehicle as she headed back to town.

Fifteen minutes later she parked up outside Weston General Hospital, a place that had become so familiar recently it was like a second home. A recent addition to the station, PC Sarah Millard, was waiting for her outside an ICU room on the fourth floor. 'Hello, ma'am,' said the uniformed officer, standing stiffly as Louise approached.

'You can call me Louise, Sarah. He's through there?'

'Yes, I managed to take some photographs of the wound before it was bandaged up. He's still out cold. His arms are littered with needle tracks and a wound to the back of his head suggests he may have been attacked.'

Sam Carrigan was a thirty-three-year-old man, though when Louise viewed him through the window of his room he looked much older. He was painfully thin, his face gaunt, and even with his eyes shut he had a haunted look. With the respirator sticking out of his mouth, he looked double his age.

'He was found at six thirty a.m., ma'am, by a golfer at the club on Uphill Road. He'd hit his ball out of bounds and was searching for it on the back of the sand dunes when he came across Mr Carrigan.'

'How long do they think he will be out?'

'Indefinite. They're running blood tests. Could be a reaction to what's happened to him, or the drugs in his system.'

Louise glanced at the thick bandage wrapped around his right arm. 'Can you send me those photos?' she said to the young constable.

Louise winced as she scrolled through the images. A symbol had been burnt into the skin of Carrigan's forearm.

The symbol looked like a distorted *S*.

'How the hell did this happen?' said Louise under her breath, as a harried-looking man approached.

'Dr Miles Bainbridge,' said the man, playing at the fringe of grey-black hair draped over his forehead. 'I wanted to see you before I finished my shift,' he added, making it clear the favour he was doing for Louise.

'Thank you,' said Louise, humouring the man as she followed him so they were out of earshot of Carrigan. 'Have you ever seen anything like this before?' she asked.

'In a manner of speaking, yes,' said Bainbridge, taking the phone from her. 'As you can probably see from the raw tissue on Mr Carrigan's arm, his skin has been branded.'

'Branded?'

'Believe it or not, people like to do this to themselves. It's an extreme form of tattooing, sometimes known as stigmatising. You burn the skin and the resulting scar leaves a permanent mark.'

'You can get this done?'

'There are practitioners of this, though I believe it is illegal at present. The idea is you burn through the three layers of skin – the epidermis, the dermis and the subcutaneous. In this case, whoever did the branding went too far and pushed through to the muscle. In addition, the wound is infected. Not surprising, given that Mr Carrigan was found face down in the sand.'

'Is there somewhere in Weston where you can get this done?' said Louise, unable to hide her incredulity that someone would do this to themselves.

'Not officially, but we've treated the odd person over the last few years when things have gone wrong. Aside from the fact that he was discovered unconscious, Mr Carrigan has severe bruising over his body, in particular on his back and around his shoulders and arms. Of course, he may have felt the need to be restrained to go through with the procedure but if you look at the ragged way the branding has been applied to the skin, and I don't wish to overstep my boundary here . . .'

Louise frowned, wishing the doctor would get to the point.

Bainbridge matched her frown. 'It's just that, I think it's possible, probably very likely, that Mr Carrigan received this mark without, shall we say, his permission.'

Louise glanced at the comatose Mr Carrigan. 'You think this man was branded?'

'I'm not one for hyperbole but I certainly wouldn't rule it out. Anyway, I'll leave it up to you, Detective. We've cleaned the wound as best we can and administered antibiotic for the infection.'

'How long do you think he will be unconscious?' asked Louise.

'He is in a coma, though he is responding to stimulus. I'd like whatever is swirling in his bloodstream to have a chance to vacate his system before I answer that. There's a reason he's in the ICU, though.'

'His condition could worsen?'

'Until we know what's in his system, we just don't know. But the combination of the infected wound, the injury to his head and the needle tracks are a concern.'

'Do we at least have an address for him?' Louise asked the constable, once the doctor had left.

The uniformed officer shook her head. 'Only ID he came in with was a driver's licence,' she said, handing Louise a clear plastic bag.

Louise glanced at the photo of Carrigan on the ID, finding it difficult to believe it was the same person as the man in ICU. 'You stay here with Mr Carrigan for now, Sarah. Let me know as soon as he comes round.'

◆ ◆ ◆

Louise glanced at her watch as she made her way back to the car. She wanted to visit the crime scene before the meeting at the station. If the mark on Sam Carrigan had been purposely inflicted, she might be able to miss the meeting altogether.

Carrigan was unconscious, and it was feasible that if he had been attacked, his attackers had left him for dead. However, there were too many other possibilities. Carrigan could have gone on a bender after having the procedure or could even have done it to himself. As it stood, her direct boss, DCI Robertson, had told her with regret that the meeting was obligatory. Inspector Dan Baker had a presentation he wished everyone in the station to see, and nothing below a dead body would suffice in excusing her from attending.

The sea was already retreating by the time Louise had made the short journey to the golf club in Uphill, leaving a trailing blanket of mud in its wake. The scene-of-crime officers, SOCOs, now sometimes referred to as the CSI, had cordoned off the area where Sam Carrigan had been discovered. The section they'd marked off stretched from the back of the grass-speckled dunes to the fringes of the golf course.

Unfortunately, there was little to see. Constable Millard had already shown her photos of Sam at the scene and her interview notes with the golfer who'd found him. The SOCOs would scour the area, but beyond finding a branding iron there was nothing of immediate interest. Chances were that Sam Carrigan had endured the procedure elsewhere, voluntary or not, and for unknown reasons had made his way to the beach.

Louise shared the photos of Sam's injuries with the lead SOCO, Janice Sutton. 'Do you know what sort of equipment you'd need to inflict something like this?' she asked.

'A branding iron and a blowtorch would be my guess.'

'So, it could have happened here at the scene?'

'Can't see why not.'

An image of scorching metal being placed on Sam's skin appeared in Louise's mind. It felt so real that she imagined she could smell the man's burning flesh.

Janice handed the phone back. 'Strange the things people do to themselves,' she said.

Chapter Three

Louise needn't have rushed back to the station. She was five minutes late but the large presentation room was still bustling with officers. After pouring herself a coffee, she joined Thomas at the rear of the room.

DS Thomas Ireland had been her closest friend at the station since her move from Bristol's MIT three years ago. Had they met under different circumstances, their relationship could have developed into something more personal. As it was, she'd made a hard rule after Finch never to mix personal and professional again. Still, she couldn't help noticing his new shirt and how fresh-faced he looked after shaving the stubble he'd been growing for the last couple of days.

'Thought you'd managed to duck out of this,' said Thomas, welcoming her with a smile.

'Try as I might,' said Louise, as Inspector Dan Baker walked into the room. 'I see Robbo isn't around.'

'He managed to sneak off to HQ,' said Thomas, as Baker took the stage.

Louise swore under her breath. She was only here on DCI Robertson's insistence and he didn't even have the decency to attend.

Inspector Baker had recently rejoined Weston-super-Mare from Devon and Cornwall. He'd had great success as enforcement tsar in Newquay, the largest of the seaside resorts in the county. His remit had been to transform the town, which had become overrun with drugs and delinquent behaviour. In a three-year period he'd managed to greatly reduce crime rates in the area and, following his success, he'd been approached by Avon and Somerset to return to Weston-super-Mare and replicate the feat.

Baker was six-four with an iron-straight back. Louise had heard the endearment *rod up his arse* on more than one occasion. Everything about him – perfectly ironed uniform, close hair-cut, and rimmed spectacles – shouted strait-laced. That in itself wouldn't have been so bad if his presentation delivery hadn't been so monotone. As slide after slide appeared on the white screen behind him, Louise tuned out of Baker's speech about cracking down on licensing laws and outside drinking, her thoughts return-ing to Sam Carrigan and the symbol so savagely emblazoned on to his skin. That someone would allow that to happen to themself was a mystery, and although it seemed a likely explanation she still wasn't convinced.

By the time Baker had finished speaking, she'd already run a quick search of licensed tattoo parlours in the area on her police-issued mobile, and she was out of the office before the inspector had time to ask her what she thought about his new plans for the town.

Louise caught sight of the Skoda Kodiaq again as she took the bypass back into town. She was impressed she hadn't noticed it when leaving the station, and the way it hung back three cars behind reinforced her feeling that the driver belonged to someone from the Ghost Squad. She eased her foot off the accelerator to try to catch a glimpse of the driver but her pursuer was wise to the manoeuvre, slowing to the same speed.

For now, Louise was content to let the other car follow. She didn't feel in any immediate danger. If the driver had been instructed to track her, then so be it. She had nothing to hide and was happy to allow the Anti-Corruption officer to waste their time.

She parked on the Boulevard, outside the block of flats in the listed building that had once held the public library. She'd lost her pursuer as she headed into the centre, but it didn't mean she wasn't still being followed. Locking the car, she waited outside for a couple of minutes before taking the short walk to the Ink tattoo parlour on Meadow Street.

Louise didn't consider herself a prude, but the thought of having a tattoo had never taken with her. She could still picture the wrinkled forearm of her grandad, the faded green of his naval tattoos distorted by his paper-thin skin. Her parents had told her as a child that tattoos were permanent and that most people who got them regretted having them. And although she'd doubted the last of those pieces of wisdom at the time, the lesson had stayed with her.

A blast of stale air, ripe with the smell of leather and disinfectant, greeted her as she opened the door to the parlour. From a side room came the buzzing sound of a tattoo gun as a young woman sitting behind the counter looked up from her book. 'You alright?' said the woman, brushing thick, black hair from her forehead. She smiled, the ring piercing on her lower lip catching a flash of sun through the windows.

'I was looking for some advice, actually,' said Louise.

'Of course,' said the woman, her smile widening. 'It can be scary coming to a place like this if you're not used to it. But what do you really want?'

'That obvious, is it?' said Louise.

The woman shrugged, the smile not leaving her face until Louise displayed her warrant card. 'It's nothing to concern yourself with,' said Louise, as the panic reached the woman's eyes. Louise noted her tattoos, surprised at the vividness of the images, the colours that swirled up her arms and the cartoon-like figure beneath her collarbone.

'You like them?' said the woman, her smile childlike in her eagerness for praise.

'They're amazing. I'd never be brave enough for that,' said Louise.

'That, I doubt. Anyway, how can I help?'

'Can I ask your name?'

'Frankie.'

'Frankie, I wanted to know if you'd ever seen anything like this,' said Louise, showing her a photo of Carrigan's wounds on her phone.

'We don't do anything like this here,' said the woman, tightening up. 'Maybe I should get Bill.'

Louise had read up on the law regarding body modification during Baker's monotone speech. It seemed to be a thriving industry that extended beyond tattooing and branding to tongue splitting, ear pointing and scarification which included branding. The law was fuzzy on the issue. The question seemed to centre on the extent to which someone could consent to allow themselves to be modified. A recent test case had determined that body-modification procedures other than tattooing and piercing that resulted in injury were deemed to be unlawful, but the guidelines set up to enforce this legal decision were at best vague.

'No,' she said to Frankie. 'Don't worry, I'm not here to check up on your operation.'

Frankie appeared to relax at this, her extended fringe falling back across her brow and covering one of her heavily made-up eyes. 'What then?'

'I was wondering what you could tell me about the mark. I know it's branding of some kind.'

'I told you, we don't do that here,' said Frankie, taking the phone from Louise. 'Doesn't look like a good job either, it's all distorted. It looks like an *S* or a two?' she said, looking at Louise for confirmation.

'Why do you think it's distorted?'

'Trying to catch me out, are you?' said Frankie, with a shy smile.

'Nothing like that.'

Frankie scratched the side of her head. 'You know it's technically illegal?'

'As I said, I'm not bothered by that. Why do you think it looks like that?'

'I don't really have any experience of it myself. With all these things, it's important to be still. This looks haphazard to me. It's not aligned properly. A real mess.'

Louise could tell Frankie was suspicious but she was clearly passionate about her subject. 'Would you ever have something like that done?'

'Not sure. Perhaps sometime in the future. Problem is, if it goes wrong, like that, you're stuck with it.'

'Anywhere round here you can get something like this done?'

Frankie took a step backwards, folding her arms. 'Not that I know of.'

'I'm not trying to get anyone in trouble, I promise. I just need to know who could have done this.'

'If I was going to get it done, I might try Bristol. London, even. No one round here any more.'

'Not even on the quiet?' said Louise, trying her best to be conspiratorial.

'I wouldn't know anything about that,' said Frankie, with a hint of a smile.

'Could you do it to yourself?'

Frankie laughed. 'Not without an extreme amount of will-power. It wouldn't be advisable.' She shook her head. 'No, I don't think it could be done.'

'Thank you, you've been very helpful. One last question, if I may. I know I must sound so naive, and out of touch, but why would anyone allow themselves to be branded like this? Tattoos, I can understand, but this?'

Louise was thankful the woman wasn't condescending. 'People have different reasons. They might simply like the idea. Others, it might be their kink. A form of masochism. There are so many reasons.'

'And you?'

'Me?'

Louise nodded towards the numerous tattoos covering the woman's skin.

Frankie smiled. 'I just love the way they look.'

'Well, they certainly look good on you. Thank you again. I'm afraid I did lie, though. I do have one final question. Do you have a back-door exit I could use?'

Chapter Four

The back door opened to a side alley leading to Burlington Street. Louise took the long route back to the Boulevard, through the pedestrianised high street. She thought about what Frankie had told her, the reasons why people would change their appearance in such a drastic way. The tattoos had looked good on her, but Louise wasn't sure she would ever be able to commit to something so permanent. She could get tired of seeing the same haircut in the mirror every day, so having something etched on her skin for ever wouldn't be for her. As for the other things, the body modifications and the scarification, they were beyond her comprehension. She couldn't imagine doing anything like that to herself, but then she guessed she wasn't the target market.

As she reached the end of the high street, she peered around the corner to the long stretch of the Boulevard, searching for the Skoda. That the Ghost Squad were possibly watching her didn't bother Louise in itself, but it was beginning to distract her from the investigation, and that was something she couldn't accept.

Walking back along the Boulevard, she found the Skoda parked further up on Stafford Place. Louise recognised the driver. Constable Amira Hood worked in Portishead. Louise couldn't remember the department Amira was attached to, but she would probably know Finch and Louise's other former colleagues. Amira was staring intently ahead, her view line taking in Louise's parked car.

Although the Anti-Corruption teams worked out of another building, Amira could possibly be working undercover for them. However, Louise thought it more likely that Finch had sent the officer to spy on her. She needed more time to think and popped around the corner to buy a bottle of mineral water from a newsagent's.

It was oppressively hot, and she drank the water in the shade of the newsagent's front awning, as she decided what to do next.

If Amira was now working for Anti-Corruption, then presumably she was watching Louise's movements. To what end, however, was a mystery. The forthcoming misconduct meeting was in relation to Louise's interference in Paul's murder investigation. In her opinion, she hadn't done anything unlawful. She had, in fact, uncovered a lead that had resulted in Paul's murderer being found when everyone else had all but given up on the case.

The more she thought about Amira following her, the angrier she became. The smart move would probably be to ignore her. Play dumb and allow Amira to continue following her. Louise had nothing to hide and if Amira, and whoever had sent her, wanted to waste their time, that was up to them.

But Louise wasn't in the mood for the smart move. She was an experienced detective with more successful prosecutions of high-level suspects than most officers in the area. That they would send a junior officer to trail her like this was at best audacious, and to Louise it felt disrespectful.

She wanted to quell her conspiracy concerns, but she'd been here before with Finch. It had started after the Walton case. Following a doomed trial experiment in the Somerset and Avon Police, both of them had been carrying police-issued firearms, and Louise had shot dead Walton, after being told by Finch he was armed. At the time, both of them had been up for promotion to DCI. Finch had claimed he'd never told Louise that Walton was armed. Subsequently, Finch had received his promotion and Louise had effectively been demoted to her current role in Weston-super-Mare. Since then, Finch had tried his best to kick her out of the force so many times it was laughable, and if Amira was here because of him, Louise would raise a complaint.

Doing a loop around the Albert Quadrant, she did her best to control her rapid pulse and the adrenaline that was fuelling her anger as she approached Amira's car from the rear. Allowing her breathing to return to normal, Louise eased down the road. Foolish or not, she wanted them to know she was on to them.

'Hello, Amira,' she said, opening the passenger-side door of the Skoda.

To her credit, the detective remained calm. Perhaps she'd seen Louise in her rear-view mirror; perhaps she had steel-like nerves. 'DI Blackwell,' she said. 'You gave me a fright.'

'Like to tell me what the hell is going on?' said Louise.

'I'm sorry. I wondered if you had noticed I've been following you. When did you spot me?'

Amira was relaxed. Louise noticed the small piercing on her nose and looked down at her arms to see if she had any tattoos. Louise fought her growing anger. 'Why *are* you following me, Amira?'

Amira took in a deep breath. 'I was going to call, but it's not something I wanted to spring on you before meeting you face to face.'

It wasn't the answer Louise had expected. 'What could possibly be so important you needed to see me face to face?' said Louise.

Amira sucked in air again, tension spreading through her body as she replied. 'It's about DCI Tim Finch.'

Chapter Five

Louise stared hard at Amira, who for the first time since Louise had got in the car appeared vulnerable. Finch had that effect on people. She was still surprised by Amira's response and was playing out various scenarios in her head. 'You're not here on his behalf?'

'God, no,' said Amira.

'You've worked with him before, though?'

'Sort of. We're in the same building at HQ but in different departments.'

'What happened?' said Louise.

'I'm afraid I fell for his charms,' said Amira, turning to look at Louise with large, unblinking eyes.

A sour taste rose into Louise's mouth. 'You wouldn't be the first,' she said, remembering her own brief affair with the man and how quickly his imagined affections had changed when a promotion was on the line. She still couldn't believe she'd been so stupid, and she'd paid the price ever since. 'I presume there's more to it than that?'

'I wanted to speak to someone who'd . . .' Amira faltered; what had seemed like unflappable confidence had all but vanished. 'I know you had some issues with him. The rumours are you were forced out of your role at MIT because of them.'

Amira was right, but Louise wasn't ready to discuss the issue with her just yet. The fallout from the Walton case had ended up being Finch's word against hers, and the only reason she was still in the job was down to the number of corpses they'd discovered on Walton's farmland. 'What do you want to tell me, Amira?'

'After our . . . I can hardly bring myself to say the word "relationship", but I guess that's what it was. After our relationship ended, and it didn't end in a very pleasant way, I started to receive these anonymous text messages. At first they were innocuous, always mentioning me by name, but nothing I couldn't handle. Then they started becoming more explicit, suggesting I should perhaps leave the police.'

Louise's heart hammered in her chest. After Finch had all but forced her to leave MIT, she'd received the same type of anonymous texts for over a year. It had driven her to the brink of insanity. He'd always seemed to know the best time to text her – when she was about to go to sleep, or when she was at her lowest. In the end, she'd almost left the force because of it. She'd known it had been Finch but had been as helpless as Amira to prove anything. 'You think Finch was sending them to you?'

'He didn't sign them, but they were obviously from him,' said Amira. 'He denied it, of course, but they continued. Every day and night. He seemed to know when I was about to fall asleep or when I'd woken up. I changed my number and they stopped for a time, but then they started again.'

Louise could tell Amira was holding something back. 'I take it you haven't reported them?' she asked, trying to make Amira get to the point.

Amira shrugged. 'I should, I know, but it's his word against mine. My career would be over if I accused Finch of sending those messages without any evidence. They're from an anonymous account – I still don't know how he achieved that – and I have no proof it was him. Also . . .' Amira looked away, colour coming to her cheeks.

'Also?'

'I allowed him to take some pictures,' said Amira, lowering her eyes. 'It was just a bit of fun and I watched him delete them. At least I thought I did.'

'I see,' said Louise. Finch had tried the same trick with her and, fortunately, she'd had enough wits about her not to oblige him. 'Did he threaten you with them?'

Amira's eyes watered. 'Not directly. He sends me them every now and then, to show me he has them, I guess. The next message suggests it's time for me to leave. And then I received this.'

Louise took the phone from Amira and read the text:

You have one month to hand in your resignation or these pictures will be seen everywhere.

'What are you going to do?' asked Louise, controlling her anger as she gave the phone back. She'd never been given the option to leave. She'd received a take-it-or-leave-it offer from Assistant Chief Constable Morley: move to Weston-super-Mare or leave the force. At the time, it had been a difficult decision. She'd spent so long building her career, succeeding in major crimes, that moving to the seaside town had felt like more than a demotion. It was only when she understood that was what they wanted her to think that she'd agreed to the move. It would be a long process, but she'd known she could rebuild her career; and despite Finch's best intentions, she'd succeeded in doing so.

'I don't know.'

'Why come to me?'

'It's been eating away at me for so long now. I'd heard about what happened to you during the Walton case. Then someone told me you're up for a misconduct panel because of your . . . brother's investigation.'

Louise lowered her eyes. 'What do you want, Amira?'

'I don't want to be forced out of my job, that's what I want. I want Finch to answer for what he's done. If he's done it to me, and I don't want to presume, but maybe he did the same to you, then he could do it to someone else.'

Louise admired the woman's resolve. That Finch had photos of her must be sickening, which made her determination that much more admirable. It also fed into Louise's guilt. She still had to work with Finch occasionally and that made it harder, but she should have tried to do something about him before now. Amira was correct: if he could do it to her, he could do it to anyone. Unfortunately, understanding that wasn't enough to make it all disappear. 'How do you think I can help?' she asked.

Amira laughed, the sound hollow in the car's interior. 'I was hoping you could tell me. If there's two of us, maybe they would take us seriously. And I know there are more. He's fucked the majority of the female civilian staff in the department. I'm sure his little power games weren't solely for me. Or us?' said Amira, looking at Louise with a dreadful hopefulness.

Louise knew Amira wanted confirmation that Finch had done the same to her. She wanted to tell her about her own sleepless nights, waiting for the anonymous texts from Finch, the way he continued to try to undermine her at every turn, but she wasn't ready to trust Amira just yet. 'Listen, if you want to go against Finch, you'll need something solid. Without concrete proof, we'd be laughed off, and probably much worse.'

'I realise that,' said Amira.

'I've been out of that office for three years but I'm still in Finch's region. I can't start a covert investigation into him.'

Amira nodded. This time she held Louise's eyes for a few seconds. 'But I can. What have I got to lose?' she said.

Chapter Six

Louise walked back to her car in a daze. Her focus was slipping. Her attention should have been on Sam Carrigan but all she could think about now was DCI Finch. Thankfully, Thomas interrupted her thought process, calling her as she reached the car. 'I've managed to track him down, Sam Carrigan, to a rehabilitation centre in Milton. I spoke to one of the managers there, David Mountson. Mr Carrigan was last seen two days ago. Apparently, the clients come and go so he didn't think it was worth reporting,' he said.

'That's working out well for them. Thanks, Thomas, I'll head there now.'

Weston-super-Mare had a long history as an area for drug rehabilitation. A mixture of private and public facilities populated the area and the town was thought to be home to at least ten per cent of all rehab centres in the UK. It was a strange claim to fame, a dirty secret the town kept from the multitude of tourists who invaded its shores during the summer.

It was a short journey to Milton, Louise travelling against a sea of cars going in the other direction, towards the centre. Only a small, worn brass plaque with the name Oaklands Lodge printed on it at the front of the rehab centre differentiated the building from the line of shabby-looking Victorian houses in the street. As Louise walked up the stone pathway to the entrance, the neighbours' front door burst open. Four children, the oldest of whom couldn't have been any older than six, shuffled into the sunlight, followed by a dishevelled woman carrying a young baby and a pushchair. Louise exchanged a nod with the woman, who looked at once exhausted and amused to find herself in such a position. Louise wondered what it must be like having to manage so many kids, when having partial responsibility for Emily was exhausting enough; and how much harder living next door to a rehab centre might make it.

Louise coughed as she stepped through the entrance, her eyes watering at the smell of bleach that hung in the air, as if the interior of the building had recently been doused with it. The place felt more like a hostel than a rehab centre. Despite the heat outside, a coldness permeated from the walls, where chipped plaster hung in clumps. She was ignored by three men sitting on a threadbare sofa playing cards as she made her way to the reception desk. She rang the bell on the desk, but no one answered. 'I'm trying to find David Mountson,' she said to the men on the sofa, who didn't look up from their cards.

'In there,' said one of them, pointing to a metal door behind the desk.

Louise stepped behind the desk and tried the door, which was locked. She rapped her knuckles on the metal and was surprised when a few seconds later the door opened. A red-haired man with matching beard, the exposed skin on his arms and neck covered in tattoos, stepped through the opening, shutting the door behind him. 'Yes?' he said, his West Country accent evident in the single word.

'DI Louise Blackwell. I'm here to see David Mountson.'

Louise noted a hint of hesitation in the man, as if he'd been caught out by her appearance. 'That's me. You here about Sam?'

'Yes, can we go somewhere to speak?' Louise peered through the door, her curiosity getting the better of her.

'How is he?'

'Still in a coma.'

The words stung Mountson. He shuddered and she thought he was on the verge of tears.

'He's not the biggest of talkers at the best of times,' he said. 'Sorry, that's inappropriate. I'm a bit shaken. You want to see his room?' said Mountson, dangling a set of keys in his trembling hand.

'Lead the way.'

The smell of bleach intensified as Louise followed Mountson up a staircase lined with a frayed carpet drained of colour.

'Your colleague mentioned something about a mark on Sam's arm,' said Mountson, leading her along a corridor of closed doors. Like downstairs, the plastering on the walls was falling apart and, behind the overpowering bleach, she noted a dank smell, signs of damp evident in the alcoves of the walls.

They stopped outside a green, metallic door at the end of the corridor. The place had the feel of a halfway house, and she wondered how anyone could come to such a place to recover. She studied Mountson as she handed him her phone, the man's eyes blinking as he saw the image of the *S* branded on to Sam's forearm. Louise wasn't sure if she was searching for something that wasn't there, but she thought she saw a hint of recognition as Mountson swiped through the photos.

'That familiar to you?' she asked.

Mountson looked up, a little too quickly. 'That? Looks bloody nasty. I've seen similar shit before. It was a craze for a while,' he said, glancing at the faded ink on his arms.

'You ever tried it?'

'Not for me,' said Mountson, not meeting her eyes as he opened the door.

Louise's heart lurched at the depressing sight of Sam's lone bed at the corner of the room. More damp was evident on the walls of the room, and aside from a scattering of dirty laundry it appeared Sam had no possessions with him.

'Funding's not what it was,' said Mountson, as if feeling the need to defend the state of the room.

'How long has Mr Carrigan been with you?'

'Two months or so now. Will he be OK?' asked Mountson, his voice soft. His concern seemed genuine. He hung his head, interlacing his fingers, as Louise moved to a desk of drawers.

'It's hard to know at this point.'

Mountson sat on the bed. His body was shaking and he'd begun crying. Louise wondered if the tears came from fear of losing his job or concern for the patient.

'Do you get on well with Mr Carrigan?'

'He's a good guy. Had a shit life, you know. He doesn't deserve this.'

'Do you mind?' said Louise, opening the top drawer of Carrigan's desk.

'I guess not. What are you looking for?'

'The doctor thinks he may have taken something recently. Have you had any problems with him?'

'We take weekly urine tests. He's always kept himself to himself. We have group meetings and the occasional one-to-one. He's quiet but he does speak. I'd be disappointed if he's using again, but as I'm sure you can appreciate, these things are rarely solved overnight.' Mountson spoke as if he was repeating a well-used script.

The drawers contained nothing beyond a few items of clothing. 'Anyone else been missing for two days?' said Louise.

'Look, at the best of times I only have two full-time staff. I simply can't keep an eye on everyone. We need at least another five full-time staff to make this work properly. I do my best to help everyone who comes here but I can't watch everyone all of the time. They're not prisoners.'

Louise sympathised. It wasn't the first place she'd seen like this since moving to Weston. Cuts were evident everywhere, and it was a wonder places like this managed to function at all. But Mountson hadn't answered her question and was behaving very defensively. 'You have a sign-in-and-out sheet, though? There must be some regulations you need to follow?'

'I'll get you a copy,' said Mountson, his arm holding the door open for her.

The card players had disappeared by the time they returned downstairs. Mountson gave her a copy of the last two days' registers. Carrigan had signed out two days ago but hadn't signed back in. Louise would have to discuss the matter with the owners of the centre, as it was conceivable Mountson should have reported Carrigan's absence.

'Will you let me know how he's getting on?' asked Mountson.

Louise gave him her card. 'You'll have to check with the hospital but you can contact me if you can think of anything else that might help. Does he have any family you could notify?'

Mountson stopped biting his lips. Eyes downcast, he shook his head.

Chapter Seven

D was her only family. He'd never wanted to return to Weston, and it had showed in his sullen features and whining tone. After finally agreeing to the move, his mood had been one of continued sulking and she'd had concerns that he'd actually go with it. Although that didn't completely change after the success of the previous night, she felt the old D was returning.

The rush of the chase had been such that she'd wanted to do it in the park, but D had told her it was too risky. Sometimes it made sense to listen to what he had to say. The park had been too public, so they'd driven to the beach, where they'd chased the man along the sand as if he were a wild animal. Yes, it had brought with it bad memories – she couldn't see the sand without her back itching – but she couldn't deny the visceral thrill of watching the man's panic as he made wild loops up and down the sand dunes.

They'd left the body in a place where it could be found. The man hadn't deserved to die. He was a warning – no more than that; his fate heralded her return. Whether or not the others understood that, she didn't care. They would find out soon enough.

And as for the branding itself.

She sucked in the hot air of the bar, revelling in that memory of lighting the iron and making that delicious mark.

Her mark.

She could still taste the burning flesh on her tongue. The man's skin and tissue had eased away as she'd placed the metal on his arm, and even his anguished screams hadn't deadened the sound of his bubbling skin.

Not that she was satisfied. If anything, the precious moments they'd spent in the dunes had only reinvigorated her resolve. She understood they had to be more organised, and certainly more careful. Their actions were public now, and they would be coming for them.

D had once again argued that they should calm things down, go back to normality for the next few months before continuing. Despite his best efforts, he didn't really understand why she had to do this. Yes, he'd been there when she needed him and enjoyed the things they did together but their reasons were far removed from one another's.

She needed to finish what was started years ago and D's argument that those responsible had already paid would always fall on deaf ears. Everything could have been prevented. A lack of kindness, or wilful ignorance, had led to this situation and that had to be rectified.

Together they watched the three women leave the bar. She scratched herself as she saw the blonde-haired one, unstable as she walked along the street. Would she recognise her if she left the car now and showed herself? Unlikely. She hadn't cared much for her then, and she doubted the woman would have the wit to see beyond her transformation.

'Are you sure we have to do this?' said D.

She lowered her eyes, pissed off at the return of the whine in his voice. 'The blonde one. I'll be waiting here,' she said.

D knew better than to argue. Sighing, he left the car.

Alone, she waited, picturing what the hot metal would do to the woman's unblemished skin.

Chapter Eight

After showering and changing at home, Louise opened the internal door in the house and walked downstairs to where her parents and Emily lived. The first thing she heard was the tapping of claws on the wooden floors as Molly came galloping towards her. The dog jumped up on Louise, tail wagging furiously, whining as if she hadn't seen Louise in weeks.

'Get down, Molly,' said Emily, following in the dog's wake. 'Hello, Aunty Louise.'

However tough Louise's day had been, seeing the smile on her niece's face always lifted her spirits. She wondered if their connection would have been so strong if Emily hadn't lost both her parents. It was as close to being maternal as Louise imagined she would ever experience, and she still felt guilty that her working life was such that Emily still had to be under the care of Louise's parents. 'Hello, darling, how was your day?'

'Real fun. Me and Grandad took Molly to the beach, and Grandad bought me an ice cream. And then, guess what?'

'What?' said Louise, matching Emily's breathless excitement.

'He bought me another one.'

'Another ice cream?'

'Yep,' said Emily, as if it were the greatest thing that had ever happened to her.

'That Grandad. I need to have a word with him.'

'No,' said Emily, embracing Louise as the dog continued jumping up and down on them.

Louise's parents were in the living room watching television.

'Hello, darling,' said her father.

'Hi, Dad. Mum. Tough day at the beach then?'

'There's some wine in the fridge,' said her mother. Louise wasn't sure if she was testing her. They'd had so many arguments about her mother's drinking over the last few months that it was sometimes a contentious issue. At Louise's insistence, her mother had seen a counsellor after Paul's death, but since moving to Weston she'd refused any further help.

'I'm OK,' said Louise. So affected had she been by what had happened to Paul, and what she could see was happening to her mother, that Louise hadn't drunk anything alcoholic in months and wasn't sure she would ever do so again. 'Just seeing if you guys are OK.'

'We're good.'

Louise wanted to hold her tongue, knew as soon as she said anything that things would go wrong, but she couldn't help but make a comment. 'Didn't fancy the beach today then?'

Her mother scowled, and Louise could tell she'd hit her nerve. 'No, I was feeling a bit tired.'

'I know, you were still in bed this morning.'

'Excuse me for resting.'

Louise ran her hand through her hair. 'I saw the empty wine bottles, Mum.'

'Not this again, Louise. I was just a bit tired, that's all. Not easy being a new mum in your seventies, you know.'

The last comment was a low blow. Her parents had been wonderful in looking after Emily, but every now and then her mother would come out with something like this. It was both a diversionary tactic and an undermining way of suggesting Louise should be taking a greater role in Emily's life. Louise glanced at her father for support, his clenched smile suggesting now was not the time to escalate the argument.

'I'm taking madam here shopping for school uniforms tomorrow, if you're free?' her mother said, after a time.

Louise appreciated the kindness in her mother's voice. Sometimes she wondered if their antagonism was one-sided. 'Busy day tomorrow, I'm afraid, but thanks,' said Louise, noting the sigh of relief from her father.

◆ ◆ ◆

Louise spent the evening on the sofa upstairs. The television was on but she couldn't concentrate on it, her thoughts moving from Sam Carrigan to her run-in with Amira Hood.

With Carrigan still unconscious, it was hard to get a real grip on the investigation. Her team had gone through the usual procedures, on the chance that Carrigan had been attacked, but what they really needed was Carrigan's version of events.

Louise wished work was something she could switch off from, and laughed to herself as she uploaded the screen shots of every anonymous text Finch had ever sent her, as a distraction.

Her early optimism about bringing Finch to justice had faded. She'd been caught up in Amira's enthusiasm, but the enormity of the task was deflating. The harsh truth was that bringing a case against a colleague would be frowned upon by many in the force. She would never normally walk away from a challenge, but her involvement made this different. Although she would have the sympathy of many, going against one's own was close to taboo. That was why the Ghost Squad and its ilk were detested by some. Clichéd as it sounded, being in the police was like being part of a family; and going against your family meant you would no longer be trusted. If she went against Finch now there was a risk she would be ostracised. She would be accused of targeting Finch, not because of what he'd done but because she was a bad loser. From the outside, it would look like she was bitter. She had been the one who had been demoted, and Finch was the one who'd been promoted to DCI.

Of course, things would be different if and when Finch was found guilty of his crimes. No one in the force liked someone who besmirched the good name of the police, and the abuse of a fellow officer would never be tolerated, but getting to that stage would be the hardest part.

She'd saved and photographed the messages Finch had sent her before, on the off chance they could one day be used in evidence. She flicked through the messages now, a spike of adrenaline hitting her bloodstream as she stopped on one particular message:

I hope you sleep well, Louise x

Louise remembered the sleepless nights she'd endured because of the messages. Not so much through fear, but because of anger and frustration that she couldn't do anything about it. He'd sent her the messages when she'd first moved to Weston, when she'd been at her most vulnerable, and had only stopped when she'd proven herself on her first major crime in the area.

She tried to look at it from a subjective viewpoint. What were Finch's crimes? He'd lied about the incident at the Walton farm, which had effectively led to Walton's death, but that had already been dealt with. Louise hadn't been listened to then and nothing would have changed. Then there was the harassment and the threats regarding the photographs of Amira. If proven, it would be enough to get him dismissed. If Amira made an official complaint now, it could have a dramatic impact on his career, especially with Louise corroborating the story. But they needed more. At the moment, it would be too easy for their detractors to describe it as two scorned women out for revenge. The only way to get Finch was by finding some hard evidence, and that seemed a distant dream.

◆ ◆ ◆

Thomas stopped her in the station car park at seven thirty the following morning. He was wearing another new shirt, a day's growth of stubble pitting his face. He smiled on seeing her, and Louise couldn't deny the uplifting effect it had on her. 'See our new tsar's been to work already,' he said, as they made their way to the entrance.

'Baker? What did he do?'

'Closed down three bars in the centre last night for serving after hours. He had plain-clothed officers in each place. Nice work if you can get it.'

'Three? He is serious. Bit of a hit to the local economy, though.'

'All three licensees have to reapply for their licences at the magistrates'. I think he's sending out a warning signal but a bit of an overkill, if you ask me.'

Louise was still undecided about Baker's approach. By all accounts, it had worked in Newquay, but she wasn't convinced his methods would work in Weston-super-Mare. It was a much smaller town, and although there was a huge influx of tourists in the summer months, there was also a tight-knit group of locals. Shutting three bars in one fell swoop risked alienating the community he'd been hired to serve.

The second they entered the CID department, they were summoned into DCI Robertson's office. Robertson was Glaswegian by birth. Although he'd lived the majority of his life in England, his accent hadn't faded. 'Where are we on this branding thing?' he said, rolling the *R* sound in 'branding'.

Louise updated him on her meeting with David Mountson.

'Do we know if this mark has any significance? What is it, a two or an *S*, or a snake?' said Robertson.

'I visited a local tattoo parlour yesterday. The law on this type of thing seems a bit muddled at the moment. Even with consent, there is a risk of prosecution.'

'If this was an attack, do we know how they managed to do it in the open?' asked Robertson.

'Some kind of blowtorch to the metal, by the sound of it.'

'Painful,' said Thomas.

'Aye, bloody painful,' said Robertson. 'Sounds like a very specific thing to do. Personal. What do we know about Carrigan?'

'He's been at the rehab centre for two months. I have a home address for him in Swindon. No landline, though.'

'We believe he is still using, yes?'

'Yes, I think we can agree the rehab isn't working at the moment,' said Louise.

'OK. Thomas, give us a minute.'

They sat in silence until Thomas had shut the door behind him. 'The date for your hearing has been set for later this month. Thought I'd give you a heads up. You have someone to represent you?'

'Do I need someone? I thought you'd said this was a formality?'

'It is, but you know how these things go. Better to have someone with you to avoid saying something you shouldn't.'

'You think I'll let my emotions get the better of me, sir?'

Robertson grinned, always an awkward gesture for him. Their relationship was close enough that she could toy with him occasionally. 'You do need to take this seriously. We got a great result thanks to your help on the case, but the fact is it was something you should have steered clear of.'

'The fact is, Iain, that if DCI Finch had given my brother's murder the attention it deserved, they would have found his killer without my assistance.'

'And this is why you need representation, Louise. You start running your mouth off about Finch, you're going to get yourself into trouble. Yes, tell them about your success in helping to find the killer, but don't turn it into an internal battle. You need to get in and out of there as quickly as possible. Bring Finch into it and it will drag on and on, and not to your benefit either.'

'I'll be sensible, sir.' Louise lifted her fingers in a salute. 'Brownie promise,' she said.

Robertson grunted and began reading the papers on his desk.

Thomas knew better than to ask what Robertson had wanted. 'Coffee?' he said, as Louise returned to the main office.

'Have you ever heard me answer no to that question?'

Thomas was one of the main positives to have come out of her time in Weston. They'd become good friends at the station and he was a strong constant she'd come to rely on. Looking his way now, she couldn't deny her attraction to him either, despite her resolution never to pursue it. He'd been married when she'd first moved to the town, going through a rough period with his now ex-wife. But his single status didn't change anything on that front. It was usually a bad idea to get romantically involved with someone you worked so closely with, as she'd learnt from her regrettable time with Finch. The last thing she wanted to do was jeopardise her strongest relationship in Weston, and Thomas hadn't given her any indication that it was something he'd ever considered. Louise was about to accept his offer of company when the office manager put through a call to her desk.

'It's a Dr Bainbridge for you.'

Louise thanked the office manager and took the call. 'Dr Bainbridge, Louise Blackwell. How may I help you?'

'Ah, Detective Blackwell. I'm surprised you haven't been notified yet but I've just arrived on duty and it appears we've admitted a young woman who has an injury very similar to that inflicted on Mr Carrigan.'

Chapter Nine

Louise asked Thomas to accompany her to the hospital. She was disappointed it had taken so long for the information to reach her when the link between the two incidents appeared obvious.

Dr Bainbridge met them outside the ward. 'She was admitted to A&E this morning. Some friends brought her in. Poppy Westfield. She's only nineteen,' said Bainbridge, showing them photos of the injuries inflicted on the woman. Bile rose in Louise's throat as the image of the girl's right thigh played on the tablet screen. This time the symbol was clearer. It looked more like the number two than the letter *S*, the tail of the *2* elongated, making it look a bit like a swan.

'We had to sedate her on admittance and she is on a morphine drip at the moment, but you can talk to her. Her friends haven't left her side.'

'At least she's conscious,' Louise said to Thomas as a nurse led them to the ward and pulled back the curtain where Poppy was recovering. Two wide-eyed teenagers, their made-up faces smudged by tears, glanced up at them as if in shock. 'Poppy, this is DI Blackwell and DS Ireland. They're going to ask you a few questions,' said the nurse.

'Girls, would you like to come with me?' said the nurse to Poppy's companions, who offered their friend guilty smiles before being led away.

Poppy sat up in bed, her face ghost-white. She looked at once older, and younger, than her nineteen years. Like her friends, she appeared to be in shock. Louise hoped it was the morphine in the young woman's system, but there seemed to be a terrible resignation in her eyes. Louise didn't want to think about what lay in store in Poppy's future, how every day she would see, or sense, the mark left on her body. It was something that would always be with her, a scar and a story she would have to share with anyone she ever became close to.

'Hi, Poppy, my name is DI Blackwell, but you can call me Louise. This is my colleague, DS Thomas Ireland. We just wanted to ask you some questions, if that is OK?'

Poppy's tongue slid out of her mouth as she closed her eyes, her head nodding in assent.

'I know this must be very difficult for you, but could you tell me what happened last night?'

'Can I have some water?' said Poppy, her voice a dry rasp as she adjusted her position.

Thomas poured her some water and the girl sipped at it as if it were nectar. Words began falling from her mouth, until she was almost rambling. 'I don't really remember. We'd been out all night, drinking, dancing, you know. It was a bit of a blur by the end. The last thing I remember is being at the club. The next thing I'm in this field and there are these people chasing me, then they caught me, and then . . .' She began crying, her hand trembling as she drank more of the water.

'Did you see the people who did this to you?' asked Louise.

'They were wearing masks, but I think one of them was a woman. It was dark, but she had that sort of figure, you know. And her voice.'

'What did she sound like?' said Louise, keen to keep the girl talking.

'She didn't say much. They were laughing lots, as if they were getting a real kick out of it.'

'Did you hear her say any names? Or the other person. He was a male?'

'I think so. He was, like, twice her size. No, I can't remember any names. I was screaming when they showed me the flame. He said something about corruption, then I don't remember anything except for the pain.'

'You're being very brave, Poppy. I'm afraid I have to ask if they did anything else to you?'

'Anything else?' said Poppy, incredulous that the branding on her thigh wasn't enough.

'Did they do anything else to you physically?' said Louise.

Louise hadn't thought it possible, but the girl went paler. 'Oh. No, not that I remember . . .'

'Do you feel that anything might have happened?'

'I don't know,' said the girl.

Louise hated having to ask the question, given the increased panic she now saw in Poppy's eyes, but it had to be asked. 'I'm going to ask someone to come here and check you over, Poppy, just to be on the safe side. Are you OK with that? We might be able to get some evidence that helps point us in the direction of who did this to you.'

'OK,' said Poppy.

'I'm sorry this is so stressful, but can you tell me what happened after they'd done this to you?'

'I'm not sure. I was in so much pain I think I must have blanked out. I remember being alone in the park. I thought I was going to die, but they'd disappeared.'

'One last thing. Have you ever seen this man before?' asked Louise, showing Poppy a photo of Sam Carrigan.

'No, why?'

'It's nothing. You get some rest. Your parents are on the way.'

As they waited for the doctor to arrive, Louise and Thomas questioned Poppy's friends. The neon glare of the hospital lights highlighted the smudged make-up plastered on their faces. They spoke to the girls individually, Louise speaking to the shorter of the two, an eighteen-year-old called Sadie.

The girl was close to hysterics and Louise spent the first five minutes trying to calm her. She'd obviously had a lot to drink the previous evening and, despite the shock of what had happened, was still affected by her hangover.

'Poppy is safe, now. It's a terrible thing that has happened to her and we want to catch those responsible as soon as we can. For us to do that, we need your help, Sadie. OK?' said Louise.

Sadie nodded, her eyes glazed.

'Tell me what happened at the end of the night, Sadie.'

Sadie looked downcast. 'We were all dancing, and then Poppy didn't come back. After a bit we went looking for her.'

'You and Elaine?'

'Yes. We thought she'd, you know, pulled.'

'Wouldn't she normally let you know if she'd met someone?'

'Usually, yes.'

'Does it happen a lot?'

'Not really, no. And not so quickly. We'd been talking to some boys earlier in the night who were at the club so we thought she'd gone back with one of them.'

'Did you know these boys from before?'

'Not really, we've seen them around but hadn't spoken to them.'

'Do you remember their names?'

Sadie nodded and recounted the names of five boys without hesitation. 'Poppy fancied Ben. She'd suggested they meet up at the club so we didn't think anything of it until we saw Ben at closing time, then we got worried, and she wasn't answering her phone.'

'What time did you last see her at the club, Sadie?'

'Must have been around midnight. As soon as we thought something was up we went looking for her. Then Elaine came up with the idea of using the Find My Phone app. We share our details.'

Louise waited for the girl to stop crying. 'Go on, Sadie, please,' she said quietly.

'Her phone was still on. Her location said she was in Clarence Park. We thought maybe her phone had been stolen but we walked there anyway and then . . .'

'She's OK, now, Sadie. She's safe.'

Sadie spoke through tears. 'I know, but when we found her I thought she was dead. And then we saw what they'd done to her leg.'

'How did you get her to the hospital?'

'We didn't know what to do. She was coming in and out of consciousness. I wanted to call an ambulance, but then Elaine stopped this car and they gave us a lift.'

Louise shook her head. She wanted to tell her how foolish they'd been not to call an ambulance and to contact the police, how idiotic it had been to flag down a passing car, which could quite easily have belonged to Poppy's attackers, but now wasn't the time for recriminations.

Afterwards, she compared notes with Thomas, who'd spoken with Elaine. The reports matched, down to the detail about Ben and the young women last seeing Poppy at midnight. Elaine had even had the foresight to take down the number plate of the couple who'd taken them to the hospital.

As the doctor arrived, Louise arranged for the crime scene at Clarence Park to be cordoned off and for the SOCOs to attend. Her next stop would be to check the CCTV footage for the town centre from yesterday evening, and in particular the nightclub, Prism, where Poppy had last been seen. She instructed Thomas to stay with Poppy and her friends and called Robertson before heading to Clarence Park.

◆ ◆ ◆

Amira was waiting for her by her car. Louise's first instinct was to tell her fellow officer she didn't have time to speak to her, but the hopeful look on Amira's face made her hold her tongue. The woman was sacrificing her time, risking her job, and possibly much more, investigating Finch. Furthermore, she had the threat of her photos being made public hanging over her, so the least Louise could do was give her a few minutes of her time. It reminded Louise about her upcoming misconduct meeting. It had been three years since Louise had worked in the same department as the man, but his negative influence was a constant she couldn't shake.

'Either you're a great surveillance officer, or I'm unbelievably easy to track,' said Louise.

'Sorry, Louise, I know you're busy. I thought it best if there is no trail of a conversation between us.'

'Don't need to apologise. What do you have for me?'

'I've found someone else who can help us. You might know her from your time at headquarters,' said Amira, showing her a picture on her phone.

'Looks familiar. She was a temp, wasn't she?'

'Terri Marsden. Worked in the secretarial pool on maternity cover. I remembered Finch being all over her one Christmas party. Should have seen her face when I mentioned him. I thought she

46

was going to keel over. She didn't want to speak at first but something similar happened to her. He went back with her that night, but she can't remember anything about it. Then she started getting text messages over the Christmas period. Unfortunately, she didn't keep any of them, but from what she tells me they were pretty nasty. Calling her all manner of names and hinting she should leave work.'

'Did you ask why she didn't come forward?' said Louise, realising the double standard of the question when she hadn't come forward herself.

'Naturally, she was scared. But he also sent her this,' said Amira, showing her a naked picture of the secretary, unconscious on a bed. 'One of many. Thankfully, she decided to keep the photos. This is the only one she would let me keep. The rest were more explicit.'

'Bastard.'

'Louise, I have to ask . . .'

Louise stopped Amira. 'He didn't take any photos of me, at least not consensually,' she said, her mind backtracking, trying to recall if there were any times where Finch could have photographed her without her knowing. They'd been very occasional lovers and Finch had only stayed over at her flat on one occasion.

'I had to ask. I imagine if he had anything on you, he would have shared that by now.'

Louise sighed and tried to control the anger rushing through her. Without even being there, Finch had managed to sow another seed of doubt in her mind. It strengthened her resolve, but she still didn't think they had enough to go on. 'Can you get all the photos from her, do you think? I know someone who could analyse them for us,' said Louise, a decision formulating in her mind.

'I'll go back and try. Why do you think he does it?'

Louise had been considering that question for the last few years. 'Finch? It's a power thing linked to his insecurity. Just look at the way he's ripped out the heart of MIT since becoming DCI. He's banished anyone who's a threat, and probably has something over those who stay,' she said, hoping her two friends in MIT – Tracey Pugh and Greg Farrell – were the exceptions. 'I didn't realise it at the time, or if I did, I chose to ignore it, but he's a classic sociopath. He treats women like that for the sport of it. Once he's made his conquest, he can't bear the idea of them being around.'

'Mummy issues?' said Amira.

'No doubt. Get back to Terri Marsden and see if she will cooperate some more. Get everything you can – the phone she was using at the time, all the images she has of the photos. I don't like it, but we have to do this incognito. Let me know when you have it all and I'll get my contact involved.'

Chapter Ten

Adrenaline still rushed through Louise's blood as she parked up by the entrance to Clarence Park. Her thoughts oscillated between rage for what Finch had done, and was doing, to regret for not fully fighting him earlier. The SOCOs had already arrived and were working from the coordinates supplied from Poppy's phone.

The park was a short walk from the seafront on Walliscote Road. A stiff breeze had reached the area, the blue of the August sky dissected by a threatening mound of shifting cloud. Louise stood on the sidelines as the SOCOs cordoned off a large area, the details from Poppy's phone not as specific as they would have liked. Louise tried to picture the scene from last night. Poppy wandering around in the darkness, her senses hampered by alcohol and whatever else was in her bloodstream, as her two attackers toyed with her. She scrunched her eyes shut as she imagined the young woman being caught, the fear and helplessness she must have felt as she'd seen the blue flame and branding iron and realised what was in store for her.

The head of the regional SOCO team, Janice Sutton, walked over, shaking her head. 'Going to be a tough one without your victim showing us exactly where it took place. The phone-tracking app is notoriously unreliable, and we're looking at a possible area of two hundred square metres at the moment.'

'My guess is this isn't something they would have done out in the open, so somewhere over there would be a good place to start.' Louise pointed to a copse of sycamore trees. 'In the meantime, I'll see if I can get her friends down here. They found her at the scene,' said Louise, as one of Janice's colleagues summoned her back over.

Janice returned a few minutes later, holding an evidence bag in front of her, a small plastic object within. 'What's that?' asked Louise.

'I think we may have found your crime scene. This piece of plastic has the logo Rothenberger on it. I ran a quick search. Rothenberger specialise in plumbing products, including blow-torches.' She showed Louise a photograph of a propane-powered blowtorch. 'See there,' said Janice, pointing to a plastic cap on the end of a curved metal tube. 'I think this could be a match. Get this tested and we could get some prints. Still be useful to get your witnesses down here.'

'I'll get on to it,' said Louise.

By late afternoon, Elaine and Sadie had arrived and identified the area where they'd found Poppy. The owners of the car that had taken them to the hospital had been questioned at the station, as had the boys they'd been talking to last night, and evidence from the scene had been sent for processing.

Louise headed back into the town centre. The ominous-look-ing cloud had burst and swathes of sun-seekers were exiting the beach, the roads out of Weston close to gridlock. Louise enjoyed seeing the town so busy. The difference between high summer and winter was stark. Louise preferred the colder months, in particular the desolation of the windswept beaches, but it was hard on the local economy. For the hospitality sector, the summer months were pivotal, the vast majority of its income derived from a few months of sun.

The downside to the influx of tourists was that parking became a major issue. Louise decided not to even try the main car parks. As the rain eased, she cut through Winterstoke Road and found a spot in Jubilee Road, a short walk from the centre.

Although Weston had changed since she'd made the day trips here as a child, sitting next to Paul in the back seat, much of it remained the same. Despite the construction of a newer cinema complex in Dolphin Square, the old art deco Odeon cinema on the corner of Regent Street was still open. Louise had spent an enchanted evening in the building with her family, watching *E.T.* on the giant screen. She could still recall the smell of popcorn, the slightly worn carpets on the staircase and the sheer excitement of the curtains being pulled back to reveal the screen. Her skin prickled as her thoughts lurched from thinking how lovely it would be to visit the cinema again with Emily and Paul to remembering that her brother was no longer around. It was a shame that the wonder of such memories was tainted by what had happened to Paul, but she tried to take some joy in remembering her brother from that time.

Working in Weston for the last three years had changed her perspective on the seaside town. In some ways, she was fonder of the place than at any other time in her life. After a tough start, she felt part of the community. She always welcomed new initiatives promoting Weston, and with Emily now at school here she was, invested in the town in a way she'd never been when living in Bristol. But she also understood better the darker side to the place. The seasonal poverty and the drug issues that had made Weston infamous. It made her think that, despite his pedantic ways, the arrival of Inspector Baker in the town might prove to be a good thing.

Further into town she was reminded of teenage years, visiting Mr B's nightclub with some friends from sixth form, each with their dodgy photo ID, when she'd been a year or two younger than Poppy and her friends were now. It was gone now, and further along Gloucester Street she came to Prism nightclub, where Poppy had been last night.

She checked the street for cameras. The nearest appeared to be on the corner by Richmond Street, but she would check what active cameras there were in the area when back at the station. The nightclub was shut now, and she banged on the boarded-up door, where she'd agreed to meet one of its managers. The club only opened on weekends in winter but had enough of a passing trade in the summer months to open six days a week. The door opened, a heavily built woman in a maroon tracksuit sticking her head out. 'Yeah?' she said.

'DI Blackwell. I'm here to see Steven Boyne.'

'Oh yeah. Follow me, love,' said the woman.

Louise followed the woman up the dimly lit stairs, the smell of spilled alcohol hanging in the air, to the main entrance of the club. The silence and lack of people robbed the place of its atmosphere and it was hard to imagine what illusion the room could magic up to make anyone want to visit it at night-time. It looked tired and run-down, the colour of the woman's tracksuit bleeding into the beer-stained carpet.

A small, balding man sat on a barstool watching Louise approach.

'Police to see you, Steve,' said Tracksuit Lady, disappearing behind the bar.

'Oh yeah. You I spoke to?' said Boyne.

Louise showed the man her warrant card. 'Thanks for seeing me at short notice.'

'I think you want this,' said Boyne, a USB flash drive in his hand. 'Last night's camera feed. I'm afraid three of our cameras are down at present.'

How convenient, thought Louise, taking the flash drive. She showed Boyne a picture of Poppy and her friends. 'Did you see these young women last night?'

'Listen, we are stringent on our ID checks. Don't even check if we think they look too young. Just send them away.'

From Boyne's defensiveness, it sounded as if he'd heard about Baker's clean-up mission. 'That's not what I asked, Mr Boyne. The women are over eighteen so you're covered.'

Boyne wrinkled his eyes and looked at the photos on Louise's phone. 'Sorry, we get hundreds of them in here. All look the same to me.'

Louise didn't appreciate the sly way Boyne dismissed Poppy and her friends so lightly. 'We're concerned that one of the girls had her drink spiked.'

That got Boyne's attention. 'Oh, come on. We do everything we can. We have a great security team; we check everyone who comes in here.'

'But three of your cameras aren't working?'

'You should still be able to see everyone in the club last night. I'll cooperate as much as I can. We don't allow any of that shit to go on in here. We have zero tolerance to drugs of all kinds. I told your boss that the other day.'

'My boss?' said Louise.

'Tall guy. DI Baker or something.'

Louise couldn't be bothered to correct the man. 'Show me the layout of this place. All exit points.'

Boyne puffed out his cheeks and pushed himself up off his seat. There was something depressing about viewing the place in the daytime. Although the windows were blacked out, light seeped through the seams, highlighting peeling wallpaper and ripped furniture. The toilets had been cleaned, but no amount of bleach could hide the underlying odours that lingered. After showing her the fire exits, Boyne guided her to the rear of the club and down an exit that led to a small car park. 'This is staff only,' he said.

Louise looked around for cameras but couldn't see any. 'Would anyone have used this exit last night?'

'Not that I'm aware of,' said Boyne.

Boyne's insistence didn't fill her with much confidence. 'I may need to speak to your staff at some point,' said Louise, making a note of the number plates of the three cars in the car park, before walking back to Jubilee Road, seconds before the clouds burst open again.

Chapter Eleven

D had moaned about coming back to the site. He'd wanted her to lie low for a few days but she wanted a closer handle on what was happening. They'd had so much fun together last night. They'd watched Poppy from afar, careful not to be seen. The club was perfect, as D knew all about the CCTV cameras. He'd told her that getting Poppy to share her drink was easy, as was guiding her outside. The choice of the park was risky, but D thought the police might have had officers hidden on the beach.

She inhaled his scent and savoured the remembered smell of Poppy's burning flesh. She would never forget those eyes. It was hard to comprehend the differing rays of emotions she'd seen in her face – the mounting terror, pleading, realisation and, finally, the terrific release of pain. It had been a shame that she'd had to wear a mask in case Poppy remembered her. She had wanted to be seen by her, wanted Poppy to appreciate the transformation she'd gone through – was going through – while she experienced a transformation of her own, but being recognised would have ruined what she had in store.

In many ways she and Poppy were alike. Poppy had been led astray. No doubt, Poppy would argue that she'd exercised free will all those years ago, but she would be lying to herself. Poppy had been a victim, even if she didn't realise it. And if it hadn't been for her betrayal, then maybe they could have grown to become friends. Either way, they were now forever entwined. Her mark was on the woman and she hoped it would do her some good.

For all his complaining, she liked being in the car with D. It was safe and compact. She felt protected both by the shell of the vehicle and his proximity. He filled out the space, his long, sinewy arms cramped against the driver's side door as if he were trapped.

As the policewoman left the nightclub, taking the back entrance, as D had predicted, she placed her hand on his arm. It was a reflex move, and she felt him tense either at her movement or at the distant sight of the dark-haired woman. 'You think she's attractive?' she asked, her fingers sliding over the thick ridge of his bicep muscle.

He smiled at that. He always enjoyed it when she pretended to be jealous.

'We need to follow her,' she said. The policewoman was an intriguing character and she wanted to get to know more about her.

D sighed again but knew not to cross her. Despite his reservations, he enjoyed their activities as much as she did. He was just that little bit more hesitant. But soon the look of reservation faded. He turned and grinned, and she caught a glimpse of the person he could be. 'No need,' he whispered. 'I already know where she lives.'

Chapter Twelve

Back at the station, Louise conducted more research into body scarification. She signed up to a number of forums, reading the many posts, trying to get a glimpse of the psychology behind body modification. But despite the attack suffered by Poppy, and almost definitely by Sam Carrigan, part of her was still preoccupied with Finch – not a mindset she wanted to be in. Thinking about him triggered a smell reflex, the scent of his citric aftershave, as real as if he were in the room. It was hard to believe she'd once been attracted by that smell. Then, he'd worn it as a subtle adornment. Now, he lathered it over himself – an unrestrained way of marking his territory – and the very thought of it made her retch.

She hoped Amira would prove to be as proactive as she'd sounded. For now, she'd left it with the young detective, who was going to contact a number of other women, both police and civilians, who'd left headquarters in the last few years. Louise had warned her to be careful but Amira knew what was at risk. Louise was in no doubt that if Finch found out what she was doing, he would be prepared to use the photos. Her rage was tinged with a continued sense of helplessness, and she could only imagine what Amira was feeling.

Louise couldn't ignore the continued feelings of guilt either. Finch was an expert at covering his tracks but maybe there was something more she could have done since her move to Weston. It was enough to cement her resolve. She'd learnt early on in her career that sometimes you had to make tough decisions. Finch had messed around with her life, and so many others', for too long. She would do everything she could to help Amira, whatever the cost.

Trying to drag herself back into the case, she was checking on the file they had on the rehab centre manager, Mountson, who had two previous convictions for affray and ABH, when a call came in from the constable stationed at the hospital.

'What is it, Sarah?' asked Louise.

'It's Mr Carrigan, ma'am. He's regained consciousness.'

Louise was back at the hospital within twenty minutes. Carrigan was sitting up in bed, being checked over by a different doctor.

PC Sarah Millard looked exhausted. 'Hello, ma'am – I mean Louise,' she said.

'Sarah. You have notes for me.'

The constable nodded and handed over her notebook. 'As I mentioned, he was a bit hyper. Kept glancing at his bandage. He looked scared as well.'

'Anyone visited him?' asked Louise.

'No.'

'How long have you been on shift now?'

'I have had some rest, ma'am, but thirteen hours.'

'OK, you should have said. Come with me to speak to Mr Carrigan and then you can go home. When are you on next?'

The PC glanced at her watch, her dry lips forming into a rueful smile. 'In about eleven hours.' Louise was pleased she wasn't looking for any sympathy and made a mental note to keep an eye out for the young constable.

In the afternoon light, Carrigan looked even frailer than the first time she'd seen him. Without the tubes and mask, his face was slack as he sipped a juice box through a straw. Tattoos surrounded the bandages on his arm. To Louise's untrained eyes, they looked less vibrant than the ones she'd seen on the woman at the tattoo parlour, as if faded through age and wear. 'Mr Carrigan, Detective Inspector Blackwell. I'm glad to see you're back with us,' she said.

'Big guns, eh?' said Carrigan, his hands shaking.

'What have the doctors said to you, Mr Carrigan?'

'Not sure. Lucky to be alive?'

Up close, Louise could see Carrigan's whole body was shaking. She'd seen similar before on drug users when they were coming down off something. The movement was involuntary, and she wondered if he knew he was doing it. 'Mr Carrigan, I'd like to go through the events of the other night, if I may?'

The shaking intensified. 'I need a fag.'

'Not sure you're in the right place for that, Mr Carrigan. Do you mind if I record our conversation?' said Louise, starting the recording app on her phone before Carrigan could object. 'I know PC Millard has spoken to you, but can you tell me what happened on the night you were admitted here?'

Carrigan shot the constable an accusing look, as if she'd betrayed a secret. 'Yes. It's all a bit fuzzy.'

'Let's start at the beginning. You were found at the back of the sand dunes next to Uphill golf course. What time did you get to the beach?'

'That's the thing, I can't remember. The last thing I remember . . .' Carrigan hung his head down. 'I don't want to incriminate myself or anything.'

'I understand. You took something? I'm not bothered about any of that, just how you came to get the mark on your arm.'

Carrigan winced at the mention of the branding, grimacing as he looked at his arm. 'The last thing I know I was in this bar, little bar by the Playhouse. I know a guy there, I was going to score some . . . anyway, he doesn't show, but when I'm outside this guy stops me and asks if I want a little something, and I bought some pills off him. I'd had a bit to drink by then.'

'You knew this man?'

'No, not this guy. So, I got a can from the offy and went over to Grove Park and swallowed the pills. Next thing I can remember I'm on the beach.'

'Are these sorts of blackouts normal for you, Mr Carrigan?'

Carrigan blushed. 'Can be. But this was different. I can't remember anything. Nothing at all. Not even a hint of how I got to the beach.'

Louise wasn't surprised by Carrigan's nonchalance about blackouts. She'd seen it in Paul too many times. 'And what happened when you got there?'

'Man, it was some weird shit. I didn't know where I was but I knew someone was following me.' Carrigan fought the tears flowing down his face, as if in war with his body. 'They weren't following, though; they were hunting me. That's what it felt like. Not even hunting me, more like toying with me. You know what I mean? They could have got me at any time but they were enjoying the chase.'

'They?'

Louise gave Carrigan time to control his crying. 'Fucking mask-wearing cowards, man. They bided their time. It was like they were herding me, getting me where they wanted. And when they did . . .'

Carrigan was shaking his head; Louise wasn't sure he would ever stop. 'When they caught up with you?' she said, keeping her voice soft as next to her PC Millard scribbled away in her notebook.

'They had this thing. Blowtorch, I guess you'd call it. They lit it up. The sound,' he said, the shaking intensifying. 'And the flame, man, it glowed blue. It was like an impossible colour. It was all I could look at. They were laughing and I thought they were going to put that flame on me.' Carrigan was trembling, sweat breaking out on his face. He looked at Louise, his lips twisting into something that might have been a smile. 'I can smell it now, you know? I can feel the *heat*. Then one of them got this iron pole out, like he was a caddy getting a golf club out of the bag.'

'Please go on, Mr Carrigan. I know this must be so hard for you.'

Carrigan wiped the tears away. 'They put the flame to the iron. Now that *did* glow. They held it in front of my eyes and I thought they were going to blind me. Then they hesitated, and for a second I thought they were going to let me go. They stood there in silence as I tried to turn away. The silence, man, it was hard to bear. The only sound was that gas thing and the heat coming off the iron. It was like they were getting off on the suspense. Then they did this,' said Carrigan, pointing to his arm.

Carrigan ran his left hand through his hair. 'I must have passed out, but not before I felt it. And I felt it.'

'Did they say anything to you? Give you a reason for what they were doing?'

'If they did, I couldn't hear anything except my own screaming. I must have blanked out. Every time I came to, the pain was so unbearable. I remember at one point I tried to crawl to the sea, but I couldn't move.'

'Can you think of anyone who would want to do this to you, Mr Carrigan?'

'What type of person would want to do this?' said Carrigan, incredulous.

'Anyone you're in conflict with. Anyone you owe money to?'

Carrigan shook his head but didn't look sure.

'The man you bought the pills off, you think he had something to do with this?'

'There were two of them. One was friggin' enormous. The other one . . . he didn't speak. It could have been the same one. Small, weedy fella.'

Louise thought about Poppy's assertion that the smaller attacker was female. 'OK, Mr Carrigan, one last thing.' Louise paused, thinking of the best way to say what she had to say. 'You've seen the mark on your arm?'

Carrigan squirmed, the shaking of his head intensifying. 'Of course I've seen it.'

'It appears to be the letter *S*, or maybe a number two. Would you agree?'

'It's a bloody big scar on my arm that will be with me for ever. I don't know what it is.'

'So you have no idea of the significance of the symbol?'

Carrigan's head moved from side to side, his whole body trembling. 'I can't,' he said, as if he were speaking to himself.

Louise feared he was about to start hyperventilating. She didn't want to push Carrigan, but they needed answers fast. The attackers weren't letting up. 'I'm afraid there was another attack last night,' she said, showing him the images of Poppy Westfield on her phone.

'Why would you show me that?' said Sam.

'We're sorry, Mr Carrigan. We're trying to get to the bottom of this. We believe the girl, Poppy Westfield, was targeted and drugged somehow. Like you possibly were?' said Louise. 'Can you remember any other details about the man you bought the pills from?'

'I don't think I'd ever seen him before. He had one of those faces, you know. Sort of nondescript. Scruffy-looking. Possibly homeless.'

'Any tattoos, distinguishing marks?'

'He had bad breath. I was out of it, man, and my memory is fucked after all this.'

Louise was about to wrap things up when she caught sight of the rehab manager, David Mountson, peering through the glass of the ward door. Catching her eye, he disappeared from sight.

'Wait here,' said Louise, sprinting for the door.

'No running!' shouted a nurse, but Louise didn't stop until she reached the ward door.

The corridor was deserted. Louise took the steps to the main reception area but if Mountson had ever been there, he'd now left.

Chapter Thirteen

The following afternoon, Thomas accompanied Louise to the rehab centre in Milton. She'd been there last night after seeing Mountson at the hospital, only to be told he wasn't due back on shift until the next day. She was given an address for him in a block of flats close to where she used to live in Worle, but there'd been no answer when she tried the door. He wouldn't be the first person to avoid talking to a police officer, but she was annoyed she hadn't got the chance to speak to him before the end of her shift.

Outside the building, the sky was now peppered completely with grey, making it feel more like autumn than the height of summer. Louise updated Thomas about her meeting with Steven Boyne at the Prism nightclub.

'Delightful place. Maybe we should get Baker down there. I'm sure he'd close it down in a heartbeat.'

'I considered that. It could do with being condemned, but we need to keep it under surveillance in case our attackers want to return to the scene of the crime,' said Louise.

'You think they were at the club as well?'

'No idea, but Poppy either met one or both of them in the club, or outside. When we get her blood tests back, I think we'll see she took something she didn't know she was taking.'

'Should we get some staff at the dunes and the park?'

Louise would have loved to deploy officers at those locations, but the department was already at straining point and, despite the severity of the recent attacks, Inspector Baker still had his pick of staff. 'Attacking Poppy at the park suggests they are switching their venues, and the area is too wide to manage at the moment. Let's see if we get anything back from the cameras.'

Next door to the rehab centre, Louise nodded in greeting to the same woman she'd seen the other day. This time she was alone, and the lack of children seemed to have taken ten years off her.

They rang the intercom outside the building, a full minute passing before they were buzzed in. Mountson stood behind the desk in the main foyer, talking to a couple of the patients. Louise caught his eye, noting his hesitancy on seeing her. He stopped talking to the patients and took a quick glance at the back office as if searching for an escape.

'Mr Mountson, good to see you again. This is my colleague, DS Ireland.'

'Thanks, guys,' said Mountson to the patients, who walked away, confused. 'How can I help you, officers?'

'Have you been to visit Mr Carrigan yet?' asked Louise.

Mountson hesitated. 'Not yet,' he said.

'I thought I saw you at the hospital yesterday evening,' said Louise, playing along. 'Any reason you didn't want to speak to me?'

'Thought you were busy.'

'I see. You've heard he's regained consciousness?'

'Yes, that's why I was there. I didn't want to interfere with your investigation.'

Louise didn't believe him, but there was little to be done about it at that moment.

'There's been a second attack,' said Thomas, placing his phone on the counter, an image of Poppy's branding on the screen.

Mountson glanced at the image, wincing as if in pain. 'I'm sorry to hear that,' he said.

'You wouldn't know anything about it, would you?' asked Louise.

'What the hell does that mean?'

Louise didn't buy the man's indignation. 'I had the feeling at the hospital that you were running from me.'

'Far from it. Hospitals freak me out, that's all. I saw you there with Sam, and that was enough of an excuse for me not to visit.'

'Where have you been for the last twenty-four hours?' said Thomas.

'My God, you're serious. I presume you talked to Sam. He would have told you I didn't have anything to do with this.'

'Where were you?'

'Drinking and sleeping, mainly. You want a list of pubs?' said Mountson.

'Thank you,' said Thomas, taking out his notebook and offering Mountson a pen.

Louise studied the man as he wrote down the names of three pubs in the Brent Knoll area. He matched the estimated height of six-two to six-three given by both Poppy and Sam, though he looked diminished today, bent over on the counter, his skin pale and blotchy. He'd told them he'd been out drinking last night, and it showed on his features. 'Aren't there rules about counsellors drinking alcohol and taking drugs?' she asked.

The question clearly stung, Mountson stepping back from the counter as if he'd been struck. 'I've made a mistake, OK?' he said.

Louise scrolled to another picture on her phone. 'Do you know this woman?'

Mountson glanced at the image of Poppy, before quickly looking away. 'Poppy Westfield,' said Louise, studying Mountson's eyes for a glimmer of recognition.

'No, sorry,' he said, not looking at her.

Louise put her phone away. Mountson wasn't being straight with them. He was hesitating and failing to keep eye contact. She needed to know what he was hiding. 'How long is Mr Carrigan supposed to be staying here now?'

'He has two more weeks left on his twenty-eight days.'

'What happens then?' said Louise.

'Then we'll see where he is. If we think he should stay longer, then we can recommend he stays, though it's not our decision finally.'

'Not to tell out of school, but Mr Carrigan has admitted to us that on the night of his attack he purchased some pills.'

Mountson shrugged. 'I'm not his minder, and he's a free man. It's not a one-stop, cure-all system. These people are addicts. They're bound to slip at one point or another,' he said, eyes downcast.

Louise handed him her card. 'Please don't go AWOL on us again, Mr Mountson,' she said.

Mountson looked relieved. 'I thought I was a suspect,' he said.

'As I said, please don't go missing on us again.'

Chapter Fourteen

'Home time?' said Thomas, as they left the rehab centre.

Louise didn't reply. If she didn't get back soon, she wouldn't get to see Emily before she went to bed, but she didn't feel right going home yet.

'Knew it,' said Thomas.

'No one is stopping you going home, DS Ireland,' she said, with a smile.

'I take it you're going to see if Mr Mountson goes anywhere this evening.'

'That is why you're the leading light in the overcrowded scene of detectives in the Avon and Somerset constabulary.'

Thomas exaggerated a sigh. 'Can I at least track down some coffee, and maybe some food?'

'Black coffee, no sugar, and I'll have whatever you're eating.'

Thomas was back at the car in thirty minutes. 'It's surprising how difficult it is to find coffee in the late afternoon,' he said. 'I'm afraid we're petrol-station-dining it tonight,' he added, handing her a sandwich with her cup of coffee. 'Any movement?'

Louise winced, the coffee still scalding hot. 'A couple of men left earlier. Other than that, nothing.'

'I heard from the station that Baker is on the warpath again. He's putting undercover officers in the bars tonight. I think half the station is out drinking tonight on expenses.'

'You've got to admire his willingness. He's doing what he said he would do,' said Louise.

'How many places can he shut down before there's a backlash? We're not exactly the same as Newquay.'

Although the town could easily survive the closure of a few bars, Thomas was correct about the comparison to Newquay. Weston relied on the summer trade. That some of it was made up of rowdy youngsters drinking their wages away was probably beside the point to many of the bar and hotel owners. It would take a major overhaul for the town to become solely a family-friendly destination. Baker had promised to look into all aspects of the area, and to Louise the greater concern was the ongoing drug problem. For that to be addressed, there had to be cooperation between the departments, not just in Weston but county-wide. Baker's enthusiasm was commendable, but closing a few dodgy pubs serving drinks out of hours wasn't going to change anything. 'I'm sure he'll soon stop when he closes Robbo's favourite drinking hole,' she said.

'You going to the shindig on the weekend?' asked Thomas.

A former officer from Weston, now a chief superintendent in Bristol, was retiring and had arranged a rather lavish retirement party at the Winter Gardens. Everyone from Weston CID had been invited, and Louise was sure it would be a good chance for Inspector Baker to be rolled out by the ACC. Despite sharing the same rank as her, Baker was something of a celebrity within the force for his work in Cornwall. ACC Morley was enamoured by him and saw it as a personal victory that he'd convinced Baker to make the move back to Weston.

'Why, you asking me out?' said Louise.

She'd said it as a joke, but there were a few seconds of awkwardness in the car before Thomas answered. 'Don't get ahead of yourself, boss,' he said, with a smile.

Louise was thankful that he was able to defuse the atmosphere so easily. 'I'd be happy for you to tag along as my plus one if you're not busy. Anything to save me from the bores.'

'You have a lovely way with words, Louise. An offer I can't refuse.'

She glanced at him, pleased to see he was smiling. 'Shut up, Sergeant, before I change my mind.'

They talked some more about Baker's plans for the town, but Louise's real focus was on the branding case. It was more than the physical damage. Again, she was reminded of how both Poppy and Sam would be forever affected by their attacks. Unlike tattoos, she imagined there was little that could be done to hide the branding scars. As well as the mental scarring from having to see the mark on a daily basis, there would be a physical reminder of what had happened to them; damage to the skin and tissue that would itch or ache on occasion.

She'd read up on human branding the night before. The procedure had a long history. It had been used during the slave trade, in religious ceremonies and as a form of punishment for convicted criminals. Gangs sometimes used it as an initiation rite and human traffickers were still using it to mark the women they forced into prostitution. With the varying possibilities, it was still hard to reconcile what the attackers' motives were. Did they see their victims as their property? Did the swan mark mean something specific? Or was it a larger comment on society in general? Were they punishing their victims for an imagined crime or for some perceived moral shortcoming?

She decided not to share her thoughts with Thomas just yet. Chances were they were simply a pair of sick-minded individuals getting their perverted kicks in a different way.

'Here we go,' said Thomas, sometime later. It was after nine, the late-summer sky darkening. A figure emerged from the front gate of the rehab centre, the stocky figure clearly belonging to David Mountson. As if he knew he was under surveillance, Mountson pulled a hood over his head. He lit a cigarette, the tip burning bright in the dusky gloom, and began walking towards town.

'Do you want me to go on foot?' asked Thomas.

'I suppose you could work off that sandwich,' said Louise, waiting for Mountson to reach the end of the road before switching on the engine.

Twenty minutes later, Louise parked up outside the Mercury building on the Boulevard. Mountson had stopped three times outside pubs on the route but hadn't once clocked that she or Thomas were following. Louise parked up and walked fifty yards or so in front of Mountson. Sam Carrigan had told her he'd bought the pills from a bar near the Playhouse Theatre and she looked around, pretending to check her phone, in time to see Mountson take the turning into the high street towards the same bar, Thomas following behind.

She called Thomas and took a back road. 'He's gone into the Uncle Sam's bar,' said Thomas.

'What's he playing at?'

'Maybe he's trying to find out who sold the drugs to Carrigan?'

If that were true, he wouldn't be the first person to interfere in an ongoing investigation. From Louise's experience, there was never a positive outcome to such actions. 'We'll have to wait it out. I'll stay down the other end, by the park.'

She walked past the Playhouse with its advance posters for the pantomime season and a special one-night-only show by a comedian she'd last heard of in the nineties. It was as if nothing had changed since her childhood and the yearly trips to the pantomime on Boxing Day, her parents eschewing the bigger shows at the theatre then known as Colston Hall in Bristol. Her skin prickled as she recalled the giddy excitement of those winter evenings; the special anticipation of eating sweets while watching the show, the eternal hope of being selected to go onstage each year. She hadn't been back to the small theatre in over a quarter of a century, and she was impressed it was still in business. She was tempted to go in now and buy pantomime tickets for this coming Boxing Day but worried about how her parents would react. It would be so lovely to take Emily to a place she'd enjoyed so much as a child, but that enjoyment had been shared with Paul and going there without him might feel like a betrayal.

She moved to the end of the road, crossing over to the entrance to Grove Park. Save for the odd car, it was peaceful beneath the murky clouds. Despite the changeable weather, the day's heat still lingered. In the distance she heard the gentle lapping of the sea signalling high tide. Every time someone walked by, she put her phone to her ear as she waited for Mountson to leave the bar.

A text came in from Thomas: *Probably drowning his sorrows.*

No one could blame Mountson for that, thought Louise, whatever his role was at the rehab centre.

We're here now. Might as well see it out, she replied.

Thirty minutes later, when her legs were restless and heavy from standing around, Thomas called. 'He's on the move towards you. There's a second guy with him, they appear to be having a quarrel,' he said, as the outlines of the two men became visible outside the lights of the Playhouse.

'You keep with Mountson. I'll follow the second guy if they part ways,' said Louise, hanging up.

She didn't need to hear them to know the pair were arguing. It was clear from their body language. Mountson was gesticulating with his arms, the second man stopping every few steps to remonstrate with him. Louise bent down, pretending to tie her shoes as Mountson followed the second man into the dimly lit park.

'I don't want to have to tell you again,' said the second man, through gritted teeth. Louise glanced up as they passed her. She couldn't be sure, but he looked familiar. He appeared to be in his early twenties, a black hoodie pulled over his head, but she thought she might have seen him before at the station, being processed.

She waited for Thomas to pass her before following the two men into the park. Hoodie was walking up the hill, Mountson raising his voice as the distance between them increased. Louise paused as Mountson stopped, Hoodie walking off into the covering of the trees lining the pathway.

Thomas continued walking towards Mountson, who must have been talking himself into action. As Thomas approached, Mountson took off towards Hoodie, his high-pitched wail indecipherable.

Louise began sprinting, as in the distance she saw Mountson attacking Hoodie. Thomas arrived before her, his presence enough for the two men, who separated and fled in different directions. Unfortunately for Louise, Hoodie had taken the uphill route.

'Go,' she said to Thomas, as Mountson skipped through the undergrowth, heading back towards town.

'Stop! Police!' said Louise, as she moved towards Hoodie. He was quick and agile but had the disadvantage of being pursued. In her experience, it tended to make people panic, and to expend their energy too soon. As long as she kept him in sight, she was sure she could catch up with him.

Thankful she was wearing her utility belt, with her expandable baton and pepper spray, she followed Hoodie as he sprang over the gate of the children's playground. He was about to jump over the other side when he lost his footing, skidding to a stop as he careered into the metal fence surrounding the play area.

'Oh,' he said, jumping to his feet. 'Just you and me, is it?'

The man's body betrayed his bravado. He had a defensive posture, his left shoulder turned towards her. But just because he was cornered, it didn't mean he wasn't a threat.

'DI Blackwell,' she said. 'I would do yourself a favour and think carefully about your next move.'

'What do you want?' said the man.

'I just want to talk to you.'

'Talk away.'

'You're going to have to come with me,' said Louise.

'No way, I ain't done nothing wrong.'

'You were engaged in a fight, and are currently resisting arrest.'

'That's bullshit.'

'Come in peacefully, answer my questions, and this doesn't go any further.'

'Fuck that,' said the man, turning towards the fence once more. Louise had anticipated the move and was on to him. Hoodie assisted her by swinging his elbow back towards her. She used his momentum against him and pulled the man's arm behind his back, ignoring his cries of pain as she cuffed him.

Chapter Fifteen

Louise drove Hoodie – whom she now knew as Ben Abbey – back to the station. The car park was busier than usual. A number of patrol cars were lined up, and Louise recognised one of the men being led inside by a pair of uniformed officers.

The foyer was pandemonium. Louise couldn't recall seeing so many people waiting to be processed.

'I've taken Mountson through to one of the interview rooms,' said Thomas, joining her.

'Look after him for a second,' said Louise, leaving Abbey with Thomas as she spoke to the duty sergeant. 'What's going on?'

The sergeant looked about him, checking he wasn't being overheard. 'Looks like our Inspector Baker has decided to lock up every drinker in the south-west,' he said.

'Don't tell me, he's shut the Prism nightclub,' said Louise, glancing over at Steven Boyne, the club's manager, who'd yet to notice her.

'Underage drinking,' confirmed the sergeant.

'Don't suppose we could jump the queue, could we? Need to interview a suspect regarding the recent branding incidents.'

The sergeant looked Abbey up and down. 'Is he pissed?'

'I don't think so.'

'Then it would be my pleasure.'

Thomas guided Abbey to the front of the queue. His hoodie was down now, revealing his oval face, a tuft of red hair sprouting from his thinning scalp. He was asked if he was holding anything, and Louise placed a bag of pills she'd removed earlier from his inside jacket on the counter.

'Personal use,' said Abbey.

'Yeah, right,' said Thomas.

Boyne recognised her as they took Abbey through to the interview room. 'Blackwell!' he shouted across the lobby area, causing a momentary pause from everyone.

'Mr Boyne,' said Louise, nodding for Thomas to take Abbey through.

The disdain was plastered over the club owner's face. 'Suppose this makes you feel big, does it? I gave you those bloody video files and then you go and shut me down.'

'This has nothing to do with me, Mr Boyne. This was a separate investigation carried out by a completely different department, though I do recall you telling me how stringent you were on not serving underage drinkers.'

'How convenient for you.'

'If you haven't been serving underage drinkers, then you have nothing to worry about, Mr Boyne. Now if you'll excuse me.'

Boyne mumbled something under his breath. Louise didn't need to hear the words to get the gist of what he was saying. She pinched the bridge of her nose, deciding she had more important things to do than get into an argument with the club owner.

Abbey had requested a solicitor so Louise had to pull some strings to get him to the front of the queue of the duty-solicitor rota, Baker's foray into the nightclub taking up all the available resources.

A harried-looking woman appeared forty minutes later and conferred with Abbey for a few minutes before the interview was ready to start. Louise didn't care about the possession with intent charge but wasn't about to let Abbey know that. She asked him about David Mountson.

'You know him?' asked Louise.

'Know of him,' said Abbey.

'Would you like to tell me what the altercation was about?'

'Not really.'

'Let me level with you, Mr Abbey. My interest here is mainly with Mr Mountson. However . . .'

'Are you planning on charging my client with anything more, DI Blackwell?'

'Your client resisted arrest, was caught in a physical altercation with Mr Mountson and had a significant amount of illegal drugs on his person.'

'Unbelievable,' said Abbey, a bead of sweat dripping down his mottled brow.

Louise didn't reply, hoping Abbey would continue talking.

The man looked at his solicitor, who nodded at him, understanding Louise's implicit offer not to take things further as long as her client cooperated.

'Jesus,' said Abbey, rolling his eyes. 'Fine, let's say for example's sake that Mountson was trying to buy off me. I'm not saying I deal, it's for personal use only, you understand?'

'We understand your view on that, Mr Abbey. Please continue.'

'Let's say then that he may have asked to buy some pills and I refused.'

'Let's not waste our time, Mr Abbey.'

'I'm not, I'm not,' said Abbey, more sweat dripping from his head.

'Get to the point, then.'

'Let's say, if I would be willing to sell the drugs, and I'm not. But if I was, I wouldn't sell to him. I told him as much and he didn't take to it kindly.'

Thomas let out a laugh and Louise matched the grin on his face. 'So if we are to cut through this bullshit, you refused to sell him the pills in your possession?' asked Thomas.

'That is correct.'

Louise scratched her forehead. 'Help us out here, Mr Abbey. We can do without the personal use stuff as well. Why did you refuse to sell to Mr Mountson?'

'Why?' said Abbey, as if the question was ludicrous. 'Because of where he works, because of that guy he hangs out with. The one with that big bloody mark on his arm, that's why.'

'You're talking about Sam Carrigan?'

'Yes.'

'You know Mr Carrigan.'

'Passing acquaintance.'

'I'm beginning to understand. You were at the bar the night Sam Carrigan was attacked?' said Louise.

Abbey was thrown by the question, glancing nervously at his solicitor. 'No. I don't even know when he was attacked.'

'You just said you know about the mark on Sam Carrigan's arm?'

'It's been in the paper, love. I know what happened, but I don't know the details.'

Louise leaned across the desk, close enough to smell the sourness on Abbey's breath. 'You've sold drugs to Mr Carrigan before?' she said, barely containing her fury.

'Wait a moment,' said Abbey's solicitor.

'You've seen Mr Carrigan before then?'

'I've seen him, yes, but I wasn't there on the night he was attacked. Check with the guys at Uncle Sam's – I haven't been in all week.'

'OK, so what exactly do you think has happened to Mr Carrigan?'

'I'm not sure exactly. I heard he was branded or something.'

'And you know who did it?'

'Fuck me. This is off the record. I'm no grass,' said Abbey, mistaking the interview for a conversation with a journalist.

'If you know who did this, you'd be best off telling us everything now.'

'It's only rumours, but . . . there's this gang from Bristol. Frenchay estate. I heard they were . . . for want of a better word, marking their property.'

'Marking their property?' said Louise.

'These aren't the sort of people you want to mess about with. Believe me. And one thing is for sure, I ain't selling to no one with one of their marks on his arm. Or to anyone who knows him.'

Chapter Sixteen

Louise didn't leave the station until after midnight. She'd been on shift for over sixteen hours. She kept her window wound down as she drove home via the seafront, the cold air helping to keep her awake. The town was desolate. With the sea at low tide, the blanket of mud stretching towards the horizon intensified the sense of isolation, as if the town's soul had gone missing.

After interviewing Abbey, they'd spoken to David Mountson, who claimed to have confronted Abbey about the attack on Carrigan. In the end, they'd released both men with a caution.

Her eyelids were drooping, the muscles in her arms taut, as she reached the driveway at her house. As she approached her front door, she looked about her, the undying loop of chirruping crickets ringing in her ears, and tried to shake off the feeling she was being followed. She'd already cracked that conundrum by uncovering Amira and told herself it was only paranoia that was making her feel this way now.

Still, she let out a sigh of relief at the sound of the lock closing on the front door. She needed sleep but valued these blissful moments of alone time. She considered pouring some vodka from the unopened bottle in the fridge, but she needed to be up in the morning and nowadays even a single drink would make her groggy.

Despite her tiredness, she wouldn't be able to sleep straight away. If she tried now, the day's events would play over in her mind. Instead, she made some hot chocolate and took out her notepad while late-night television played in the background. She'd found that making notes before she went to bed aided her sleep. She made a list of what needed to be achieved tomorrow, underlining the names Poppy Westfield and Sam Carrigan, as if she could possibly forget that they were the true victims, before heading to her room and collapsing on her bed without taking off her clothes.

An operetta of squawking seagulls woke her the following morning. So dark had it been in her room last night, she hadn't shut her curtains. Now she battled the early-morning sunshine, the sound of her alarm clock piercing her ears and overloading her senses.

Emily was usually a sound sleeper and wasn't up. Louise had grown used to seeing her niece on a daily basis, and although she'd seen her yesterday morning it felt like too long a time period had passed. One thing she hadn't considered when agreeing to share a house with her family was how lonely it could be living in the same building but going days without seeing them. Pouring coffee into her travel flask, she dropped a short note through the dividing door before heading out.

Thomas was waiting outside his house in Worle as if waiting for a bus. 'You're keen,' she said, as he got into the car.

'You're five minutes late, boss.'

'It's six fifty,' said Louise.

'Late is late.'

'I'll get you to pick me up then next time,' said Louise, with a playful scowl.

They had an early appointment with Louise's old work colleague and friend DI Tracey Pugh, who was currently working with the Serious and Organised Crimes Unit at headquarters.

'I could hardly sleep,' said Thomas, as Louise drove down the feeder lane on to the M5. 'Kept waiting for the call saying there'd been another victim.'

'Small mercies on that front,' said Louise.

'Maybe Baker banged the attackers up by accident. I'm sure half of Weston was in the nick last night.'

Louise recalled Boyne's appearance the night before at the station. After the interview with Abbey, she'd found out that Boyne hadn't taken kindly to his club being shut down and had caused enough commotion to receive a caution. She'd yet to check through the CCTV personally but had been told by her colleagues that the images from the nightclub had been all but useless. 'We can go through the list when we get back,' she said, her mind wandering to the night when Poppy had been in the club and the sickening wound inflicted on her thigh sometime later.

They made good time to Portishead, and Tracey greeted them with coffee and pastries. Tracey had been with Louise during her time at MIT. She was a brash character with a heavy head of thick, curly black hair and never failed to cheer Louise up. The office was already busy with staff and, hating herself, Louise couldn't help wondering if DCI Finch was in and would make an appearance.

As if sensing her unease, Tracey led them to an interview room. She pulled the blinds down as they took their seats, Louise catching the scent of Tracey's perfume as she sat down before them.

The situation could have been awkward. Tracey and Thomas had slept together when Tracey had been seconded to Louise's first major case in Weston. Thomas had been married at the time, albeit going through a difficult period that had eventually led to him getting divorced, and the dalliance had caused friction for some time. In retrospect, Louise wondered if her concern had been tainted with a hint of jealousy. She'd been pleased that both of them had managed to move on from the situation and knew she could rely on them both to be professional.

Louise had called Tracey the previous evening, relaying the information Abbey had provided.

'We're monitoring three potential rival gangs in the Frenchay area at the moment,' said Tracey, uploading images on to the screen in the room. 'Same shit, new faces,' she added, as Louise read through the notes she'd prepared.

'I take it no branding incidents?' said Thomas.

Tracey shook her head, a loose strand of hair falling over her face. 'No one has started marking their customers, as far as I'm aware.'

'Seems counter-intuitive to us as well, but the dealer we pulled in last night was spooked by something,' said Louise.

'There is this,' said Tracey, uploading a series of disturbing images. 'We had a spate of acid attacks in the last six months. Mainly attacks between the gangs, but a couple of civilians were caught in the crossfire. Merrill Joyce, twenty-eight,' said Tracey, an image of a scarred woman appearing on the screen. 'A known user on the estate. Roger Atkins, twenty-five, same estate. As you can imagine, both were reluctant to speak to us. Our intelligence suggests that both victims usually bought their gear from the same dealer in Frenchay, affiliated to the O'Connell family. Both claim they were warned off from buying from the O'Connells again before they were sprayed with the acid. Kind of fits in with Abbey's theory.'

Louise shook her head as she studied the images on the screen. At least with the branding, the scars could be hidden. The lives of the unfortunate people on the screen had been destroyed, most likely because of a pointless war they had little or no part to play in.

'If it was an attack on the O'Connells' clients, do you have an idea who would be responsible for such an attack?'

'As I said, there are two other rival gangs that we know of. The feeling is that the O'Connells are still trading, so the attacks could have been a tit-for-tat thing. Possibly some dispute having to do with these two poor sods.'

Louise knew as well as anyone that managing the drug situation in the city was a cyclical problem that would probably never go away. Dealers came and went. Low-level arrests were made but, as an old boss of hers had once stated, *you can't arrest your way out of a problem*. As soon as a gang of dealers was put away, a new group would appear within days. Because of this, the main goal for investigating teams was finding the large suppliers who smuggled the drugs into the country.

'I've got teams ready to start looking into this for you. We know rumours of these brandings are already circulating around the city. I'll get our team on the ground, start looking for something more concrete for you.'

Although a joint investigation had become almost an inevitability after the second attack, Louise could have done without the involvement of MIT, but if she was going to liaise with anyone, she was pleased it was her old friend. Tracey walked them to their car, the three of them exchanging pleasantries – about Emily, Thomas's son and Tracey's ongoing relationship with a young officer from HQ.

As Thomas got into the car, Tracey pulled her aside. 'Forgot to tell you, I'm coming to that retirement do on Saturday down your way. Please tell me you're going,' she said.

'Three-line whip,' said Louise. She wanted to ask Tracey about Amira but didn't want anyone else involved at this stage.

'Good. Let's meet up for a drink beforehand.'

'Deal,' said Louise, embracing her friend as she heard in the distance the words 'DI Blackwell, a word if I may.'

Tracey pursed her lips. 'Do you want me to stay?' she mouthed.

'It's fine, see you Saturday.'

'Sir,' said Tracey, moving off as Louise turned to face DCI Finch.

'Tim.'

'Louise, a joy as ever. Getting a taste of a real police environment for a change.'

The comment was so petty and childish, but Louise struggled not to react. She could sense Thomas looking at her from the car.

She sighed, involuntarily inhaling a whiff of Finch's aftershave, which made her want to retch. 'What do you want, Tim?'

'You seem to have an interesting case on the go at the moment. You here for our help?'

'DI Pugh was giving us some drug-gang-related advice.'

'Was she now? I heard about that poor girl. Poppy Westfield. Nasty business. Public-relations nightmare. You'll be glad to know I'll be speaking to Assistant Chief Constable Morley this afternoon. See if we can free some staff up for you. How's that niece of yours?'

The onrush of adrenaline in her bloodstream was not welcome. Louise could feel herself shaking and didn't want Finch to know he could provoke such a reaction in her. From anyone else, the last question would have been innocuous. From Finch, it was laced with malice. During the last investigation they'd worked together in Cheddar, Finch had all but threatened the safety of Emily. He'd used the phrase *it would be horrible if something happened to her* with a relish that had resulted in her almost attacking him. She knew it was a game, a ploy to make her lose her cool and do something she shouldn't. But she lost all sense of composure when it came to Emily. She clenched her fists, pulling in air through her nose. Finch wasn't above doing anything if it served his purpose and knew that she understood this.

'Are you worried about something, Timothy?' she asked, trying to wrong-foot him.

The smirk slipped from Finch's face, re-forming a split second later. 'And what have I to be worried about?'

They could have been talking about Louise's forthcoming misconduct meeting. Louise was reminded of Robertson's warning not to bring Finch into the discussion, but the truth was the DCI had let the investigation into her brother's murder slip and if she pushed the point, it could prove problematic for him. The only thing stopping her doing so was the arbitrary nature of her evidence. Finch wasn't stupid enough not to have covered himself, and the fact that they'd eventually found the culprit, albeit because of her, meant that, technically, he had been successful. But was Finch even referring to the hearing? She hated the paranoia he could provoke in her, but she couldn't help wondering if he'd found out that Amira had contacted her. Either way, she wasn't about to get into a debate with him.

'You tell me, Timothy,' she said, opening the passenger side of the car, Finch's smirk remaining fixed on his face as Thomas drove away.

Thomas kept his eyes on the road as Louise controlled the rage storming her body. She told herself not to fixate on Finch. It was what he wanted and she needed to get her mind back on the case. 'What do you think?' she said, as Thomas pulled on to the motorway.

Thomas opened his mouth but didn't say anything.

'About what Tracey said.'

Thomas's shoulders dropped. 'Hard to say at the moment. Same principle, I guess, but I'm not convinced the acid attacks and the branding are related. Do we know if Poppy Westfield is a user?'

'Her friend, Sadie, says they've tried Ecstasy on a few occasions, but nothing beyond that. I guess it's conceivable they tried to buy something that evening. Hopefully we'll get something back from the wider CCTV images later,' said Louise. Like Thomas, her initial thoughts were that the acid attacks and branding weren't linked. The acid attacks were brutal but haphazard, akin to a drive-by shooting. Whereas the branding attacks seemed more personal. There was a terrible intimacy to the attackers' actions. Not only had they taken their time torturing their victims, they'd made a procession of the event. They'd all but hunted Sam Carrigan through the sand dunes and had done the same to Poppy in the park. The idea that their attackers were part of a drug gang warning users only to buy drugs from them didn't ring true. The attackers had taken joy in what they'd done and Louise was convinced there would be more to come.

Louise's police-issued phone rang as they pulled off the M5 into Worle, a number she didn't recognise. 'DI Blackwell,' she said, answering via the car's speakers.

'Suppose you think this is funny, do you?' said a half-familiar voice.

'Mr Mountson?'

'Yes, it's bloody Mr Mountson. What the hell do you think you're playing at?'

'Please calm down, sir, and tell me what the issue is,' said Louise, glancing at Thomas, who was frowning. Like her, it appeared he had a sinking feeling about what Mountson was about to tell them.

'Don't play dumb with me. I have your idiot friends here, trying to close our centre down.'

'Baker,' said Thomas, to himself.

'Tell me exactly what has happened, Mr Mountson.'

'They came here about an hour ago. Had some sort of warrant to search the premises. They now claim to have found drugs within. Dubious to say the least. Now we're told we have to try and rehouse our patients. This is because of last night, I take it? I was just trying to help.'

'This has nothing to do with me. Can you confirm that Mr Carrigan is still at the hospital?'

'I knew this was to do with him. Yes, he's not set to return yet. Won't be able to now.'

'It's not that, Mr Mountson, I just need to check he is OK.'

'This smacks of police targeting to me. One of our patients gets attacked, and days later you're doing a search of our premises? Come on, what's going on?'

'I'm on my way. Please hold tight,' said Louise.

'What the hell is Baker playing at?' she said to Thomas, once she'd hung up.

'It's one hell of a coincidence.'

'Closing the Prism club, and now this? Next he'll start closing all the tattoo parlours in town.'

'You jest . . .'

'Don't,' said Louise, as Thomas turned down the street of the rehab centre, where there was already a strong police presence.

'Is Baker here?' she said to one of the uniformed officers posted outside.

'Through there, ma'am,' said the officer, pointing to the entrance, where Louise saw Baker in a heated conversation with Mountson.

'Here we fucking go,' said Mountson, as Louise and Thomas approached.

'I've already warned you about your language, Mr Mountson. DI Blackwell, DS Ireland,' said Baker.

Baker dwarfed Mountson, who himself was over six feet tall. His body language was particularly severe today, his back so rigidly straight it was as if he were wearing some sort of corset.

'Can I have a word, Dan?' said Louise, nodding to the side of the front garden.

Baker looked surprised by the request but dutifully followed Louise to the spot. 'You know I have an active investigation involving one of the patients here, don't you?' she said.

'Mr Mountson has pointed out that fact, yes,' said Baker.

'You should have already known about it, Dan. Weston isn't that big a place and this is our most high-profile case. Sam Carrigan was attacked the other evening and was branded by his attackers. Don't you think you should have consulted me before raiding the place where he was staying?'

'I apologise if there was an oversight on my part, but we were following a number of tip-offs. This is the second place we've searched today. We have strong evidence to suggest dealers are using this centre to sell their wares. A lead supported by the amount of drugs we have already uncovered, on a simple preliminary search.'

'You found drugs in a drug-rehabilitation centre. Not sure that's happened before,' said Louise, unable to hide her sarcasm.

'You're upset,' said Baker.

Louise took in a deep breath, incredulous that he was trying to patronise her. 'Yes, I'm upset, Dan. Last night you closed the nightclub where Poppy Westfield was last seen before her attack. This morning you're closing the rehab centre housing the first victim. You noticing a pattern here?'

'Coincidence?'

'I don't think so, and even if it is, that's irrelevant. You should have informed me you were coming here.'

'As I said, an oversight. I don't wish to fan the flames, but this does tend to suggest our departments aren't perhaps working together the way they should.'

Louise shook her head. She'd come across similar career officers all her life. Baker was an expert politician, turning an error on his part into something much wider, but she wasn't prepared to put up with it. 'Don't shift the blame, Dan. This is your mess. Where did you get the tip-off?'

'Anonymous.'

'How convenient.'

'It's on record,' said Baker, nonplussed. 'Same person called in last night regarding the Prism nightclub.'

'And what's going to happen to this place now?'

'It will be shut down immediately, following a further investigation.'

'And my victim?'

'Mr Carrigan? He's still at the hospital, I believe.'

'And when he's discharged?'

'We're looking into getting everyone relocated today. If not, they can stay here under our supervision until a place has been found for them.'

Louise wasn't sure if Baker was trying to provoke her. His face was unreadable, his narrow eyes and thin lips hardly moving. She had to remind herself they were on the same team. Baker had been right to follow up his lead, and if the evidence pointed to drugs being sold on the premises, he had to shut the place down. But there was a way of working, and his oversight was causing her concern. For now, she decided to take a collaborative approach, though she was unable to hide her continued anger at the situation. 'We should sit down and talk, Dan. I have some information about the attacks that may be of interest to you,' she said.

Baker's lip twitched, a smile forming. 'That would be wonderful, Louise. And again, please accept my apologies if I have adversely affected your inquiry.'

Chapter Seventeen

She couldn't stop thinking about last night.

Coming back to Weston had been a necessity, a means to close the bad feelings that threatened to hold her back, but watching the policewoman, Louise Blackwell, last night, she'd felt something change within her.

The plan had been to keep a close eye on the woman. Blackwell was obviously the lead detective and they both thought it prudent to keep abreast of her movements. She'd read up on the officer's impressive history and, despite having seen her working on a few occasions since branding Sam Carrigan in the dunes, it was watching her unguarded that had changed her opinion of the woman.

D had driven them to Sand Bay, and together they'd walked through the woodlands until they were in sight of Blackwell's house. At first, she'd pretended they were chasing someone, missing the buzz from the other nights. Imagination was great and everything, but she wanted to hear that rapid breath of the hunt, to feel the anticipation of capturing their prey and the glorious moments that would follow. But soon a different type of elation came over her. Her skin prickled, heat rushing through her body, at the thought that Blackwell was unaware she was being watched.

Louise had arrived back late. The clouds had darkened by then and they'd been able to see little beyond a shadowy outline, but there was something about the way the woman made her way across the pebbled driveway and into the house that captivated her. She'd savoured the tingling of adrenaline in her bloodstream as she'd watched the silhouette of the woman in the top-floor window and imagined the beautiful mark she could place on her skin.

She could have stayed there all night, and if it hadn't been for D she probably would have. Watching was more than an illicit thrill. She couldn't explain her growing obsession, but it had felt right to be there.

And it felt right to be here now.

He'd asked her if she'd wanted to be strapped in, but she'd refused. It would only remind her of what happened, and she was beyond that. She lay down on the massage bed, reluctantly accepting the gag he offered.

Four of the five branding marks on her body had been given by D, each at her request. She told him to put this one beneath those four; the other mark merely scar tissue on her upper-right shoulder, now covered by the tattoo on her back.

Sweat broke out of every pore on her body as D lit up the blowtorch. 'Are you sure?' he whispered, like the child he could sometimes be, like he didn't know her at all. There was a risk in adding a new mark so soon. The mark D had given her after the night at the dunes was still healing, but she couldn't wait any longer.

'Do it,' she said, her body shaking involuntarily as he heated the iron, the delicious smell of burning metal filling the enclosed space of their bedroom.

She screamed as he placed the metal on to her flesh, the tears flooding her face almost as hot as the branding iron, as the pain sent her into a delirium. She withdrew deep into herself, her body an outer shell where every nerve ending was on fire.

She must have passed out, for when she opened her eyes the pain was a distant thud on her lower back.

'I gave you something. You were hyperventilating,' said D.

She was too tired to argue. She was still on her front, D tending to her back like a nurse. 'How does it look?' she said, breathless.

D arranged the mirrors so she could see. She grimaced as the faded L symbol on her shoulder came into view, only to smile when he showed her the new mark, her mark on her lower back beneath the others. It was red-raw now but would soothe into something beautiful. She would only have to touch it to be reminded of Poppy, and that wonderful night in the park.

The thought sent a shiver through her body. She pushed herself off the massage chair and said, 'Let's get ready for tonight.'

Chapter Eighteen

Louise stopped at a garage on her way back to the station. The forecourt was filled with SUVs, day tourists making the most of the August weather. Two children, dressed in swimsuits and lathered with sun cream, were ahead of her in the queue, their hands filled with sweets. As she ordered her second ready-made sandwich in as many days, Louise realised she had no idea what Emily and her family were up to today. She'd grown used to having a more active role in Emily's upbringing, and was thrown by her ignorance. She wanted to call her parents and tell them she would be home for a family dinner that evening, but with the way things were progressing, she couldn't offer any false hope.

Still reeling from her meeting with Baker and her earlier confrontation with Finch, Louise called the family-liaison officer who'd been looking after Poppy Westfield and her family.

'She seems physically better but she hasn't left her room. As you would expect, the parents are going through it, especially the mum,' said the FLO.

Louise tried to remain detached. Being professional meant not getting personally involved, but the incidents with Sam and Poppy were having a harder-than-normal effect on her. She'd seen much worse than this before, but something about the terrible intimacy of the branding resonated with her. It was effectively torture, and the long-lasting effects, both physical and psychological, would be immense. 'Are they speaking to you much?'

'As much as you'd expect. You can sense the tension in the house, as if they're about to turn on each other and possibly me.'

Louise thanked the FLO and hung up. Nursing her first coffee since being at headquarters, Louise considered speaking to Robertson about Baker's behaviour. She didn't want to tell tales and knew such action risked making her appear weak in Robertson's eyes, but she wondered if her concerns needed to be put on record. In the end, she decided to give Baker the benefit of the doubt. He'd asked that they work more closely together and she was willing to give him that chance.

As for her concerns over Finch, they too were better left for another time. Finch wanted her to kick up a fuss and she wasn't about to make it easy for him. For now, ignoring him was the best move. Something had rattled him, and she was happy to wait and see what he would decide to do next.

She turned to her massive to-do pile, dismissing everything not linked to the branding case. She began by reviewing the CCTV images her team had worked through. As she'd been informed, the videos from the club were all but useless. The low-definition images weren't even in colour, and she couldn't make out any of the figures. She stopped it at one point, thinking she might have seen Poppy talking in a huddle with her friends, but it was impossible to tell.

The team had managed to collate some images of Poppy and her friends in town, walking along Regent Street. The young women had already listed the bars they'd been to and the owners and staff had been questioned. A list had been compiled of known criminals who'd been in the area that evening and the team were questioning everyone they could, but it still didn't feel enough.

The manner of Sam's and Poppy's attacks suggested that the attackers knew their victims, or at least had singled them out for targeting. Blood tests had been returned and traces of the date-rape drug Rohypnol had been found in both Sam's and Poppy's bloodstreams. It suggested that both had been drugged and then somehow transported – Sam to the beach, Poppy to the park. That took some planning. It also meant that the attackers had to have been nearby. In Poppy's case, Louise thought that at least one of them had to have been in the club with her.

Unfortunately, she couldn't rule out another possibility: that a third person, possibly the man who'd sold the pills to Sam, was also involved. Abbey had denied being present at the bar on the night of Sam's attack, and so far witness reports from the bar, and Sam's testimony, backed this up.

Thomas brought her over another coffee as she viewed double-speed footage from the cameras situated on the roads leading to the club.

'I've been doing some research on this scarification stuff,' said Thomas, sitting on the edge of her desk. 'I might have found somewhere in Bristol that offers branding as a service.'

Louise paused the video and looked up at Thomas, the darkness beneath his eyes suggesting his sleep had been as deprived as Louise's. 'I'm pretty sure we're still viewing this activity as illegal?' she said.

'That seems to be the guidance. The place doesn't out and out say they do it, but there are images on their site.'

'Show me,' said Louise, standing so Thomas could access her laptop.

The website images appeared generic to Louise. There were examples of tattooing, piercing, ear modification and branding she was sure she'd come across during her own research. 'I know I must be way out of touch, and shouldn't judge, but why would anyone do this to themselves?' she said, viewing an image of a woman with elongated ear lobes that dangled to her shoulders, her tattooed neck leading to a branded image of the word *LOST* on her breastbone.

'It looks quite extreme to me as well,' said Thomas. 'I guess we're past it, boss.'

'Speak for yourself.'

'Shall I set something up?'

'Let me finish up here and we can pay them a surprise visit together.' She took one last look at the image on her screen. She tried to see some beauty in the raised skin on the woman's breastbone and took some comfort from the fact that the woman was smiling and that she'd had the modifications because she'd wanted them.

Reloading the CCTV images, Louise paused when she caught sight of a man entering Richmond Street at 11.30 p.m. on the night of Poppy's attack. The image was grainy and she couldn't make out his face, but the two seconds she caught of the man's gait reminded her of David Mountson. She called Thomas over to verify.

'Well, he's got a beard, I'll give you that,' said Thomas.

Louise scratched the back of her head. Was she looking for something that wasn't there? Thomas was correct, of course, but that didn't make it easier. 'You can get me another drink for that,' she said.

She watched the video again after Thomas had returned with a lukewarm coffee. Perhaps she was searching for something that wasn't there, but the man in the footage moved like Mountson, as if he wasn't completely confident in his body, in particular his towering height.

She called a member of her team, asking them to forward the research that had been conducted on Mountson's social accounts. Mountson wasn't particularly active but he had a Facebook account with images that went back over the last ten years. Louise scrolled back through his timeline, trying to find some connection between the static images and the blurred video that might have been of the man.

The beard was a constant, as was his awkwardness in front of the camera. Most of the images were of him with other men, mainly with a similar dress sense. For someone who managed a drug-rehab centre, there were a surprising number of pictures with people drinking alcohol. In one photo, Mountson was arm in arm with another man, both of them holding huge steins of lager. The picture was dated three years ago, within the period Mountson had been managing the centre.

'Are we going then, boss?' said Thomas, waving his car keys in front of her.

The noise of the jangling metal distracted her and she almost missed it. Scrolling back further, she caught another image of Mountson with a man. She zoomed in. The resolution wasn't great, but it was clear enough for her to be sure. 'Look at this,' she said, turning the laptop round so Thomas could see.

'Whose arm is that?' said Thomas, looking at the L shape branded on to the forearm of Mountson's friend.

'I don't know,' said Louise. 'But I'm sure Mr Mountson can help us find out.'

Chapter Nineteen

Mountson wasn't at the rehab centre, or at the address they had for him. 'An odd thing for him to have omitted,' said Louise, scrolling through the images on her phone as Thomas drove them to Bristol.

'I suppose it's not really the kind of thing you forget,' said Thomas.

'Your friend having a branded symbol on their forearm? No, not something that would slip your memory, especially if a person under your care has just had the same thing forcibly done to them.'

Louise called the station and requested that Uniform watch Mountson's building and notify her as soon as he returned. She was trying to reconcile the information they had on the man. It wasn't unusual for counsellors to be former addicts – in fact, it was common – but it was unusual for them to be drinking alcohol. A concern intensified by the fact that Mountson was temporarily AWOL.

'You thinking Mountson may have been dealing drugs out of the rehab centre?' said Thomas.

'It's a question I'd like to ask him.'

They made good time to the tattoo parlour, situated down a side road in Bedminster, south Bristol. The man who greeted them as they entered the building reminded Louise of a club doorman. He was a good six-four, his rounded chest merging with his stomach to create a giant mound of flesh that, despite him being overweight, looked solid. She wasn't surprised to see he was covered in tattoos. The skin of his left arm was a canvas of ink. Louise was impressed by the image of a rose entwined with a lion, the piercing blue eyes of the lion in stark contrast to the dark colours on the rest of the design. His right arm was more of a hotchpotch of designs, the faded colours and inferior detail suggesting they were much older. Like the photographs she'd seen on the website, he had discs in his ears known as flesh tunnels; his earlobes stretched down three or four inches. Folding his thick, muscled arms across his chest, increasing his already considerable size, he destroyed the tough-guy look by beaming a smile at them. 'Good afternoon, how may I help you?' he said, his accent broad Bristolian.

The smile faded as Louise and Thomas introduced themselves. 'I was wondering if we'd get a visit from you at some point. What's this about?'

'Why did you think you'd get a visit from us?' asked Louise.

'Happening all over. Councils trying to close us down 'cause they don't understand.'

'We're not here to close you down. Some of the procedures you advertise on your website are of questionable legality, though,' said Thomas.

'Questionable legality,' said the man, as if the words were new to him.

'You may have read about the incidents in Weston?' said Louise.

The man lowered his eyes. 'Awful. That man, and that poor girl. I just read about her in the *Post*. Some monsters out there.'

'You offer branding services here?' said Thomas.

The man frowned. 'What you getting at?'

'Nothing,' said Louise. 'We're looking for some advice. See what we're working with here. You're not going to incriminate yourself, but you've offered scarification before? Branding, in particular. Perhaps before the law changed?' she added, trying to keep him onside.

'To consenting patrons, yes.'

'Can you tell me a bit more about it? Why do people have it done? Is it painful, that sort of thing?'

'May I?' said the man, taking off his shirt to reveal a torso with no visible untainted skin. The motif from his arm was repeated, the image of a lion filling the man's torso. 'What can I say, I like lions,' he said, turning around to show them the branding marks on his left shoulder blade. 'My initials. I know, not very original. I was trying to be ironic. You know, when your mum used to write your name in your coat, that sort of thing. You can touch it if you want.'

Louise stared at the raised skin, the initials MB protruding like a growth, but declined the offer to touch. 'And what is your name, sir?'

The man put his shirt back on, his endearing smile returning. 'Mason Brown. My wife did it, before you ask. We did consider putting her initials on me, but it felt a bit disrespectful, you know.'

Louise shook her head. 'Not exactly, no.'

'Well, branding has been used on humans for centuries. Criminals used to get branded so you knew what they'd done, that sort of a thing. Round here, of course, we used to have a horrendous slave trade. Colston, and all those wankers. They used to brand their slaves. Utter bastards. Didn't seem right to put someone else's initials on me, so did my own. I love them.'

'If you don't mind me asking, why do it?'

'It's like the ink. People do it for various reasons. For me, it's partly an identity thing, but it's also like a shield. It changes me, both on the outside and in. Every time I have something done, it's like a barrier to the outside world. Probably doesn't make sense if you haven't had it done,' he said, mirroring the words Louise had heard from the woman at the tattoo parlour in Weston.

'Must be painful?' said Thomas.

The man shrugged. 'Different pain thresholds. I may or may not have used a little anaesthetic,' he said, offering Louise a smile.

'I realise it's an awkward question, but have you ever heard of this being done to someone without their consent?'

'Not since the slave owners, no. I've never met an artist who doesn't take their work seriously. Even more so with those who work on modification, scarification in particular. We knew the consent issue would be a thing at some point so everyone was always meticulous. And why the hell would you do this to someone if they didn't want it to happen?'

Mason Brown's last response played through Louise's mind as they made their way back to Weston. As Thomas drove, she conducted more research on historical branding. She'd read up before about the use of branding on criminals, and in the slave trade. She also knew that similar procedures were used in modern-day human trafficking. Victims were often tattooed with identifying marks, like cattle. It made the theory espoused by Ben Abbey – that the drug dealers were marking their customers – sound almost feasible. Maybe if they were doing it as a warning to others, she could buy into it, but it still didn't ring true. Sam Carrigan had told her how his pursuers had been laughing. And although this didn't rule out the possibility that a drug gang was responsible, she still felt that the attacks were more personal in nature.

'Drop me back at the station. And then you should head home for some rest,' she said to Thomas, as they reached the outskirts of Weston.

'Is that what you're going to do?'

'Not exactly.'

'Maybe you should go home and see your lovely niece?'

Louise sighed. 'That would be nice. But I want to track down Mountson and find out about this photo.'

'Then why don't we do that together?'

'You sure?' she said.

'There'll be time enough to rest when we're dead,' said Thomas.

Louise was pleased he'd agreed to help. The early days of these types of cases were usually the most pivotal. She put guilty thoughts about abandoning Emily and her family to the side. When they'd lived in different towns, weeks would often go by without her seeing her niece, even though she'd tried to see her at least every weekend; she was sure she would be forgiven for not seeing her for a couple of days.

As Thomas searched for a spot outside the rehab centre, Louise's phone rang. It was Amira. The letters AH appeared on the screen of the in-dash computer. Louise declined the call on her phone. Thomas didn't take his eyes from the road.

Louise trusted Thomas implicitly. She'd decided not to tell him about Amira's plans as she didn't want to burden him. The less he knew, the better. Time was running out for Amira, and she would do everything in her power to help, but the second Thomas heard about her plans, he would be complicit, and the last thing she wanted was to risk his career.

She sent a text to Amira after leaving the car, suggesting they talk later, before walking up the path to the rehab centre, where she recognised the uniformed officer, Sarah Millard, who'd been monitoring Sam Carrigan at the hospital.

'You here alone, Sarah?'

'Inspector Baker asked me to monitor everyone leaving. Waiting on one more person, ma'am.'

'They didn't waste any time. Has David Mountson returned at any point?'

'No, ma'am. He'd left by the time I came on shift but I was told to call you if he returned.'

Louise tried Mountson's phone, but there was no answer.

'His flat?' asked Thomas.

Louise nodded. Hindsight was wonderful, but she wished she'd searched through Mountson's social-media files sooner. Unsurprisingly, he wasn't at his flat, so with Thomas's agreement they headed for an address Louise had obtained for Mountson's parents. 'This, then we're going home for the night. I can't face another forecourt sandwich for dinner.'

'Deal,' said Thomas.

It took them twenty minutes to reach the Mountson household, a quaint, detached cottage in Uphill village. 'Not what I was expecting,' said Thomas, as he knocked on the front door.

The sea was visible from the cottage's porch. The sun was setting, fiery colours settling over the rippling water. It was a peaceful place, the breeze light with the scent of the distant water.

'They're on holiday,' came a voice from behind the hedge to the side of the building. 'Sorry, the Mountsons, on holiday.' The source of the voice, an elderly man with thinning grey hair, stuck his head out from behind the hedge.

'Anywhere nice?' asked Louise, introducing herself and Thomas.

'Greece. Should be back in a couple of weeks.'

'We're actually trying to locate their son, David,' said Louise.

The man frowned. 'What's he done now?'

'Oh, nothing. We just needed his help on something.'

'Well, I'm not sure if that's really the case, but I'm afraid I can't help you anyway. I'm good friends with Linda and George – the Mountsons – and they haven't seen their son for a number of years. Estranged, I believe the term is. Breaks your heart, it really does.'

'I'm sorry to hear that, Mr . . .'

'Groves. Tragic, really. He was such a lovely boy. I remember the day he was born, would you believe? To see them go from being all innocent to what became of him.'

'And what became of him, Mr Groves?'

'Classic story of joining the wrong crowd. I was a school-teacher. A head teacher, in fact. Seen it all. You can never know for sure the path they'll take. In David's case, it didn't matter that he had such wonderful parents. They couldn't stop it happening to him, and they tried, believe me.'

'And what did happen to him?'

'Drugs. You probably know better than I do, but the town's aflood with them. I don't know the specific details – I don't like to pry, you know – but he got in trouble at school to begin with. Then he started missing days, and before you know it he was a full-blown addict. A junkie, they call it.'

'He was at your school, Mr Groves?' asked Thomas.

Groves recoiled as if Thomas had sworn at him. 'Heavens, no,' he said, as if anything so unbecoming could happen under his watch.

'Mr Mountson got his life back on track, though, didn't he?' said Louise. 'He works at a rehab centre now, helping people who'd suffered the same problems as him.'

'What same problems? He chose what he did.'

'It's not as simple as that, Mr Groves,' said Louise, regretting getting into a debate with the man. 'This is a bit of a long shot, but would you happen to know the other person in this photo?' she added, handing Groves her phone with the image of Mountson and the second man with the branding on his arm.

Groves frowned, clearly unhappy about being corrected. He pulled out a pair of spectacles from his top pocket and looked at the image, mumbling to himself.

'What was that?' asked Thomas.

'Yes, I know him. He went to my school until he was expelled. I tried to warn the Mountsons about him. He was here all the time, leading young David astray. Goes by the name of Laurence Dwyer. Nasty piece of work.'

'What was he expelled for?'

Groves clenched his teeth. 'He was selling drugs in the school. The second we found out about it, he was gone,' he said, as if personally affronted by these past events.

'Do you happen to know where Dwyer lives?'

'Haven't seen him for years. I heard he's still up to his old tricks, though. Now, if you don't mind, my dinner is on the stove.'

'You're going back into the station, aren't you?' said Thomas, as he dropped Louise at the station car park.

'Quick check on this Dwyer character, then I'll be straight home, promise,' said Louise.

'I was going to suggest we go for a drink,' said Thomas. 'Been a tough day.'

'Oh,' said Louise. They'd often gone for a drink together after work, but there was something in the way that he spoke this time, a slight hesitation that suggested it might be more than just drinks. 'That's a great idea, and normally I would, it's just I need to find out some more details or I won't be able to rest,' she went on, hearing how flustered she sounded as the words left her mouth. Maybe it was all in her imagination, but she'd felt closer to Thomas over the last few days. She reminded herself of the promise she'd made to herself not to get directly involved with anyone in work but still felt her cheeks redden. 'I'm still on for Saturday, though,' she blurted out, hoping she sounded more composed than she felt.

Thomas lifted his hands up and smiled. 'Do you want me to come and help?'

'No, no. One of us gets an early night. I'll see you in the morning,' said Louise, leaving the car before he had time to object.

Chapter Twenty

Andrew Thorpe couldn't believe his luck.

Up until this point, the whole evening had been a washout; his fault really, for going anywhere in Weston on a Thursday evening. Even at the height of the season, a Thursday was usually a lost cause. They still came out, but he always felt as if they were holding back, as if waiting for the weekend.

Not that he hadn't got close. He'd been chatting to a couple of them in the pub, and they'd come with him to the club. One was a minger, but her mate was fit. He'd danced with them for over an hour before realising they were more into each other than they were into him. That hadn't stopped him persevering, but he could spot a lost cause, and gave up. He spent the last hour of the night hitting shots and chasing any girl he could find.

He'd left the club alone and was consoling himself that the weekend was still to come when he spotted her sitting alone by a shopfront on the Boulevard. 'You don't want to sit there all alone this time of night,' he said, stopping, his arms stretching across the width of the opening.

'You're probably right,' said the girl, standing upright.

'Hey, don't I know you?' he said. The girl was pretty. Short, but pretty. She had the leather, punk-type-look going. Purple hair, heavy make-up, but she was definitely a looker. Maybe it was the alcohol talking, but her eyes were huge and welcoming. She seemed to be appraising him back and seemed to like what she saw. She looked familiar, but so many girls did nowadays.

'I don't think so.'

He studied her further. Something about those eyes, and her full lips. Had they slept together before? It wasn't inconceivable. He'd been playing this game for so long now that it could have happened. 'You were in the Boar earlier?'

'I was. Didn't know I had an admirer,' she said, with a sly smile.

Thorpe focused on the ink on the woman's neck. 'What's that?' he said, pointing to the tattoo snaking up from her collarbone.

'A manitou,' she said.

'What's that mean?' said Thorpe.

'Walk me up the road and I'll explain.'

Had she explained? He couldn't quite remember. They'd stopped at a chicken shop, where she'd convinced the guy behind the counter to sell them some cans of lager. He'd made a note of the place – a handy reference for the future – and once again he had the feeling that he knew her from somewhere.

The next thing he knew, they'd been sitting in the back of a taxi. At least, he thought it was a taxi. He couldn't remember ordering it. That was right, she had an app on her phone and the cab had appeared after a few minutes. When he'd asked what app it was she'd just given him that smile that was at once seductive and reminiscent.

'Here, drink some more,' she said now, handing him one of the cans and rushing him back into the present.

'Where are we going?' he asked.

'Back to my place, silly,' she said, her eyes locked on to his as he took a swig of the warm lager.

Thorpe looked outside, but his eyes were blurred. The windows were tinted, and all he could make out were shadowy outlines of trees. 'Where do you live?' he said, his neck craning to get a look at the driver – the glimpse of the man's eyes in the rear-view mirror enough to make him sit back in his seat. 'What's going on?'

'What do you mean, sweetie?' said the girl, as the car swerved to the right and took an off-road track.

'I think I'd like to get out now,' said Thorpe, a weakness coming over him that he feared wasn't linked to the copious amounts of drink he'd consumed that evening.

'In a minute,' said the driver.

The driver pulled the car to a stop and turned to look over at him. His face was half-covered behind an unkempt beard, but in the half-light of the car the man's skin looked discoloured. Thorpe wasn't sure what he was seeing but there was something off about his face. He wasn't sure if the man was scarred, but there were lines on his face that weren't . . . natural. Then he remembered where he'd seen the man before.

The driver smiled. 'Nice to see you again, Andrew.'

'What's that?' asked Thorpe, as the man took out a canister from the boot of the car.

'This is your salvation,' said the man.

Thorpe considered running, but every time he moved he felt dizzy. 'What do you want?' he said to the girl. The smile was still there, but the seductiveness – if it had ever been there – had faded from her eyes.

Thorpe didn't much care for its replacement.

'It's not what we want, Andrew, it's what you want,' she said.

'What does that mean?' said Thorpe, a feeling worse than fear rushing his body at the sight of the blowtorch.

'You like young girls, don't you, Andrew?' said the man.

'Come on, man, I'm in my twenties.'

'You're twenty-nine, Andrew.'

'So?'

Thorpe didn't know what the hell the man was talking about, but he understood the tone. Had he finally pissed off the wrong person? He tried to think back to the girls he'd slept with recently, but the names never stayed. He'd got into scrapes before. Jealous boyfriends, husbands even. Once he'd stayed at a girl's house, only to be attacked in the morning by an irate father, who'd, thankfully, been restrained by a mortified-looking wife. But this – never this. 'Whatever I've done, I'm sorry. I never meant to hurt anyone,' said Thorpe.

'How about Poppy Westfield?' said the man.

'Poppy?' Poppy, he did remember. She was stunning and . . . How long had that been – two, three years ago? 'What about her?'

'You tainted her, Andrew, and now you'll have to pay,' said the man, lighting the blowtorch.

The sound of the blue flame was enough for Thorpe to soil himself. He fell on his knees and pleaded to the girl, who placed her hand on the man's arm. 'Thank you,' said Thorpe, looking at the woman as the man switched off the flame.

'You don't even remember me, do you?' said the girl.

This got Thorpe's attention. If only he could remember, he could understand what he did wrong. If he knew that, maybe he could get out of this situation. 'I'm sorry. You look familiar, but . . .'

'I'm a bit older now, maybe that's why. But I was always invisible to you, wasn't I?'

'I'm sorry if I ever did anything to hurt you. But . . .' Thorpe felt the heat seep down his legs as the woman glanced at her watch.

'This is the bit I like best,' she said. 'Shall we say five minutes?'

'I don't understand,' said Thorpe.

She pointed to the woods, to the unfathomable darkness he struggled to focus on. 'You've got five minutes, Andrew. Best start running.'

Chapter Twenty-One

Louise was pleased to see that the CID department was deserted. Being alone in the open-plan office usually filled her with optimism. It reminded her of being the first to arrive in the morning, the day filled with possibilities. Now she had to deal with the familiar sense of frustration. Things felt like they might be starting to fall into place, but they still knew too little. What she feared most was a third attack – that was why she was working so hard – though she had to concede it was all but inevitable, unless they found those responsible.

At the moment, the closest they had to a suspect was David Mountson, and that still felt like a long shot. Perhaps he might fear retribution, but surely Sam Carrigan would have noticed that one of his attackers was the manager from his rehab centre, even if he was wearing a mask.

She logged on to her laptop and scanned her messages. Tracey had sent a message with an update on her investigations into the O'Connell gang. She'd attached details of the acid-attack victims they'd discussed that morning. The images were no less harrowing viewed for a second time. The parallel between these attacks and the branding was obvious, but Louise wasn't convinced they were related. The acid attacks were haphazard and disorganised, whereas what had happened to both Sam and Poppy appeared meticulous and planned.

The uneasy truth was that there didn't necessarily have to be a reason behind the attacks. They could look for motive all they wanted, but sometimes people did horrendous things to each other for the sake of it, for some twisted satisfaction that couldn't be imagined, as with Max Walton. If that was the case, then the investigation would prove to be even harder than it was at present.

Louise called Amira as she ran a search on David Mountson's friend, Lawrence Dwyer. 'Sorry I couldn't answer earlier,' she said.

'No problem. I wasn't sure if you were still on duty,' said Amira.

'Everything OK, Amira?' said Louise, noting a sense of despondency in the young officer.

'Terri Marsden has pulled out.'

'Pulled out?'

'She no longer wants to go ahead with pursuing Finch.'

'She's probably just a bit scared. Talk to her again,' said Louise.

'I did. I spent all afternoon with her. You're right, she is scared. She told me that bastard had sent her another text a few hours after meeting us.'

'What was on it?'

'It was one of the pictures he'd taken of her. Nothing else, but sent to her phone. She opened it up when she was out having coffee with some friends. He must be on to us,' said Amira.

With everything going on, this was the last thing Louise needed. She felt guilty for thinking like that, even more so to be relieved that Finch didn't have any photos of her. Did he know they were on to him, and had he known when she'd seen him at HQ? 'Has he sent you anything?'

'No, but this can't be a coincidence.'

Louise rubbed her eyes. She needed to sleep, was no good to anyone in her current lacklustre state. 'I agree. But let's think about this rationally. If he's warning her off, it means he's at least a little bit afraid. Did Terri keep the message on her phone?'

'Yes. It was mortifying for her, but she said she would keep it for now.'

'OK. Go and speak to her tomorrow and see if you can get the phone from her. I know someone in Tech who may be able to help us.'

Louise left her desk. Despite the late hour, she made some coffee, trying to distract her mind. She hated the visceral reaction she had just thinking of Finch. Her mind should have been fully focused on the branding case but now all she could think about was him. She could almost smell his citric aftershave in the air, and she wouldn't be that surprised if he appeared from the shadows. It felt inconceivable that Terri receiving a message shortly after Amira had met with her was a coincidence. And if he was on to Amira, it was likely he knew Louise had some involvement. Louise wasn't bothered by that in itself, but it would make things harder. After what had happened at the Walton farm, she knew there were no lengths to which he wouldn't go to protect himself.

After pouring coffee, she called Simon Coulson, one of the techies from MIT, and arranged to meet him on Saturday morning. Coulson had proved himself reliable and discreet on a number of occasions, and she felt able to trust him. All she had to do now was decide whether to get Tracey involved.

The warning Finch had given Amira meant there was just over three weeks until Amira had to hand in her resignation or face the consequences. It was such a limited timeline that Louise considered calling Finch's bluff. But it wasn't pictures of her that he was holding.

Coulson was a tech wizard. If anyone could find some evidence on Finch, then Coulson was the person to do it. She told herself there was little she could do until then and turned her attention to the branding case, running searches on Laurence Dwyer.

It didn't take long for the matches to flood in. As the old schoolteacher had suggested, Dwyer had been getting into trouble since his teenage years. He had a string of arrests to his name. Although mainly possession charges that had resulted in cautions, five years ago Dwyer had been charged with GBH for a glassing incident at a bar in the Westbury area of Bristol, though the case had eventually fallen through.

She read the reports, but the words had stopped making sense. The coffee was only serving to make her hyper, and she shut her laptop off after printing up an address for Dwyer's parents in Whitchurch, south Bristol.

The pubs were kicking out as she drove home. A few rowdy revellers were making their way to the clubs, or at least those establishments Baker had yet to shut down. They looked younger every year, the girls in their short skirts, the boys in their tight jeans and sockless shoes. Louise wasn't envious of their youth, but as two young couples made their way in front of her at the pedestrian crossing opposite the Grand Pier, she was taken by how carefree they were. Giggling and bouncing along the road and down on to the beach.

Maybe she should have accepted Thomas's invitation earlier, whatever the potential difficulties. It was an old argument she seemed to continually be having with herself. Everything was so centred around her career it was as if her real life was on permanent hold. For someone so willing to take risks at work, her private life was one lacking in adventure. She liked Thomas and was attracted to him, but was it enough to jeopardise their working relationship? Or was it another complication she could do without?

It was no way to live. She was always putting things off, telling herself that once a case was over she would try something new. But there was always another case, and the time had come to move on with her life.

By the time she reached home she barely had the strength to leave the car. The last few days had taken their toll and she briefly considered sleeping behind the wheel. In the end she dragged herself outside, enjoying the sense of peace in the quiet surroundings of the house. In the distance she could hear the sea, the sound of the gentle lapping water bringing her a sense of optimism.

Inside the house, she went straight to her room and collapsed on the bed. When her phone rang five hours later, she was still fully dressed.

Chapter Twenty-Two

Louise's fears about the branding case escalating into murder had been realised. It took a ten-minute drive to reach the crime scene, the body conveniently placed in the car park of Weston Woods in Worlebury Hill Road. The area had been cordoned off, a tent erected over the body, the SOCOs in their white suits already at work.

Louise was the first member of CID at the scene. She didn't wait for Thomas, changing into a SOCO uniform so she could view the victim without a risk of contaminating the scene. As she was pulling the full-body suit over her clothes, Janice Sutton walked over and showed Louise a wallet, wrapped in an evidence bag, retrieved from the victim. 'Andrew Thorpe, aged twenty-nine,' she said.

'Do we have an idea of cause of death yet?' asked Louise, taking the bag, the smiling face of a young man, possibly of Mediterranean heritage, looking back from the plastic prison.

'I can confirm it's one of your branding victims,' said Janice, turning her camera around to the view screen.

It was hard to reconcile the smiling man with the lifeless images Louise scrolled through. She zoomed in on the image of the man's face and turned to Janice for confirmation.

Janice nodded. 'He's been branded on the forehead,' she said. 'It looks like a two to me.'

'This wouldn't have killed him?' said Louise, horrified but unable to look away from the images on the screen.

'Probably not in itself. But the trauma may have triggered something else. We haven't seen any other possible causes yet. Obviously we'll know more when Dempsey arrives.'

Dempsey was the county pathologist. Louise had had a one-night stand with the man when she'd first moved to Weston, and ever since their working relationship had been strained.

Following Janice into the tent, Louise took some deep breaths, fighting the initial feeling of claustrophobia she always experienced in such close confines. The scene was being videoed by a second SOCO, Thorpe going through the final indignities of being processed by the team.

'He was found on his back like this?' asked Louise.

Janice squinted. 'A dog walker, would you believe?'

It was somewhat of a cliché, but the truth was it was so often a dog walker who found murder victims. Louise had once been part of a multi-departmental search for a murder victim involving specialist air and ground teams only for a dog walker to find the victim, many miles away from the area they'd been searching.

'He said he didn't touch or move the body,' added Janice, as Louise looked down at the corpse.

Even in death, the mark on Thorpe's forehead looked painful. The wound appeared deeper than the others, as if the attacker had been pushing the branding iron through the skin and flesh, aiming for the bone. 'He was alive when this happened to him?'

'The bleeding around the wound suggests it was ante mortem, though Dempsey will have to confirm,' said Janice.

'And this was the cause of death?'

The SOCO shrugged, suggesting Louise should know better than to ask for hypotheticals. Louise stared at the corpse, trying not to imagine the panic the man would have experienced as the branding iron was brought towards his head. 'Any signs of restraint?'

'Not that we can see. Were the other victims drugged?'

'Traces of Rohypnol.'

'That could be your answer, then. If he was given something it could have had a paralysing effect.'

'So he was unable to move while that thing was made on his forehead?'

'Depends what he was given. Not enough to try and prevent it, by the looks of it. Any idea of the significance of the two?'

'Not yet, only that it's a constant. Not sure if it's a two or a swan symbol.'

'Could be a swan, I suppose. Signing their work?' said Janice.

'If I had a suspect with a name beginning with an S, I'd be on to a winner,' said Louise. 'That said, at this stage, any real suspect would be a bonus.'

Janice gave a supportive nod of the head before placing the camera to her eye to take some more photos.

The body wasn't removed from the scene until the afternoon, Dempsey's arrival delayed by two hours due to a suspected suicide he'd attended on the other side of Cheddar. By the afternoon, an incident room had been set up in the station. The Thorpe death was now an active murder investigation. The picture of Thorpe took centre stage. Beneath his photo were smaller images of Poppy Westfield and Sam Carrigan alongside images of the matching branding marks.

'Strange to think they're the lucky ones,' said Thomas, handing Louise a coffee.

'We need to visit them both again,' said Louise. Sam and Poppy had each claimed not to have known the other, and Louise needed to know if either had a connection to Andrew Thorpe.

'I can go and visit Carrigan now in his new centre, if you're happy visiting Poppy?' said Thomas.

Louise nodded. 'See if anyone has heard from David Mountson at the rehab centre when you're there as well.'

Finding Mountson was now a priority. That he'd gone AWOL so close to Thorpe's death was more than a worry, especially considering the image they'd uncovered of Mountson's friend, Laurence Dwyer, and the branding mark on his arm. It wasn't the sort of thing that would have slipped Mountson's mind, and Louise could only assume he'd purposely withheld the information from her.

'Let me know once you've questioned Carrigan. I'd like to pay Laurence Dwyer a visit before the end of the day, if we can find him.'

Louise was about to leave when Inspector Baker buzzed through into the office. The effect was of a headmaster appearing in a classroom. A hush descended over the room, as if everyone could sense the tension between Louise and the new inspector. 'Everything OK, Dan?' said Louise.

'Hi, Louise. I heard about your latest victim. I wanted to see if I can offer my help in any way.'

Louise fought the childish urge to accuse Baker of being nosey. 'I appreciate that, Dan,' she said, sighing inwardly as Baker moved towards the crime board with the images of the victims.

'Terrible business,' he said, shaking his head. The man towered over her, Louise not even reaching his shoulders. 'Some sort of vigilante?' he asked, not looking away from the board.

Again, Louise had to bite her tongue. She always welcomed the assistance of everyone in the station. By their very nature, these cases were a cross-departmental affair. Intelligence could come from the unlikeliest of sources and Louise enjoyed being part of a larger team, but something about Baker's manner irked her. It was as if he was placing himself at the centre of everything when, in reality, this wasn't part of his job, and the closure of the nightclub and the rehab centre still grated. She considered saying, 'Maybe you should return to closing down the local bars, Dan', but knew it would make her sound weak and paranoid. Instead, she said, 'What makes you think it's a vigilante?'

Baker stuck out his bottom lip. 'It was just a thought, really. The first victim is a drug dealer?'

'No, he's a drug addict. And the other two victims, including Mr Thorpe, don't have a criminal record.'

'My mistake. Do we know the significance of these marks, though? You know that up to the late nineteenth century we used to brand criminals. Maybe there is some significance there?'

'Maybe, Dan. It's one of many angles we're looking at right now.'

Baker slowly turned towards her. 'I see. Well, don't let me take up any more of your time.'

Louise walked him back to the office door as if to make sure he was going to leave.

'Couldn't have come at a worse time,' said Baker, as he buzzed open the door.

'Not for Mr Thorpe, no,' said Louise.

'Insensitive of me, I know. It's just with the gathering tomorrow, it's a shame that the attention will be on these attacks and not on the good work we're doing here as a station at the moment.'

Louise didn't comment as Baker walked stiffly away. She wasn't sure if he'd meant to be antagonising, but it was hard not to take what he'd said as a barbed comment.

Louise tried to put Baker's remark to the back of her mind as she left the station. Friday afternoon, and the weekend tourists were already making their way into the town centre. Louise envied their ignorance. Maybe it was her lack of sleep, but the recent events were playing on her mind. In her role, she'd trained herself to become professionally detached from events, but it wasn't always that easy. She found herself struggling to get past the horrendous injuries inflicted on Sam and Poppy; the branding inflicted on Thorpe's forehead felt to her like the final insult. Thorpe's parents had turned up at the scene, and she'd been helpless as she'd watched their reactions. The indelible mark would last for ever in their memories and there was a risk that the image would become a matter of public record, that Thorpe would be remembered as the man with the mark on his forehead; whatever that mark meant.

She'd seen so much in her time – faces and bodies mutilated beyond recognition – that these events shouldn't be having the effect they were. But when the door to the Westfield residence was opened and she saw the haunted, distant look in the eyes of Poppy's mother, it reiterated the lasting damage the attacks were causing.

'Mrs Westfield, I'm so sorry to bother you again, but I need to speak to Poppy.'

There was a genuine despair to Mrs Westfield's response. As if Louise was threatening to force the woman's daughter to go through the ordeal again. 'Can't you leave her alone for a bit? Please. She won't leave her room and . . . and we don't know what to do.'

'I am so sorry, Mrs Westfield. If there was another way. I won't take too long, I promise.'

The Westfield house was a pretty Victorian terraced property a couple of streets down from the seafront. Mrs Westfield led her across an immaculate wooden floor towards the staircase. She looked back, red eyes pleading, as Louise followed her up the stairs, past walls filled with family photographs. She was sure the Westfields would one day move on with their lives but understood only too well how bleak and far away that future must look now.

'Poppy, dear,' said Mrs Westfield, knocking on the door. 'Louise is here to see you. Can she come in?'

'OK,' came a brittle voice from the other side of the door.

'I'd like you to stay, if that's possible. Is Mr Westfield home?'

Mrs Westfield shook her head. 'What is it?' she said, the sadness in her eyes replaced by something wilder, a kind of mounting terror that made what Louise had to say all the more difficult.

Poppy was sitting up in bed, her duvet pulled up to her neck. Her wide eyes peeped out at Louise, innocent and lost.

'There's no easy way to say this, but there has been another attack,' said Louise, feeling helpless as Poppy let out a small shriek, matched in tone and pitch by one from her mother, who rushed to her side.

'It's OK, Poppy, you're safe now,' said Mrs Westfield.

Louise wondered if she'd made a mistake. She needed Poppy's response but was concerned the girl wasn't up to it. 'Your mum's right, Poppy. We simply need your help so we can catch those responsible. I wanted to show you a picture of the victim. Is that OK?'

At that moment, Poppy appeared to have more resolve than her mother. She moved herself straighter in the bed, a glint of determination on her face. 'I don't want to see the . . .' she said.

'No, this is a photo of him before the incident,' said Louise. She handed Poppy her phone, the girl's face draining of colour as she looked at the image of Andrew Thorpe.

'Mum?' said the girl.

Mrs Westfield glared at Louise before looking at the image. 'Oh no,' she said.

'You know the person in this photo?'

'Mum?' repeated Poppy, her anguished, high-pitched voice making her sound much younger.

'We know him. We had a little problem with him that's been resolved,' said Mrs Westfield, putting a shielding arm around her daughter.

'Can you tell me his name?'

'Andrew Thorpe.'

'You had a little problem with him?' said Louise.

'Can we talk outside?'

Ever since Louise had shown her the photo, Mrs Westfield's determination had returned. Poppy wrapped herself tighter in the duvet as Louise stepped outside the room.

'What's happened to him?' said Mrs Westfield, once they were out of Poppy's earshot.

Louise showed her the other image of Thorpe, the crude branding on his forehead above his lifeless eyes. Mrs Westfield lowered her head. 'Oh my God. I must admit I wanted something bad to happen to him, but not this.'

'I don't understand. How do you know Andrew Thorpe?'

Mrs Westfield sighed. 'Poppy and this Andrew were seeing each other for a time, if you know what I mean.'

'They were sleeping together?'

'Yes. The thing is, Poppy was only fourteen at the time.'

'I see. So this was when?'

'About five years ago now. Andrew was twenty-four at the time. We didn't know anything about it. We put a stop to it straight away, but they continued seeing each other for a bit. In the end, Greg had to go and see him.'

'Greg, your husband?'

'Yes. We had to warn him off. Told him we would go to the police if we ever saw him again.'

'And did you see him again?'

Mrs Westfield shook her head.

'Where is your husband now?'

She looked confused. Louise could almost see the thought process working through her mind, reflected in her changing facial expressions. 'Don't be ridiculous. He wouldn't have anything to do with this. Look at what happened with Poppy.'

'Please just tell me. Let's get this sorted.'

'He's at work. He's a teacher at the comp.'

'Schools aren't back yet,' said Louise.

'They have him back in already, setting up for the new school year.'

'Thank you, Mrs Westfield. If he gets back here before I see him, tell him to call me immediately.'

'This is ridiculous.'

'Please, Mrs Westfield.'

'Fine.'

Louise climbed into her car. Glancing back, she saw Mrs Westfield, arms crossed, staring back at her as if everything that had transpired was her fault. She called Thomas and updated him on the new information.

'OK, I'll try to make my way over there now. However . . .' said Thomas.

Louise began shaking her head. 'Don't however me, Tom.'

'It's Sam Carrigan. Why they didn't tell us sooner I don't know.'

'Told us what, Tom?' said Louise. Thomas was the last person she wanted to lose her patience with, but she didn't like the hesitancy in his voice.

Thomas's sigh was audible on the other end of the phone. 'He's discharged himself and we have no idea where he is.'

Chapter Twenty-Three

She closed her eyes at the memory, shuddering at the pure sensation she'd experienced: her hands on his as the iron had melted Thorpe's forehead. How she'd kept pushing, guiding those shaking hands, until Thorpe was convulsing.

And then the needle.

She hadn't told D about the tattoo needle – he would only have objected, moaning that killing Thorpe would only bring more attention on them – but she'd had no intention of letting Thorpe live.

At first she'd thought D was going to stop her. She'd seen the reluctance in his eyes when she'd produced the needle, and she'd been forced to ease his hands away as she'd moved the needle to Thorpe's eye.

Marking Thorpe was never going to be enough. He was just like the other three from her past, and deserved the same retribution. They had each taken turns watching her, so she had taken away their means of watching.

Back then, Thorpe had been with Poppy. That had made her think that maybe he wasn't all bad, but she knew better now. If it hadn't been Poppy, it would have been another girl. He was a sleaze and a predator, and when it came to it she'd had no qualms about sticking the needle through the soft jelly of his eyeball.

Afterwards, she'd made D drive her to the policewoman's house. Mountson had gone missing and something about being near the policewoman, even if she couldn't be seen, eased her.

And that was in part why they were here now, sitting in the car waiting for DI Blackwell to leave Poppy's house.

She had to be careful. The police would soon make connections between the victims, and that meant danger. And perhaps the biggest threat was the policewoman herself.

She enjoyed watching the woman, unseen. She'd never seen someone carry herself the way Blackwell did, as if she were completely in control of her environment – of everyone and everything around her.

And she conceded she was a little envious. No doubt the woman had her problems, but from what she'd seen, DI Blackwell lived an idyllic life in her shared house with her parents and darling niece. She'd never experienced that, having to move from care home to care home until she'd managed to escape.

But now she wondered if she could get a taste of that life. She still had work to do, but maybe, after, she could have what Louise had. Even if she had to take it for herself.

Warmth flooded her at the thought. She looked down the street to Poppy's house, wondering what the soft flesh of her thigh looked like now. Did the young woman feel their connection? Did she understand the significance of the mark that would forever link them? Soon Blackwell would tell her what had happened to Thorpe. She wished she could be there for that moment, to savour the torment and confusion. Would the mum be able to hide her glee, she wondered, as eventually the policewoman left the house.

Blackwell had an enviable grace to her. She seemed to be completely contained, as if devoid of self-consciousness, as she walked away from Poppy's grieving mother.

She couldn't wait for Blackwell to be part of her family.

'We shouldn't follow her,' said D.

'What if she goes to see Mountson?'

'We'll find him, don't worry, but we can't risk her recognising the car.'

He sensed it as well as she did, the shift in their relationship. Last night had taught her she wanted more and that already he was struggling to keep up. For now she needed him, and she agreed with his assessment.

She watched Blackwell – Louise, her Louise – driving away, and shivered with loss and anticipation. 'You're right,' she said, her hands all over him. 'Let's get home as soon as we can.'

Chapter Twenty-Four

The school Mr Westfield worked at was on the other side of Weston, near the station in Worle. Louise arranged for a patrol car to sit outside the Westfield house as she dealt internally with the incompetence of the rehab centre. Hindsight was a pointless thing, but she blamed herself. She should have kept a tighter rein on Sam Carrigan, should have checked in on him as soon as Thorpe's body was discovered. Now she had a missing victim and a missing suspect, and her confidence was low that Mr Westfield would be waiting for her at the school.

The school was at the top end of Worle, close to the motorway. Louise had driven past the playing fields on numerous occasions but had never had reason to visit before. The building looked desolate in the August sunshine, only two cars in the tarmac car park. The area felt isolated, despite its proximity to the motorway, the buildings and fields that much vaster for the lack of people.

The front door of the building was locked. She buzzed, but no one answered, so she took a walk around to the rear of the building. That she was desperate for Mr Westfield to be there highlighted how quickly the investigation was deteriorating. With both Carrigan and Mountson AWOL, the last thing she needed was another potential suspect on the loose. If Mr Westfield had gone missing as well, then the minimum she would expect would be an ear lashing from DCI Robertson. And with seemingly the whole of Avon and Somerset Police congregating in the area tomorrow, as Baker had suggested, it was the wrong time for things to be slipping out of control. But worse still was the worry that a killer, or pair of killers, was out there somewhere and could strike again at any time.

To the rear of the building, two men crouched together, looking down a drain to the side of a netball court. Neither looked up as she approached. One of the men, unseasonably dressed in a full business suit, jumped up as she announced her presence. 'Don't do that to an old man,' he said, smiling as he grasped his chest in pretend shock.

She recognised the other man from the hospital. 'Hello again, Mr Westfield. It's nothing to worry about, but I needed to have a quick chat with you,' she said.

'My office is open,' said the suited man, offering Westfield a sympathetic smile.

'What is it?' asked Westfield, as they left him and made their way across the tarmac.

'It's Greg, isn't it?' said Louise.

'That's right. Is this about Poppy? Is she OK?'

'Everything is fine, Mr Westfield. Let's get inside and we can talk.'

Westfield led her to the rear of the school building and through the sports hall. Despite it being the summer break, Louise could smell the familiar odours of school lunches and sweaty trainers as if they were ingrained in the fabric of the building. Their footsteps echoed on the hardwood of the gym floors, the sound accompanying them as Westfield led her along the desolate corridors to his office.

He beckoned her to sit. 'What's happened?' he said, his pale face blotchy with red marks from the heat.

'Poppy is fine. I've just seen her. I'm afraid there's been another incident. Last night, a man was attacked. Like Poppy, he was branded by his attackers.'

Mr Westfield closed his eyes at the mention of branding. He'd started to tremble, and Louise gave him a few seconds to regain his composure. It was the less considered side of violent crime. For every person attacked and injured, there was nearly always another subset of victims – partners, parents, family and friends – who suffered the fallout. In many ways, Poppy's parents would suffer the after-effects of Poppy's attack as much as the young woman herself. It would live with them for ever. She'd seen it in the way her parents dealt with Paul's murder. It was evident in her mother's drinking, but she saw it in her father as well. The occasional faraway glance as though he was lost in thought, the way he sometimes choked up when Paul's name was mentioned. However irrational it would appear to the outside world, she was sure the Westfields would blame themselves for the attack on Poppy; would live with the guilt of not being able to protect her until the day they died. Louise would have told them it wasn't their fault, but it wasn't her place, and nothing she could say would have any impact on their thinking.

'After talking to Poppy and Mrs Westfield, I believe you knew the victim.'

Mr Westfield looked up sharply at her. 'Who was it?' he said.

'I'm afraid the victim died, most likely due to complications from his attack. Andrew Thorpe,' said Louise, showing Mr Westfield the image of Thorpe at the scene, the branding mark red-raw on his forehead, hoping to provoke a reaction from Poppy's father.

'Jesus Christ,' said Mr Westfield, looking away.

'Tell me about him,' said Louise, surprised by his visceral reaction. His face had reddened even more and he was staring at Louise with a fierce intensity.

133

'This is your fault,' he said, his eyes not leaving Louise.

'I don't follow, Mr Westfield.'

'We came to you about this and you did nothing.'

'You reported Mr Thorpe's relationship with your daughter?'

He turned away, tears forming. 'No, we didn't. What would the point be? You wouldn't have done anything.'

'That's not true, Mr Westfield. We take cases like this very seriously. If you thought Andrew Thorpe was engaged in sexual activity with your daughter, he would have been arrested.'

'Bullshit.'

'Please, Mr Westfield, this isn't helping anyone. Start from the beginning.'

'I'll start from the beginning,' he said through gritted teeth. 'When Poppy was about to turn fourteen her behaviour started to change. She was always such a good girl,' he said, turning away again as he lost his train of thought.

'And then what happened?'

'It was nothing at first. She started coming home a bit late from school, then we found cigarettes in her room. We weren't overly concerned to begin with. We put it down to usual teenage behaviour. Hasn't my wife told you all this?'

Mr Westfield frowned as Louise shook her head. 'That's about right. She acts like it never happened. So . . . then, one night, Poppy didn't come home until after midnight. It was a Saturday, but obviously we were beside ourselves. She'd just turned fourteen at this point. She wasn't answering her phone and when she finally did come home, it was as if it wasn't of importance to her. As if staying out till midnight was a normal thing for a fourteen-year-old to be doing.

'This became a regular thing. Her schoolwork began to suffer. Some days we couldn't get her out of bed in the morning. We were pretty sure she was taking drugs of some sort. I started following her after school, and found she was hanging out with some older kids. They had cars. I didn't know what to do,' said Mr Westfield, surprising Louise again as he started to cry.

Louise let him, not wanting to risk him clamming up.

'Eventually, we went to your lot,' he said, the rage returning as he wiped the tears from his blotchy face. 'For all the use that was. A lot of useless platitudes about teenagers being teenagers. In the end, I pestered them so much that they took some action. They followed Poppy to the beach in Brean. Gave out a few warnings over underage drinking, possession of drugs – that sort of a thing – but not much else. Told me they were trying to scare Poppy out of the group.'

'It didn't work?'

'No, it didn't work. For a couple of weeks it was better, and then the same patterns started replaying. We were going to go to social services when her mum found contraceptives in her bag. She was fourteen. We confronted her, which, as you can imagine, didn't go down very well. She told us she was in love and it was none of our business.'

'Andrew Thorpe?'

'Yes, Thorpe,' he said, emphasising the man's name as if Louise were a disruptive pupil who wasn't listening closely enough. 'I found him. He denied everything, and there was nothing we could do. What they did to my little girl. She was all but an addict. I tried to warn Thorpe off, but he laughed in my face.'

'What did you do?'

Mr Westfield stared at her, his eyes boring into hers with sadness and rage. 'We all but destroyed our family. We took her out of school and moved her to her grandparents in Devon. I knew it would end up being Thorpe's word against ours, and Poppy thought she was in . . . Anyway, I needed to act quickly. It was the only way. Thankfully, it worked out. She got her GCSEs and A levels. We were worried when she returned, but she's made some good friends and we'd thought this group had moved on. Now you're telling me that Thorpe is dead?'

'I have to ask Mr Westfield, where were you last night?'

His face reddened as it dawned on him what her question meant. 'You think I did it?' he said, not hiding his incredulity. 'I wish I had. I would have gladly taken that little fucker's life.'

'Please don't say that, sir. Where were you?'

'I was here until five, then I went home. We ordered some takeaway at about eight. Online, see,' he said, thrusting the delivery note on his phone in front of her.

'Thank you. We asked you before if Poppy knew the first victim, Sam Carrigan?'

'If she says she doesn't know him, she doesn't.'

Louise showed him a picture of Carrigan. 'Maybe he was part of the group Poppy was hanging about with?'

Mr Westfield shook his head, repeating the gesture when she showed him the image of David Mountson.

'How about him?' she said, showing Mr Westfield the image of Mountson's friend, Laurence Dwyer.

Mr Westfield clenched his jaw. 'He was there, definitely. Mouthy little sod. I got the impression he was the leader of the group.'

Chapter Twenty-Five

It was a short drive back to the station, but Louise hadn't reached it by the time a call came in from the pathologists with an urgent request to attend the mortuary. Mr Westfield's heartfelt recollection was still fresh in her mind as she turned back towards the A370, the mortuary a thirty-minute journey away in Flax Bourton. Although she hadn't been in Weston during the timeframe mentioned, Westfield's accusations about the police stung. She understood his pain and hadn't even considered arguing against him. No parent wanted to hear excuses from the police. The sad fact was that there weren't the man hours available to react to every case of a teenager going wild. A fourteen-year-old girl staying out late was low down on priorities for the police, and social services were so stretched in all regions that it would usually take something more than this to get involved beyond a rudimentary basis.

That the parents suspected Poppy was sleeping with the much older Thorpe was a different matter. If they'd only come to the police about that, Thorpe would have been arrested, and if any evidence had been found, he would have been charged with sexual activity with a child.

Sadly, it was too late to worry about what could have been. Thomas still hadn't been able to locate Sam Carrigan, who, along with David Mountson and Laurence Dwyer, was a person of interest. Louise could picture the patronising face of ACC Morley tomorrow evening if they didn't find at least Mountson and Carrigan. Inspector Baker's arrival in Weston had set departmental tongues wagging. The threat of Weston's CID team being merged with HQ in Portishead was a constant cloud hanging over the station, and any screw-up in the investigation – which was now effectively a murder inquiry – would provide the ACC with all the ammunition he needed to get what he wanted.

Louise put the idea of working alongside Finch again to the back of her thoughts as she parked up outside the mortuary. Dempsey had a lair in the basement of the grey building that even with the sun glaring down on it looked cold and unwelcoming – a feeling that intensified as she descended the staircase into the cold, windowless corridors of the lower floors.

Much like in the school hall, the smells of the mortuary – the formaldehyde and the lingering smell of blood – clung to the walls. Despite what was often portrayed on television and film, not every police officer managed to become accustomed to such places. Louise was glad she still felt out of place in these cold surroundings, that the sights and smells turned her stomach. It was one thing being hardened by what she saw – that was inevitable – but the day she was fully accepting and it stopped bothering her would be the day she needed to leave the police for good.

Putting on a gown and mask, she peered through the glass of the viewing area and saw Dempsey standing next to a body covered in a plastic sheet. 'Hi, Louise. You should come through, this is very important,' he said.

Breathing through her mouth, as if she could stave off the smells of the examination room during her time there – she pushed through the doors.

The skin around Dempsey's eyes creased and she could tell he was smiling beneath his mask. She knew he still had a thing for her. She regretted the way she'd handled the fallout of their night together. She thought now that perhaps she'd misjudged him. He was a sweet enough guy, even if he wasn't right for her, and she could have treated him with a bit more kindness and patience the few times he'd asked her out since.

'Thanks for coming so quickly. I readjusted my schedule the second Mr Thorpe arrived. I was studying the mark on his forehead when I noticed something I'd missed at the scene, something fascinating. I'll start the post-mortem shortly, but thought you'd like to get a heads up on this. Pun intended,' he added, shining a torch on Thorpe's head, the light hitting the branding mark, which appeared faded and worn.

'See?' said Dempsey, with the overenthusiasm of a child. 'That pinprick mark on the side of his right eye.'

Louise peered closer, holding her breath again as she tried to ignore Thorpe's lifeless eyes. 'I see it – what about it?' said Louise.

'At first I thought it was innocuous, and I wanted to see you before I go further, but I'm pretty sure that puncture wound goes all the way through into the unfortunate Mr Thorpe's brain.'

Chapter Twenty-Six

Louise couldn't contain her annoyance when she returned to the station to find Inspector Baker loitering in the incident room. Her reaction was disproportionate. With his recent work in the town centre and the rehab facilities, it made sense to get his input, but something about the way he stood – the rigidness of his long, straight back, his feet too close together, as if he were permanently standing to attention – aggravated her. She put her reaction down to tiredness and forced herself to say hello.

'It's becoming quite a case,' he said, keeping the same stifled stance as he turned to look at her.

Louise had sent updates to Thomas after staying with Dempsey for the post-mortem. She was still coming to terms with the pathologist's insight regarding the hole in Thorpe's eye. A sharp metal rod, less than a millimetre in diameter, had been inserted through Thorpe's eye and directly into his brain. Dempsey had sounded almost gushing about the precision required to make the insertion successful and hadn't been shy to congratulate himself on noticing the pinprick mark in the first place.

The new evidence changed everything. Thorpe's death appeared to be premeditated and not simply a complication from the branding to his forehead. Patterns were emerging, but Louise accepted she was struggling to connect everything. Poppy and Thorpe were linked, and she was sure if they could locate Sam Carrigan they could prove a further link between all three victims. Along with David Mountson and Laurence Dwyer, finding Sam Carrigan was a priority. That they'd let both Mountson and Carrigan slip away was an error she didn't wish to consider at that moment.

Unsurprisingly, DCI Robertson wasn't so forgiving. He summoned her into his office, along with Thomas and Baker. His arms were folded, his eyebrows furrowed. 'So, three people of interest are missing?' he asked, his accent at peak Glaswegian as he glared at each of them in turn.

Louise wasn't about to open her mouth in response to the rhetorical question.

'We have a patrol car stationed outside Poppy Westfield's house,' said Baker, as if it had been his idea.

'Let's hope we can keep hold of one victim then,' said Robertson, placing his hands on his face. 'Right, give me the room with DI Blackwell,' he added.

Thomas tilted his head towards Louise as he left, questioning if she was OK. She nodded back as Baker filtered out and closed the door behind him.

'You know what I'm going to say, don't you?' said Robertson.

'"I know you've worked these types of cases before, with continued success, DI Blackwell, so I trust you to handle this one in the way you see fit?"' said Louise, with mock optimism.

Robertson snorted. 'No one's doubting your credentials, Louise, but I have to get MIT's support on this. We have one murder victim and two victims with serious injuries. One of whom is currently missing. With Farrell having left us, we don't have the resources any more. And with this stupid bloody do tomorrow night, I need to act now.'

DS Greg Farrell had been part of the CID team in Weston until Finch had seconded him to MIT. She knew Robertson was right.

They simply weren't equipped to work this sort of case on their own, and everything about the investigation so far suggested that the attacks were far from over. The attackers had killed now, and the escalation suggested they were far from finished. The team needed help but, even so, it was hard for Louise to accept she couldn't keep full control; harder still to acknowledge that she would once again be faced with working in the same team as Finch. Louise wondered what Amira would think about her working alongside the man again, with the knowledge of the threat looming over her.

'If there was another way, you know I would do it,' said Robertson. 'It goes without saying that you would remain SIO and would report directly to me. MIT would be here to help us, but we do need their help.'

Louise had heard the same words before; it seemed every time a case reached a certain level in Weston, then headquarters' help was requested. This was beyond Robertson's control. He trusted her and she knew he would leave the investigation in her hands if he could. Even if he didn't show it, he would be feeling equally frustrated. MIT's involvement would also reinvigorate the growing suggestion that the departments be merged, and if that happened, no one's job would be safe.

'Is that it?' said Robertson, as Louise stood to leave.

The one thing neither of them had mentioned was DCI Finch. With the internal hearing coming up, having Finch in the station would make things even more difficult, but anything she said to the contrary now would sound petty. 'Do you want me to argue, Iain?'

'A little bit,' said Robertson, with a twitch of his lips that she recognised as a smile. 'Get some sleep, Louise. I know you've been working non-stop on this.'

'Do I still have to go to this ridiculous thing tomorrow night?'

'I've told you before, Louise. You have to play the game sometimes. Stick your head in, make an appearance. I know you're busy, but if you don't show, it will only set the wrong tongues wagging.'

'Maybe the wrong tongues would understand I'm working on a murder investigation,' said Louise, loitering by the door's entrance.

Robertson's face twitched again, this time forming into a frown. 'Just pop in for one drink. Hell, I'll buy you one myself.'

'My God. If you're paying, then how could I miss it? Goodnight, sir.'

Robertson lowered his eyes and returned to the pile of papers at the edge of his desk.

Chapter Twenty-Seven

Louise stumbled to the bathroom and drank from the tap, dehydration making her lethargic. It was just after 6.30 a.m., and too many things had been on her mind last night to rest properly. It wasn't just the threat of MIT joining the investigation. Robertson had been right – they needed at least two more officers to help with the case – but everything felt so up in the air at the moment. She'd kept glancing anxiously at her phone, waiting for the call informing her that another victim had been discovered, until at some point she must have drifted to sleep.

She turned away from the glare of the early-morning sun as she opened her curtains, catching a glimpse of the muddy sea creeping into shore. Pouring coffee, she unlocked the dividing door and went downstairs. The scratching sound started immediately, Molly's claws clicking on the wooden floors as she bounded her way towards her. Louise hadn't seen the dog in three days and Molly was even more excited than usual. She jumped up on Louise, her tail driving her body as she whined in greeting.

'Hello, girl,' said Louise, stroking the dog's head. It was comforting to see Molly running loops around her as she followed Louise to the living room, where Emily was curled up in a ball watching morning television.

'What are you doing up already?' said Louise.

Her niece didn't look away from the television as she held her arms out in front of her for a hug.

'I could stay here for days,' said Louise, snuggling in beside the girl as Molly joined them on the sofa, desperate not to be left out. 'Have you had any breakfast yet?'

'Pancakes, please,' said Emily, with a sideways glance and a little grin.

Molly accompanied Louise to the kitchen, where Louise made pancakes from scratch, adding some blueberries she found in the fridge. She took such joy in these small pleasures, knowing that soon she would be back at work, dealing with the fallout of recent events. Despite herself, she checked the recycling bin and saw two empty wine bottles. They were white wine, something her father didn't touch, and so both bottles had to belong to her mother.

When the pancakes were ready, Louise had to forcibly drag Emily from the sofa to the table, the girl's eyes glued to the television.

'So, what have you been up to the last few days?' she said, placing the girl on to one of the kitchen chairs.

'Not much. I've been out with Grandad most days,' said Emily, between mouthfuls of pancake and syrup.

'Just Grandad?' said Louise, with a sigh.

'Grandma has been tired quite a lot,' said Emily, matter-of-factly. 'Where have you been, Aunty Louise?' she asked, the faintest hint of accusation in her voice.

'I'm sorry I haven't been around, Emily. I've been so busy at work.'

'You don't have to go back in today, though, do you?'

'I'm afraid I do.'

'But it's Saturday, isn't it?' said Emily, waving her fork in front of her, a dribble of maple syrup falling on to the table.

'Criminals work on the weekends, I'm afraid. However, I was thinking we could take Molly for a quick walk before I have to leave,' said Louise, the dog bounding over with a comical look of expectation on her face.

Ten minutes later they were sneaking out the front door, Molly's tail bouncing off the walls, her lead held in her mouth as if she were taking herself for a walk. The sky was cloudless, but there was a cold snap in the air. 'You sure you don't want your coat?' asked Louise.

'I'm fine,' said Emily, grabbing the lead from Molly's mouth and sprinting ahead with the dog.

Times like this always made Louise question her career in the police. These moments with Emily were precious and she feared she was missing her niece growing up. There was no end in sight to the investigation, and chances were high she would be spending the next few weeks working non-stop. She promised herself she would try to make time for Emily, but conceded it was probably another hollow promise.

Emily took a shortcut through the woods to the beach, for a short time out of Louise's sight. Louise fought an irrational panic and sped up her walk as the sound of the sea drew nearer. 'Emily, wait up,' she called, her heartbeat easing as Molly ambled towards her, a branch at least four times the size of the dog in her mouth.

'What have you got there, girl?' said Louise, catching sight of Emily in the distance, leaning against a tree.

Sand Bay was deserted in the early morning, and it was as if they had their own private beach waiting for them. Emily skipped down the slope to the wet sand, Molly sliding down to join her.

Louise could have spent all day there, Emily stumbling over the pebbles and rocks, Molly never more than a few feet away from her, the dog's nose glued to the ground, sniffing at the new and exotic smells.

'How are Grandma and Grandad?' asked Louise, as she caught up with her niece.

'They're fine,' said Emily, bending down to pick up a flat pebble and throwing it into the sea. 'Grandad showed me how to skim stones, but I can't do it. You try.'

Louise recalled her father showing her how to skim pebbles into the sea as a child and had to fight her sadness that Emily's father, Paul, would never be able to share these moments with his daughter. She found a round, smooth pebble and launched it towards the sea, surprising herself by making it bounce three times along the water.

'Wow,' said Emily.

'Beginner's luck. You try.'

Emily tried again, and squealed with delight as her pebble bounced once over one of the incoming waves.

'What's Grandma been doing?' said Louise, as they walked back towards home.

'She just stays inside, watching the television,' said Emily.

Emily was perceptive for her age and, with everything that had happened in her short life, there wasn't much that got past her. Louise tried to formulate a question. She wanted to know how much her mother had been drinking recently, but it wasn't fair to bring Emily into the discussion.

'She's been a bit poorly as well,' said Emily.

'Oh really, in what way?'

'Normally in the morning. She gets up very late and never wants any breakfast. Yesterday she wasn't even out of bed before me and Grandad left for the day.'

Although counselling sessions had helped her mother, the drinking hadn't stopped completely. Louise wasn't sure there was a middle ground, and every time she tried to broach the subject with her mother, they would fight. Her father didn't want to admit there was a problem, despite the years of anguish they'd gone through with Paul. Her mother's drinking had intensified after Paul's death and, although she drank much less now, it would always be a concern for Louise. It made her think of the now-abandoned rehab centre in Milton. Her mother was lucky she had family to support her, but even that wouldn't protect her in the long run.

It was feasible that there was some propensity to alcohol problems in the family, and Louise knew from bitter experience with her brother that things were likely to get worse. It was at the stage now that it could be overlooked, dismissed as her mother letting off steam, but Louise was worried about the long-term effect it would undoubtedly have – on her mother's health, on her father's wellbeing and, most worrying of all, on Emily.

Her father was up by the time they got back. He hugged her as she walked through the door, his face changing to mock outrage as Molly bounded in, her coat still wet and muddy from being in the sea. 'I presume you're not going to leave me to sort this out,' he said.

Louise glanced at the kitchen clock. 'That's what grandads are for,' she said, kissing her dad on the forehead. 'I'm really sorry, I have to go in.'

'But it's the weekend,' said her father, repeating Emily's complaint.

'Bad guys don't stop at the weekend, Grandad,' said Emily.

Louise bent down to hug her niece. 'You should listen to her,' she said. 'She knows what she's talking about.'

It was hard saying goodbye to her niece. The main reason her parents and Emily had moved to Weston was so that Louise would get more opportunity to spend time with the girl. After Paul's death, Emily's behaviour had changed. For a time, it was as if her innocence had been destroyed. She'd misbehaved in school – had even been suspended for biting another pupil – and had become almost too much for her grandparents to handle. That behaviour had all been eradicated following the move, but it was still within her. Occasionally Louise would see the girl staring off into the distance, and it worried her to think what thoughts were running through her niece's mind. 'I'm so sorry I can't stay with you today, Emily. When this case is over, I promise I'll spend much more time with you,' she said.

'I enjoyed going for a walk with you today,' said Emily, her eyes shining.

'I think that was by far the most enjoyable thing I've done all summer. I wish all days could start like that. Now, you get back inside and enjoy your day with Grandma and Grandad. I'll see you this evening.'

Chapter Twenty-Eight

Louise drove along the Kewstoke Road towards town. On her left were the woods where Andrew Thorpe's body had been discovered. Today would be the perfect day to get some news, even if it was a location for one of the three missing people. She was desperate to get back to work, but she'd agreed to meet Amira and Simon Coulson. She'd come close to cancelling it, but she'd made a promise to Amira and felt she had a duty to give her some of her time.

A water-skier was braving the waves beyond Marine Lake as Louise made her way along the seafront. In the distance, the island of Steep Holm jutted from the mud-coloured water and, recalling her first major case in Weston, Louise was reminded of how much she'd achieved in the town since her arrival. At the traffic lights, she watched the water-skier flip over his skis, falling head first into the water. She could just make out the laughter from the driver of the speedboat before she had to pull away. Little incidents like that reinforced her growing love for the town, and she felt a surge of optimism as she parked up and crossed the road to the Kalimera, a restaurant she'd frequented every day when she'd first moved to Weston; days when any sense of optimism had been hard to find.

The beautiful owner of the restaurant, Georgina, greeted her in her usual sardonic style. 'You grace us once again,' she said.

'Always good to see you, too, Georgina.'

Georgina turned and began making Louise a black Americano without being asked. 'They're already waiting for you. I'll bring it over.'

Louise checked her watch as she walked over to the table by the window where Amira and Simon Coulson were sitting. 'I see you've met,' she said, taking a seat.

'We've just got here,' said Amira, her right hand gripping the table for support.

Louise waited until Georgina had brought over her coffee before getting into their reasons for being there. 'Thanks for coming over, Simon,' she said. 'On a Saturday, as well.'

Coulson shrugged. 'You know my social calendar. This is the highlight of the week. How can I help?'

Louise had asked Coulson there on the pretence that she needed some help on the branding case. She'd told him to keep it to himself and she trusted him to do just that. 'You two know each other?' she asked.

'We were just discussing that. We've seen each other around,' said Amira.

Louise sipped at her coffee. 'OK. I'm afraid I misled you, Simon. I need some off-record help, but it could be risky for you.'

Coulson had been instrumental in a number of cases Louise had worked on in Weston since leaving MIT. He shared her disdain for Finch, but it was still a big ask to request he work against the man. He sat stony-faced as she told him what had happened to Amira, and the other woman, Terri Marsden, leaving out the threat Finch had levelled at Amira. For a second, she thought he wasn't going to help, then he asked, 'You have the phones with the photos on?'

Amira, who was still clinging on to the table, nodded. 'This is my phone,' she said, handing over an old iPhone. 'Terri allowed me to borrow hers, but she would like it back.'

Louise understood how embarrassing it must be for Amira to pass over her phone to a man she hardly knew. Coulson nodded but didn't touch either phone. 'You believe he sent these photos to you through an anonymous account?'

Amira nodded. 'He did.'

'Not an easy thing to achieve, especially without leaving a trace,' said Coulson. He still hadn't touched either phone and Louise was growing concerned he wasn't going to help.

'What is it, Simon?'

Coulson looked downwards. 'I'm sorry to ask this, but what has he got on you?'

'On me?' said Louise.

'I know it must be embarrassing. I'm sorry . . .'

'No, no, you're right to ask. You know what happened with the Max Walton case. Our differing recollections of what happened that night?'

'Of course.'

'Well, that wasn't enough for Finch. He wanted me off the force. Possibly because I was a reminder of the lies he'd told, but more likely because I was a risk to him. Forcing me out of MIT to Weston wasn't enough for him. He began harassing me. He used to send me messages every night, trying to undermine me.'

'I'm presuming these were anonymous too?'

'I'm afraid so. I made a record of every message – date, time and message.'

'You have the phone?'

Louise reached into her bag and produced her old phone, hesitating before handing it over. As much as she trusted Coulson, the phone was her only real evidence against Finch and she was reluctant to let it out of her sight.

'Photos?' he asked, struggling to meet her eyes as she placed the phone next to the others.

'He didn't take any of me.'

Coulson let out a blast of air, as if he'd been holding his breath. 'OK, leave it with me,' he said, eventually picking up the phones and bagging them. 'I can get going?' he added, already standing, apparently desperate to get away.

'Thanks, Simon,' said Louise. 'I really appreciate this.'

'We both do,' said Amira, as Coulson left. 'Thanks for sorting this, Louise,' she said, once he'd gone.

'You don't need to worry, he can be trusted,' said Louise, wondering if she'd ever fully felt that way about Finch. Yes, they'd been partners and had shared a bed on more than one occasion, but it wasn't just hindsight that made her think he wasn't trustworthy. Of course, she'd never expected his eventual deceit to be as grandiose as it had been. They'd both been ambitious, but she would never have expected him to go to the lengths he had, just to secure a promotion.

Finch had told her that Walton was holding a weapon, and because of that she had shot him and Max Walton had lost his life. Louise was now convinced Finch had taken a perverse sense of pleasure, both from the act and his subsequent denial that he'd ever told her Walton was carrying a gun. Only then had she understood the extent of his sociopathic traits. In retrospect, the clues had been there all along, and to this day she wasn't sure what bothered her the most: that he'd duped her or that she hadn't realised sooner what he was all about.

'We need to keep Terri onside. She was so reluctant to hand over her phone. Now I can really understand why,' said Amira.

'The photos will be safe with Simon, and if anyone can prove a link with Finch, it will be him.'

'I imagine this is the last thing you need at the moment,' said Amira. 'I've been reading about the branding case. It's a murder investigation now?'

Louise finally understood Amira's agitation. 'MIT will be helping us, and I know Finch will be in Weston tonight if he isn't here already. Maybe best to go home for the weekend? Leave Simon to do his work.'

Amira visibly shook at her announcement, as if she feared Finch was about to walk through the door. 'I don't know how you can deal with him on a daily basis. It makes my skin crawl just thinking about him.'

'Has he messaged you again?'

Amira nodded and showed her a snapshot of the latest message.

I hope I don't have to share these with your parents, read the text, beneath a compromising photo of Amira.

'We've still got time. I know Simon. He will be on to this immediately. Let's see what he comes back with and we can go from there.'

It wasn't even 11 a.m., yet Louise felt she'd already worked a full day. She'd spent the last thirty minutes updating members of MIT on the case. She was thankful that Finch had sent her former colleague Greg Farrell to assist, and that Tracey had been seconded from Serious Crimes; more grateful still that Finch had yet to show.

Tracey updated the team on the O'Connell family and the acid attacks that had taken place on the Frenchay estate. The known members had been questioned all week and had naturally denied all knowledge. Tracey was struggling to find any link to the Weston attacks, which backed up Louise's feeling that they weren't related. Tracey confirmed that the Serious and Organised Crimes department would continue the investigation into the gangs, but for now Louise filed away the line of inquiry from the branding case. The connection between Poppy and Andrew Thorpe was enough for

Louise to believe the branding attacks were personal in nature and extended beyond the rivalries of warring drug gangs. But until she located the three missing men, it would prove hard to know for definite.

With tasks allocated, Louise poured herself what must have been her fifth or sixth coffee of the day and returned to her desk. The crime board was visible from her seat, the photos of Mountson and Dwyer beneath the large images of the three victims, with the corpse of Andrew Thorpe taking a macabre centre stage.

Dempsey had emailed a preliminary report confirming his findings from yesterday. Thorpe had been branded before the needle or wire was inserted through his eye. Louise squirmed in her seat as she wondered how much the victim would have known about what was happening to him. For his sake, she hoped that the pain from the branding had knocked him unconscious. She wasn't squeamish about much, but incidents involving the eyes always turned her stomach. Years ago, she'd worked as part of a task force in Bristol into a serial killer dubbed the soul jacker who'd had a penchant for removing the eyes of his victims, and the images from those days had stayed with her. She had to close her own eyes as she pictured Thorpe lying on the ground, restrained, staring at his attackers, the sharp metal needle that would end his life inching closer and closer.

'Coffee?'

Louise almost jumped as she looked up to see Thomas standing in front of her desk. 'Don't do that to me,' she said.

'What? Ask if you want a coffee?'

'You move like a cat burglar, I swear it. No, I'm fine for coffee. I have the caffeine shakes as it is.'

Thomas nodded but didn't move.

'Anything else, Sergeant?' she asked, pleased to have a few minutes of respite from thoughts of needles and punctured eyes.

'Probably not the most appropriate time, but I was wondering if you're still planning to go this evening?'

Louise wasn't sure if she'd imagined the hint of hope in his voice. The last thing she wanted to do was lead him on, but she didn't know if it was all in her imagination. They'd agreed to go together and maybe all he was doing was getting verification. 'Like I said, it's a three-line whip for me. You could still escape, though,' she said, regretting her choice of words, which she feared made it sound like she didn't want him to go.

If he was deflated by the comment, he hid it well. 'I have my suit pressed and everything.'

'Well, in that case . . .'

'Leave here at seven?'

'Sounds good to me,' said Louise, turning away as her pulse quickened.

'There is one more thing,' said Thomas, switching to professional mode. The quick change in tone took Louise off guard. It made her wonder again if she was making something out of nothing, that Thomas's attraction to her was all in her imagination. 'I've been looking back at the old files on Poppy Westfield. I'm waiting for some reports from social services, but we have records of her parents making complaints about local kids they claimed were drug dealers. They even reported her missing once,' said Thomas, handing her a file. 'She'd only been gone a few hours and turned up at two am.'

Louise scanned the file. There were reports of youths loitering outside Poppy's old school, the one where Mr Westfield now worked. Some cautions for possession of Class C drugs. Nothing out of the ordinary.

'There was some action taken, as you can see on page eight,' said Thomas.

Louise turned to the page. A report showed that a group of youths suspected of dealing drugs had been monitored at a beach in Brean, which supported Mr Westfield's claim. After two days, the surveillance was shut down. Officers had given the group some warnings about anti-social behaviour – late-night drinking, loud music, possession of Class C drugs – but no action had been taken.

Louise skimmed down the sixteen names, stopping at Andrew Thorpe and Poppy Westfield. 'Two of our victims. But no Sam Carrigan,' she said.

'No, but Laurence Dwyer is also on that list. However, you might think the list of supervising officers is interesting. Purely coincidental, I know, but . . .'

Louise flipped to read the sign-offs, looking up at Thomas as she read the name Dan Baker. 'Our own Inspector Baker, or Constable Baker, as he was then.' Louise checked the dates. She hadn't realised how quickly Baker had progressed through the ranks, going from constable to inspector in four years.

'The notes suggested he wanted more action taken,' said Thomas.

'That would tally. He isn't renowned for his love of partying.'

'Do you want to speak to him about it?'

Louise was sure Baker wasn't hiding anything. Lots had happened in his career in the last four years, and there was no reason he should remember the names of some local kids from that period, but it still felt like a bit of an oversight on his part. 'Get the team to go through this list one by one. I hope to God I'm wrong, but this could be a list of potential victims,' she said, just as DCI Finch arrived.

Chapter Twenty-Nine

It didn't matter that he'd died. The mark was the same. D placed it on her back, like the others, as she experienced the transformative effect of the metal searing her flesh.

As before, the pain made her dizzy. It filled her body in a way that was incomparable. She was lost, her body convulsing as she was transported, her blood on fire as it spread the pain through her in a delicious wave.

Minutes passed in the lost reverie. She'd dallied with body modification long before that first mark was forced upon her. Even at that young age, she'd taken delight in transforming herself. They'd called it self-harm at the care home, but they never really understood. Yes, it was a way of escaping the mundanity of her life, the bullying both at school and at the home, and thoughts of the parents she'd never known. But every time she hurt herself – a deep scratch from her fingernails, a pinch of skin from nail clippers, the time she'd cut open her flesh with a school protractor – she sensed the change deep within herself. Each wound was an extra layer of protection from the outside world, a shield she enhanced with the tattoos spread across her flesh.

But the brandings were different. The first had taken away her power, but the rest had brought it back with interest. She'd understood when the three of them had held her down – after doing the things they never should have done – and placed that searing hot metal on her skin, that they'd changed her in a way she could never have envisaged. For a short period of time, it had been as if they'd owned her. Not in the way a farmer owned the cattle he branded, but something much deeper. For although they'd branded her, they were as much connected to her as she was to them.

They were family. A connection only death could sever.

The greatest irony of it all was that she would have probably said yes if they'd only asked. Not to the first part. That she hadn't wanted. But she would probably have accepted the branding on her shoulder. She'd wanted to be changed and it had changed her, but not in the way she'd expected.

D looked worried as she came back. 'This can't be doing you any good,' he said, showing her the third new mark he'd emblazoned on her skin in less than a week.

She wasn't worried. The mark was with her now, an added layer of armour beneath her clothes. She would take it with her tonight, even if the pain had yet to subside.

Whether they knew it or not, she was different, and one thing was for sure: she wouldn't stop until her body was a kaleidoscope of marks.

Chapter Thirty

Louise sensed everyone in the office stopping as Finch walked over to her desk. He'd been at the station many times before, but that didn't take away the edge of having him here, especially after her earlier meeting with Coulson and Amira. 'DCI Finch. To what do we owe this honour?' she said, emphasising 'honour' with as much sarcasm as she was able to muster.

'The honour is all mine, Louise, as always. I thought I'd offer my personal help on this case, due to its severity,' said Finch. His attempts at displaying his authority – the wide-leg stance, the formal tone of his voice – were as blatant as his overpowering aftershave.

Everyone might have returned to their work, but Louise knew they were still listening. Finch had all but declared he was here to save the day, but Louise refused to be provoked in her own station by him. She took solace from her earlier meeting with her two colleagues. For once, she knew things Finch didn't and, hopefully, very soon his interference would be a thing of the past.

'I have somewhere to be, Tim, but Greg and Tracey can update you,' said Louise, enjoying the frown of displeasure that crossed Finch's brow. 'I'm sure they could assign you a task,' she added, as a parting shot.

◆ ◆ ◆

She savoured the small victory as she made the short journey out of Weston. Of late, every place Louise visited felt like it had a history relating personally to her. Brean Down was no different. Nine miles out from Weston, the area brought back a number of memories she'd rather forget. On the main road into the town, she passed the gaudy holiday park with its glittering lights and substandard fairground rides where she'd interviewed a succession of lonely seasonal workers. Not far from there was the house where she'd confronted a now-convicted killer. And worse was to come. As in Weston, the sunshine could hide a multitude of sins. As she pulled into the National Trust car park at the foot of Brean Down, she saw the seasonal effect on the tourists and day trippers. The sea was out, but that didn't deter them. Like ants, they trailed up the steep incline of the cliff side. Perhaps they knew and chose to forget. But when she looked at the sheer drop at the top, all she could see was the wrecked body of the young woman who'd been forced to jump from its heights the previous year.

Climbing down the stone steps to the beach, she fought the urge to return to her car. Sometimes she had to work this way. Others would probably see it as a waste of time to visit the place where a group of kids had been told off years ago, but she wanted to experience the area for herself. If nothing else, it gave her a chance to clear her mind and organise her thoughts. It was a common feeling, having multiple avenues of investigation going on at the same time. The trick was to eliminate the clutter. For now, she had to trust Coulson was getting on with his job looking into the phones, and she had to focus her energy back on to the murder investigation.

Thomas was supervising the team looking into the list of names from Baker's old police file. The report had been so standard it could have been an instructional template. Louise knew the devastation anti-social behaviour could cause to a community. Sometimes it was easy to put it down to kids having fun, but this often neglected the effect it had on others. Baker had been a subordinate officer in the surveillance on the gang of kids. There were reports of late-night drinking, some minimal drug use, but no evidence had been uncovered for suspected drug dealing. In the end, Baker's team had taken some of the kids' names and warned them off, despite Baker's noted reservations. It was the type of shock that would resonate with most kids. On the face of it, they had done little more than get a little rambunctious – their greatest crime being possession of illegal substances and underage drinking. In Louise's opinion, Baker's team had done the right thing by letting them off with a warning, and Thomas hadn't found any further reports of anti-social behaviour by members of the group.

Of course, things looked different when you considered that two of the sixteen people on the beach that night had been branded, one of whom was now on a slab in the mortuary.

She continued walking along the beach, fighting the images of Thorpe's desecrated body, the needle approaching his eye, from her mind. She played over the facts from the case, focusing on the anomaly of Sam Carrigan. He was the first victim, his only link to Andrew Thorpe and Poppy Westfield being the manager of the rehab centre, David Mountson. Yet, try as she might, Louise couldn't see Mountson being responsible. Even if he'd been wearing a mask, she was sure Carrigan would have recognised him, and there was something about Mountson's demeanour – a lost, almost confused countenance – that suggested to her he didn't have the ruthlessness to make the attacks.

Further along, she passed a large family group protected by colourful windbreakers staring out towards the mud as if willing the sea to come in. Like Weston, the coastline in Brean was subject to a severe tidal range. It sometimes struck her as odd that people would spend hours at the seaside without there actually being any sea, save for the distant puddle separated from them by a carpet of thick, brown mud.

A hundred yards further on, a group of teenagers were swigging from large, plastic bottles of cheap, clear cider; some playing football, others huddled together, getting burnt by the sun. They looked to Louise like bored locals and she wondered how the disparate group would compare to the group of sixteen who'd loitered on the same stretch of sand five years ago.

She was about to call Thomas for an update when her phone rang, the number not allocated to her address book. 'DI Blackwell,' she said, answering.

'Yes, DI Blackwell, this is Charles Groves, neighbour to Mr and Mrs Mountson. We spoke on Thursday.'

'Mr Groves, how may I help?'

'Well, you see, I heard some noises last night, didn't think much of it at the time, but I noticed this morning that some of the flower beds at the front of my house have been destroyed. I considered it may have been local wildlife, but one of the flowerpots outside Linda and George's house has been smashed.'

'Are the Mountsons back from their holiday?'

'No, no, no, that's my point. I think someone has broken into their house. I was going to call the police, then . . . well, you are the police, I suppose.'

A myriad of thoughts played through Louise's mind. She didn't want to jump to conclusions – coincidences occurred – but already she was picturing the next branding victim somewhere in the Mountson household. 'OK, please don't touch anything, Mr Groves, I'll be there in fifteen minutes,' she said, then ended the call and rang Thomas before setting off back to Weston.

◆ ◆ ◆

Thomas was waiting outside the Mountsons' house, where Mr Groves was watering his plants. 'I hope I did the right thing, calling you. If I'd known for sure, I would have called last night, but it was late and I was a bit groggy,' said the retired head teacher.

'What time did you hear the noises?' asked Louise, bending down and scratching her finger on the chipped porcelain of the Mountsons' broken flowerpot.

'Three thirty-seven a.m.,' said Groves.

Thomas glanced sideways at Louise as he looked over the damage. 'Very precise of you,' said Louise.

'I glanced at my clock radio. I was a maths teacher, so I'm good at remembering simple numbers,' said Groves, obviously pleased with himself.

'Did you get out of bed?' asked Thomas.

'I'm afraid not. I wasn't sure what I heard, and it was only this morning that I saw the broken flowerpots.'

'Thank you, Mr Groves, we'll take it from here,' said Louise. 'I'll take the back,' she said to Thomas, once Groves had returned to his gardening.

A path ran between the two houses, and the back gate to the Mountsons' garden was open. Louise sneezed as she opened the creaking door. The garden was immaculate. The lawn was mowed to perfection, a wondrous array of flowers surrounding the border. She was about to move towards the back of the house when she noticed the bi-fold doors that led out to the garden were open. Her first thought was that the Mountsons had hired gardeners to maintain the place while they were away, but as she crept nearer she caught the outline of a body through the opening.

She called Thomas and told him what she'd found. 'Do you want me to come back there?' he said.

'No, wait there in case anyone tries to leave by the front door,' she said, edging forward across the lush lawn, her extendable baton in her hand.

A faint musty smell greeted her as she stepped into the house, the drop in temperature triggering goosebumps on her exposed skin as she made out the figure of Sam Carrigan on the floor of the Mountsons' kitchen.

'I'm going in,' she said, checking around her before stepping through the threshold. She gagged as she narrowly missed a puddle of what appeared to be fluorescent vomit and placed her hand on Carrigan's neck.

'Thank God,' she said, feeling the steady thrum of the man's breathing as she turned Carrigan on to his side, only for the looming figure of a second, much larger man, to appear in the entrance of the kitchen.

Chapter Thirty-One

'Mr Mountson,' said Louise, loud enough to make sure Thomas could hear on the other end of the phone, as she got to her feet.

'Yes, that's right. What the hell are you doing in my house?' Mountson looked little better than Sam Carrigan. He was wearing only boxer shorts, his torso all but invisible beneath a canvas of ink. His eyes were sunken and he reached over to the kitchen worktop to gain his balance.

'Would you like to sit down, Mr Mountson?' said Louise, as Thomas joined her, coming through the bifold doors.

'I'd like you to tell me what you're doing in my house,' said Mountson with a lack of conviction, as he slumped down on one of the kitchen chairs.

'It's not your house, though, Mr Mountson, is it?' said Louise.

'Is he OK?' said Thomas, bending down to check Sam Carrigan's pulse.

'Too much booze,' said Mountson, lighting up a cigarette. He took a drag of his cigarette, sighing, as if he were drawing oxygen into his lungs. 'And it is my house.'

'It's your parents' house.'

'That makes it mine,' said Mountson, his hand trembling as he took another drag.

'That's not quite how the law works. Do your parents know you are here?'

'Don't know.'

'Did they give you permission to be here?'

'Yes,' said Mountson.

Louise sat down opposite the man, the metal chair scraping on the hard floor as she pulled it away from the table, an unwelcome blast of cigarette smoke reaching her nose. 'Would you like to tell me what's going on here, Mr Mountson?' she said, indicating to Thomas with a twitch of her head that he should take a look around the rest of the home.

Mountson went to object, his mouth flapping open, then shut, as the energy deserted him. 'What do you mean?' he said.

'What I mean, Mr Mountson, is that around the time a murder victim was discovered in the woods, with the same injury as Mr Carrigan suffered, first you disappear and then we find out Mr Carrigan has discharged himself from hospital. Now I find you both in a house you may or may not have permission to be in. Furthermore, Mr Carrigan was until the other day under your supervision at a drug-rehabilitation centre. And correct me if I'm wrong, but you are both extremely hung-over.'

'Fuck me, I need some coffee,' said Mountson.

'Doing a bit of house clearing?' said Thomas, returning to the kitchen area.

'It's my stuff.'

'The flat-screen television and stereo system are yours?' said Thomas.

'Yep.'

'Put the kettle on, will you, Thomas? Mr Mountson is about to give us an explanation for all this.' Louise shot Thomas a questioning look. He shook his head, meaning there was no one else in the house.

'I guess I've lost my job anyway. I don't think you understand the impact these last few days have had on both of us.'

'I can imagine, Mr Mountson, but that's not an explanation.'

'Black coffee,' said Mountson, receiving a withering look from Thomas. 'With Sam being moved out of the centre, and the news about that murder, it all became a bit too much.'

'If I'm reading this correctly, you're saying that the last few days got too much for you so you decided to go on a bender with someone placed in your trust. Someone who has just gone through severe trauma and shouldn't be touching intoxicants of any kind?'

'Coffee, sir?' said Thomas, slamming a cup down on the table, brown liquid spilling on to the tabletop.

Mountson frowned but took the drink. 'We're friends.'

'That doesn't quite cut it, does it, Mr Mountson? Your job is to prevent those in your care from taking drink and drugs. And you're supposed to lead by example. You must see that?'

'I said I've all but lost my job, didn't I?' said Mountson, raising his voice.

'What's going on?' said Sam Carrigan, getting to his feet with the agility of a new-born giraffe. He'd been sleeping on his side, and only now was the branding visible on his arm, red-raw and prominent, drawing everyone's eyes.

'It's nothing, Sam,' said Mountson.

Sam rubbed his eyes as if not trusting what he could see. 'It's you two,' he said, staggering to his feet before falling on to a chair with a comical bounce.

'It's not his fault,' said Mountson.

'What aren't you telling us, Mr Mountson?' said Louise.

He placed his head in his hands. 'We're more than friends, aren't we?'

Louise sat back in her chair, letting out a deep breath of air. 'You're in a relationship?'

'That's a lovely way of putting it, but yes,' said Mountson, wincing as he drank his coffee. 'Obviously, I couldn't tell you before, or I would have risked losing my job. I think it's a moot point now.'

'That's why you were at the hospital, and why you ran away when I saw you?'

'You've got me. It just sort of happened. Not proud of any of this,' he said. 'I wanted to protect him, you know? When that body was found, we needed to get out of here. We went drinking, and one thing led to another and we ended up back here.'

'It would have been a lot easier if you'd told us to begin with, Mr Mountson. The details of the victim haven't been released yet. I know your stomach may not be up for it, but would you take a look at the victim for me?' said Louise, showing him a photograph of Thorpe before the murder.

If it were possible, Mountson's face went paler than before.

'You know him?'

'Andy,' said Mountson. 'He's dead?'

Louise glanced at Thomas before scrolling through to the next photo. She wanted to provoke Mountson into a reaction and got just that when she showed him the photo of Thorpe's corpse with the branding on his forehead: Mountson stumbling from his seat and vomiting over the dishes in the sink.

Chapter Thirty-Two

Mountson declined the offer of a solicitor. Louise had yet to make contact with the man's parents, and for now had given him the benefit of the doubt regarding his appearance at their house. She'd made it understood that part of that deal was that he returned to the station and answered some questions.

'Where's Sam?' asked Mountson, as Louise and Thomas entered the interview room.

Louise placed a coffee in front of him. She'd allowed him to shower and change, but he still wore his hangover like a shroud, every word and movement appearing to be a great effort. 'He's fine. He's in one of the other rooms. He's even eating something. Can we get you anything?' said Louise, recalling the mess Mountson had made of his kitchen.

'I'll pass.'

Louise went through the normal preliminaries before uploading a picture of Andrew Thorpe on to the screen in the interview room. 'You recognise this man?'

Mountson lowered his eyes. 'Andrew Thorpe.'

'You understand what has happened to Mr Thorpe?' asked Thomas.

'Don't show me that picture again, please,' said Mountson.

'The body of Andrew Thorpe was found in the Weston Woods car park yesterday morning. His death is being treated as murder. A branding similar to the one inflicted on Sam Carrigan was found on his forehead. What can you tell me about this?'

'What can I tell you? I can tell you it sickens me to the stomach. As you saw.'

'You knew Andrew Thorpe?'

'In passing.'

'How did you know him?'

'There was a group of us. Used to hang out over Brean way. Goes back four or five years. I didn't really know them that well. I was a lot older than most of them.'

'Did you sell them drugs, Mr Mountson?' said Louise, trying to throw Mountson off course.

He paused, not as incredulous as Louise had expected. 'No,' he said, without conviction. He shrugged his shoulders. 'I'll admit the majority of them were probably taking some shit, but they weren't getting it from me. I'd only join them on the odd occasion. I was high most of the time, and there was nothing else to do.'

'You were on talking terms with Andrew Thorpe?' asked Thomas.

'There wasn't much deep conversation going on, but yes, we knew each other.'

'When was the last time you saw him?'

'I don't know. I've seen him around town now and again, but we're just nodding acquaintances, you know? Haven't stopped and talked to him since those days on the beach.'

'Why did you stop meeting up?' asked Louise.

'I imagine you know that. We were warned off hanging out there and the group sort of disbanded. As I said, I was hardly there.'

'And Mr Carrigan?' asked Thomas.

'What about him?'

'Was he ever part of this group?'

Mountson snorted. 'I only met him a couple of months ago. What is this shit?'

Louise had to concede this point, as so far they couldn't link Carrigan to Weston prior to him attending the rehab centre in Milton. 'Do you know this woman?' she said, loading a picture of Poppy Westfield on to the screen.

Mountson pursed his lips. 'Pretty. She looks familiar, but . . .'

Louise loaded the next image, of the branding on Poppy's thigh.

'Jesus Christ, warn me if you're going to do that,' said Mountson.

Louise scrolled through to another image of Poppy from five years ago. 'That clear things up for you?'

Mountson rubbed his face, his hands shaking. 'Oh fuck,' he said.

Louise looked out the side of her eye towards Thomas. She didn't say anything as she waited for Mountson to continue.

'She used to go there too.'

'To Brean?'

'Yes. Can't remember her name. I was always a bit concerned about her because she was that bit younger. Penny?'

'Poppy,' said Thomas. 'Poppy Westfield.'

'Poppy, of course.'

'Why did you swear when you saw her photo?' asked Louise.

Mountson bit his lower lip. 'She was seeing Thorpe, wasn't she?'

'You tell us.'

Mountson turned his hands up, palms facing towards the ceiling. 'What is it you want from me? I hardly knew those kids. Thorpe was what, early twenties? It's not great, but it's not my responsibility to stick my nose in everywhere. She was old enough, wasn't she?'

Louise leaned in forwards. 'No, she wasn't, Mr Mountson. She was fourteen at the time.'

Mountson's skin lost his colour. His head flopped on to his chest. 'I feel sick,' he said.

'You must understand how this looks, Mr Mountson. First, Mr Carrigan, who we have subsequently found out you're in a relationship with, is attacked. Then Poppy Westfield, a girl you used to know – who was having underage sex with an associate of yours, which in this instance is a crime of sexual activity with a child – is attacked in a similar way. And finally, Andrew Thorpe, the person committing this offence, another of your former cohorts, is found branded and murdered. Only one person links all three victims, Mr Mountson, and that person is you.'

Louise was surprised to see Mountson's eyes redden as tears formed. 'What is this?' he said. 'I haven't got anything to do with this. I was devastated when it happened to Sam. All the rest of this . . . You can't really be serious.'

Louise paused and exchanged looks with Thomas. It wouldn't be the first time a guilty person had broken down in tears in front of her. Sometimes it happened because of remorsefulness or fear, often it was an act. Louise could only guess at this stage. At that moment, she didn't know if Mountson was directly involved. She agreed that Sam Carrigan would have recognised Mountson had he been his attacker, and from what she knew of him she didn't believe he had the mental strength to carry out the attacks on Poppy Westfield and Andrew Thorpe. That didn't mean he wasn't hiding something from them.

'What names can you remember from those times on the beach?' asked Louise.

'From Brean?' said Mountson, wiping his eyes as if surprised to realise he'd been crying. 'It was five years ago, and I was out of my mind most of the time. There were a couple of guys I knew. I see them around now and again.'

Louise placed a paper and pen in front of him. 'As much detail as you can,' she said.

Mountson wrote two names and handed the sheet back. Neither was the name Louise had been hoping to see – Laurence Dwyer. 'We've been doing a little snooping online. I was wondering if you happen to know this guy,' said Louise, uploading the picture of Mountson with Dwyer. She kept her eyes rooted on Mountson as the photo came on the screen. He would make a terrible poker player. His eyes twitched, his hand rubbing his beard.

'You know this man?' asked Thomas.

'Knew him,' said Mountson.

'Knew him?'

'Laurence. Haven't seen him since those times.'

'Surname?'

'Dwyer.'

'Laurence Dwyer. From what I understand, he used to hang out with the group in Brean?'

Mountson's eyes darted from side to side. 'Perhaps.'

Louise lifted up the piece of paper. 'He doesn't appear on your list.'

'I forgot.'

'Tell me about Mr Dwyer.'

'What's to tell? We were mates. Used to hellraise. You know how it is.'

'Mr Dwyer has a criminal record for selling illegal substances.'

Mountson shrugged. 'He wasn't an angel.'

'You keep talking about him in the past tense,' said Louise.

'What can I say? He disappeared four years ago. He was getting some heat and upped and left without a word.'

'Any idea where?'

'Nope. He was a bit in love with America. You could try out there.'

Louise nodded. 'One last thing,' she said, uploading the close-up of the *L* branding on Dwyer's arm.

Mountson lowered his head on to his hand, his eyes closed.

'I don't think you have been completely upfront with us, Mr Mountson,' said Louise.

Mountson stared into the corner, refusing to look at either of them. Louise waited. It was clear the symbol on Dwyer's arm was a similar branding mark. She needed Mountson to come out and admit it. They sat in silence for an uncomfortable period until Mountson finally spoke. 'Can I show you something?' he said.

'Yes,' said Louise.

Mountson stood and began undoing his belt. 'Whoa, cowboy,' said Thomas.

'I just want to show you something, it's on my lower back,' said Mountson, turning around to display the *D* symbol branded on to the pale and blotchy flesh above his coccyx.

Chapter Thirty-Three

Louise arranged for photographs to be taken of the mark on Mountson's lower back. Mountson had explained that he and Laurence Dwyer had dared each other to get a branding mark, each choosing the initial of their first name. After confessing to that, he'd shut down, as if the last few days had finally caught up with him. Louise decided to give him some space and sent him to the holding cells to cool off.

DCI Robertson arrived in a cloud of aftershave. He was wearing a three-piece suit, his jacket very snug across his ample stomach. 'You're not going like that,' he said, in a dismissive growl.

Louise had all but forgotten the retirement event that evening. She'd brought a dress with her, but the thought of attending now drained the energy from her. As if reading her mind, Robertson interrupted her before she had a chance to speak. 'Unless the attacker has someone captive at this precise moment, you can both spare a few hours. That's why we have a team here, as well as MIT,' he said.

Louise updated him about the branding mark on Mountson.

'Good, we're making some progress. Let's put a notice out on this Dwyer fellow,' said Robertson, looking up from his desk. 'And don't be late,' he added, before leaving.

'Don't think we're going to be able to have that drink before-hand,' said Louise to Thomas.

'Not sure I can face all that lot without at least one drink,' said Thomas.

'Let's stick to coffee for now,' said Louise.

'Is that a hint?'

'Sure is, Sergeant.'

David Mountson had been given some food and drink and was looking more composed by the time he returned from the holding cell. Louise asked him once more if he wanted a solicitor before questioning him about the symbol branded on to his back.

'What does it mean?' she asked.

Mountson shrugged. 'Doesn't mean anything. It's my initial.'

'What about the mark on Carrigan?' asked Thomas.

'What about it? That's completely different.'

'You both have branding marks on your bodies now. That must mean something.'

'Sam didn't choose to have that mark. What Laurence and I did was a bit of fun. He was into ink, so was I. The branding was something different. We decided to give it a go.'

'Where did you have it done?' asked Louise.

'I don't want to get anyone in trouble,' said Mountson.

Louise uploaded the photograph of Andrew Thorpe on to the screen on the wall, her patience fading. 'It's a bit late for that, Mr Mountson, don't you think?'

'It was somewhere in London. Catford, I think. Place doesn't exist any more.'

'Why did you have yours done on your back?'

'I wasn't sure I wanted it to be visible.'

'And Laurence Dwyer?'

'Laurence wasn't one for reservation. He didn't care. He liked being separate from the crowd, you know? He wore it as a badge of honour.'

'I have to ask, David, what was the extent of your relationship with Laurence?'

'We were friends, nothing more.'

'Are you sure? Seems a very committed thing to do together,' said Thomas.

'We were friends. We fooled around now and again, but Laurence would fuck anything that moved.'

'Where is he?' asked Louise, trying to catch Mountson out.

'I don't know and I don't want to know.'

'Why's that?' said Louise.

'Look, I was friends with him but, in the end, he was too much for me. He was wild. Unstable, you know? I got hooked because of him. He introduced me to everything. It was only when he went that I was able to start thinking about getting my life together.'

'He sounds like he was a bit of a bully,' said Louise.

Mountson bit his lip. 'You could say that. It wasn't obvious at the time, but he had a way of making you do things, you know?'

'Like that?' said Thomas, pointing to the picture of Andrew Thorpe's corpse still on the screen.

Mountson looked at the image and winced.

'You think Dwyer could do something like that?' asked Louise.

Mountson glanced at them one at a time. 'If I'm being honest, I don't really know.'

Chapter Thirty-Four

Mountson's hesitation in the interview was enough to suggest that he thought Dwyer was capable of the attacks. They questioned him for another twenty minutes, but Louise felt they were moving in circles. In the end, she decided to keep both Mountson and Sam Carrigan in custody for the night. It made sense to keep them under observation. They were potentially a risk to others, though at present Louise was more concerned that the two men were potential victims and felt keeping them locked up for the night was the best way of protecting them.

Reluctantly, she went downstairs and grabbed a quick shower before changing into a black dress. It had been some time since she'd worn it and she was pleased it was still a good fit. By the time she returned to the CID office, Thomas was also suited and waiting for her. She hadn't seen him in the suit before. He'd been dressing well of late, and a curious part of her wondered if any of it could be for her benefit. Since moving to Weston, she'd tried to ignore her attraction to him, especially when he'd still been married. But even now after his divorce, it was something she felt unable to act on. She reminded herself that, as with Farrell at MIT, Thomas was effectively her professional partner in Weston and that was something she couldn't risk jeopardising – however good he might be looking that evening.

'You scrub up well,' he said.

'Not too shabby yourself. Do you want me to drive? I'm not going to be drinking tonight.'

'You're planning on going to one of these things without drinking? You have been to these before? You'll be the only sober person there,' said Thomas, sounding genuinely incredulous.

A few years ago, she would never have dreamt of going to such a function without drinking, and Thomas's jest about being the only sober one there would no doubt prove to be accurate. But after Paul's decline into alcoholism, and with the same fate threatening her mother, she wanted to avoid temptation as much as possible.

It already felt wrong to be going to some fancy get-together when the town was facing the crisis of two murderers being loose. Anyone in the police not going to the retirement party was out working. She had teams stationed outside Poppy Westfield's house, and close to the crime scenes. With Baker's help, a number of uniformed officers were working undercover in the town's bars and nightclubs, and messages had been sent out via local media outlets that people should behave with extra vigilance. But she still feared that wouldn't be enough. The attackers were specific, and most likely had their next target in their sights. Louise wanted to be ready to act and intended to spend the bare minimum amount of time at the party that evening.

Louise called Tracey as she drove to the centre, arranging to meet her at the Winter Gardens, rather than for pre-drinks, as they'd discussed. It was still light as they approached the seafront. The tide was in and the setting sun glistened on the rippling water. With the terraces of the local bars and hotels filled with people, the day's heat still carrying in the air, Louise could have mistaken the town for a

Mediterranean hotspot. A vision that was dispelled as she took the turning to the tired grey of the shopping-centre car park.

'You sure we have to do this?' she said to Thomas, as they parked up and took the concrete staircase – ripe with smells of nicotine and urine – to the high street.

'There are just some aspects of the job they don't tell you about,' said Thomas, as they walked through the ornamental gardens to the back entrance of the Winter Gardens.

Louise declined the offer of champagne as they entered to a cacophony of noise in the main ballroom. It was as if the whole of Avon and Somerset constabulary were in the room. As she glanced at the art deco design of the curved walls, she again thought how wrong it was to be here. She pictured Mountson and Carrigan back at the station, nursing their hangovers, Andrew Thorpe's parents mourning their son, and the Westfields at their home, trying once more to come to terms with how their lives had been devastated. What would they think about her being here, when the murderers were still on the loose?

She smelled Finch before he appeared. It couldn't have been more obvious than if he'd pissed in the corner, his citric aftershave somehow managing to fill the air despite the hundreds of people in the room. She wasn't surprised to see ACC Morley and his wife accompanying the DCI. However, the fourth person in their party caught her off guard.

As was protocol, the ACC spoke first, introducing his wife to Louise and Thomas. Morley had about as much time for Louise as Finch did, but no one would ever have guessed from his effusive introduction.

Then it was Finch's turn. 'You two know Natalie, I'm sure,' said Finch, introducing the elegant woman standing next to him as if they were all best friends.

Natalie Gurgenstein was the head of the Crown Prosecution Service in the area. Louise had worked with her on a number of cases. She was highly intelligent, attractive and good company. Louise smiled as she shook hands with her, wondering what on earth would make her attend the event with Finch.

She'd gone out for the odd drink with Natalie after busy work days, but she couldn't ever recall Finch being mentioned. Even so, she must have known about his reputation. Louise supposed that she had once fallen for Finch's charms, so it wasn't inconceivable that someone else would. It was taking all her willpower not to take Natalie to the side and tell her about Amira Hood and Terri Marsden, about her own terrible relationship with the man. She felt that she had an obligation to warn her, but there was no conceivable way she could think of doing so without coming across badly.

Louise noticed the narrowing of Finch's eyes, as if he were trying to read her thoughts. Did he know she was on to him? Terri had pulled out because he'd sent her a reminder photograph, but that could have been a coincidence. Either way, Simon had the phones now and was hopefully making some inroads. What she wouldn't give to be able to wipe that smirk from his face.

'If you'll excuse us,' said Thomas, rescuing everyone from a silence that was rapidly growing uncomfortable.

'You OK?' he asked, once they'd reached the relative safety of the bar area.

Normally, she would have taken umbrage at Thomas feeling the need to drag her away from Finch and Morley – she didn't need protecting and was loath to show any weakness in their presence – but at that moment she was simply glad to be away from them.

'Sure I can't get you that drink?' said Thomas.

Louise was tempted, but there was a risk that one drink might lead to too many others and she was painfully aware that somewhere in town the attackers were still active. All she wanted now was to show her face for an hour, go home and get some sleep, and be up and ready to continue the investigation tomorrow morning.

Thomas was of another mind. As she moved through the room, exchanging small talk, she noticed his frequent visits to the bar. Where she was struggling with the situation, Thomas appeared to be in his element. Getting drinks for people and conversing with everyone as if the whole event had been staged for his benefit.

'DI Blackwell.'

Louise cursed under her breath, turning to face the person who'd called her name. Inspector Dan Baker was standing behind her, his body impossibly straight, as if he'd been stalking her. 'You gave me a fright there, Dan,' she said.

Baker smiled but remained rigid, as if he were stuck in place. 'Let me introduce my wife, Rebecca. Rebecca, this is the illustrious DI Blackwell. A bit of a star around these parts,' he said.

Such was the space Baker occupied, Louise had almost not noticed the petite woman standing next to him. Rebecca barely came up to Baker's chest height. She was a pretty woman with red hair and looked to be a good ten years younger than her husband. She was holding Baker's hand tightly, but they still looked like an odd pair with their height and age differences. And despite herself, Louise couldn't help but glance at the prominent tattoo that snaked up from the woman's chest to her shoulder. 'You are being too kind, Dan. Very pleased to meet you, Rebecca,' she said, trying not to stare. Ever since the case started, she'd been alert to people with tattoos. Until now, she hadn't appreciated how ubiquitous having a tattoo appeared to be. Even so, seeing the tattoo on Baker's wife surprised her, as if she couldn't have imagined the wife of someone so strait-laced being adventurous enough to get something like that done.

'Likewise,' said Rebecca, letting go of Baker's hand and shaking Louise's, holding her gaze with a surprising intensity. 'I understand you're working on that horrible murder case I've been reading about in the papers,' she said, her eyes locked on to Louise's.

'That's correct,' said Louise.

'Now, now. No shop talk, Rebecca,' said Baker.

'That's OK. I'm sure everyone is thinking about it,' said Louise.

'Such a terrible business. With the branding and everything. Horrible,' said Rebecca.

Louise nodded, though she saw more excitement than disgust in Rebecca's eyes. 'How are you finding moving back to the area?'

'Oh, it's fine. I have family here anyway so it's not that much different. So tell me, any possible suspects?' said Rebecca, lowering her voice, as if they were conspirators.

'We're working on it.'

'Come on, Rebecca, I think DI Blackwell is probably taking some pleasure from having a few minutes off from the case. Can I get you anything from the bar, Louise?'

'No, thank you,' said Louise, as Baker all but dragged his wife away.

Louise spent the next thirty minutes doing her duty, shaking hands with more people and pretending to enjoy herself. Networking was an aspect of her career she'd never been great at. It had been pointed out to her on numerous occasions that this was holding her back. Maybe if she'd been more willing to play the game, she could be a higher rank by now. Finch was a master of it, and that was why he was currently in conversation with the assistant chief while she was left wandering the ballroom alone. But did she really want that? The Peter Principle often rang true in the police force. She enjoyed the day-to-day challenge of an investigation and, although she was sure she could get a more senior management position, she wasn't suited to such a role. DCI Robertson was all but desk bound and that wasn't something that interested her. Not that a promotion was imminent. It had been left unsaid, but her enforced move to Weston had been a kind of retirement. Like a horse sent to pasture, she was sure that Finch and Morley had expected her move to Weston to effectively end her career. No doubt they'd hoped that the change of pace in her new environment would make her question her role in the police force. What they hadn't counted on was her resilience, and with her misconduct meeting approaching it made her wonder what they had in store for her next.

'What are you doing on your own?'

Louise turned around to a smiling Thomas, who was holding two full glasses of champagne. His eyes were glazed, and he had slurred. She took one of the glasses. 'You seem to be having a good time,' she said, placing her drink on the bar.

'You have enough of these, anything can be fun. Everything OK with you? I imagine there are a few people here you'd rather not see.'

'Are you my knight in shining armour now?'

Thomas frowned, and she realised she'd been a bit sharp with him.

'Sorry, Tom, I appreciate your concern. I hate these things and yes, there are a few people I'd rather not see.'

Thomas opened his mouth to speak and, for a second, she thought he was going to mention Finch. A flash of indecision reached his eyes and Louise leaned over and took the second glass from him. 'Let's get you home,' she said.

They walked back alongside the seafront, a light drizzle in the air, the sea's retreat towards the dark horizon almost complete. 'You heard the rumours?' said Thomas, as they crossed the road towards the car park.

'Have you been gossiping again, Sergeant?' said Louise.

'Me?' said Thomas with mock outrage. 'Well, maybe a little.'

'Go on then. Tell me what sinister plan you've uncovered.'

'It's not good news, I'm afraid. It seems they're definitely going to shut us down.'

'How many of those champagnes did you have?'

'It's true. The plan is to amalgamate all CID departments to headquarters.'

Louise had heard it all before. Ever since Baker's appointment, such theories had started circulating around the station again. Her hope had been that the department's recent successes in high-profile cases would prevent such a move, but theirs wouldn't be the first department to be centralised. Portishead was only a twenty-to-thirty-minute drive from their station in Weston, and although it would logistically be harder to work cases from headquarters it wasn't inconceivable. Much of their work was conducted out of the office and being in Portishead meant they could cover a greater area than present. 'You'll forgive me if I don't dwell on that at present.'

'Did you see Baker's wife?' said Thomas, as they reached the car.

'She seems nice.'

'She's about half his height.'

'Can't say I noticed.'

'Yeah, right.'

Louise recalled the woman's interest in the branding case as she made her way down Locking Road towards Worle. It was only five hours ago that she'd been at the station interviewing Mountson, but for now the case felt like a hazy memory. If she wasn't so exhausted, she would have dropped Thomas off and gone straight to the office to continue working.

'I expect you in bright and early tomorrow,' she said with a smile as she pulled up outside Thomas's house. Until her recent move from her bungalow in Worle, they'd been all but neighbours, Thomas having moved to the area following his divorce.

'I'll see what I can do,' said Thomas, not leaving his seat. He was laughing, the fresh air on the seafront having accelerated his intoxication. 'Listen, I've been meaning to say something . . .'

Louise's pulse quickened as Thomas leaned towards her. Her mind began playing tricks on her as he tried to kiss her. It told her this was something she wanted, at the same time warning her that this was the wrong time, and most definitely the wrong moment.

In the end, she turned her head in time for Thomas's lips to brush against her cheek. He pulled back as if sobering up in an instant. 'I . . .' he began, his eyebrows lowered in regret.

Louise gave him what she hoped was a reassuring smile. 'Get some sleep,' she said. 'I'll see you in the morning.'

Chapter Thirty-Five

She was different. Although invisible to everyone else, the branding felt as if it were burning its way through the fabric of her dress, as though she was carrying Andrew Thorpe's death on her flesh. She wanted to free herself to display the marks on her body – so they would know, so they would fear her – but now wasn't the time. For now, she was content to move among them unknown, the symbol on her body a secret she was willing to keep for the present.

The evening was glorious. It was as if the quaint and forgetful town she'd left behind had been transformed in her absence; revitalised and born again in the same manner as herself. The residual heat helped, as did the number of people filtering through the town. The seafront felt alive in a way she'd never experienced before. The Grand Pier took centre stage, stretching into the sea, as people ate and drank outside the cafés and restaurants. Winter would change all that, but she wasn't prepared to wait until then. This was her town now and she'd only just begun making her stamp upon it.

They'd danced and drunk their night away. She liked D in action. His easy charm, the way others deferred to him, as if sensing his power. That they didn't give her as much respect was understandable. She was content to remain hidden for now, to allow him to soak up the attention. None of them knew of the branding, red raw on her flesh. They didn't know what she'd done or what she had in store, and that brought with it a power of its own.

Afterwards, she'd insisted they drive to Louise's house. She had one more target, but she couldn't stop thinking about the woman, and her ready-made family. D wasn't keen on being there. He wanted to go for the last target, to finish what they'd planned. But her plans had changed. She didn't regret killing Thorpe – he had deserved to die, and using the needle on him was a potent reminder of her past, but there was no benefit to having her mark on a corpse.

Marking Mountson's boyfriend had changed her outlook. Him, and that stuck-up little bitch, Poppy, would wear her mark for the rest of their sordid lives. But why stop there? The town was littered with hundreds of potential connections, metres of flesh she'd yet to call her own, and the most precious of all belonged to Louise.

She'd sensed it the first time they'd met and these last few days watching her had cemented the feeling that their paths were intertwined.

'Why are we here?' asked D, moving towards her, his hands close to her latest branding mark.

She couldn't explain it to him. She owed him for how he'd helped her, both now and in the past, but he would never really understand what she wanted. He was already jittery about being here. If she told him she wanted Louise to be part of her family, he would probably run a mile. 'Don't you enjoy the power of watching? She thinks she's safe, thinks her family are safe, but we could change that with a click of our fingers,' she said, appealing to D's baser needs.

'It's an unnecessary risk,' he said, as a light switched on and off on the top floor, where Louise slept.

Unfortunately, such comments were becoming typical. She was frustrated that they still couldn't locate Mountson. She'd wanted to follow Louise in the morning, but D had said it would be impossible, that she would be trained to notice stalkers.

'If we can't locate Mountson by tomorrow, we'll find other targets,' she said, producing a penknife from her bag. She took one last look up at the house as she rolled up the sleeve on her shirt and made a delicious slice across the flesh of her upper arm before heading back to the car.

Chapter Thirty-Six

It was such a beautiful morning that after letting Molly out into the garden Louise decided to take her breakfast – black coffee and the extravagance of a chocolate croissant – outside. Everyone else in the house was still asleep, and the dog kept running off and returning to her, checking she hadn't been abandoned.

Of all the things she'd expected to happen last night – a confrontation with Finch or ACC Morley being most likely – the last thing she'd expected had been for Thomas to try and kiss her. And despite the strains of the ongoing case, it was all she could think about.

She hoped they could put it down to a drunken mistake, but she couldn't shake the fact that despite the clumsy advance, and her own soberness, she'd come close to kissing him back. These things happened all the time. When you worked in such close proximity, particularly in such tense circumstances, it was natural to seek out comfort and pleasure where you could. Thomas and Tracey had had the briefest of flings in the past so perhaps she shouldn't have been as surprised as she was by last night's events.

She was sure they would be able to get past the incident. It would probably be awkward for a day or two and be forgotten. But if she was being true to herself, she wasn't sure she wanted to get past it. She'd been attracted to Thomas from the first day, and though she'd tried to fight it her feelings for him had deepened. The objections she placed in front of herself – he was married, then following his divorce he was too vulnerable – were now obsolete. However, they still had to work together and for now that was one obstacle she couldn't see beyond.

She was the first from the team to arrive at the station. Those not at the event had been working through the night, and the duty sergeant informed her that Baker's team had shut down another bar last night for serving after hours.

Even DCI Robertson, who at times seemed to live in the office, was absent. She'd spoken to him a couple of times the previous evening and he'd looked about as pleased to be there as she'd been.

She brewed a fresh pot of coffee and took the report from the night shift into the incident room. Carrigan and Mountson were still in custody and Louise called the patrol car stationed outside Poppy's house to check there had been no activity. Everything seemed to point towards the group of teenagers from five years ago, and Louise looked up the report with Dan Baker's name on it once again. The names Poppy Westfield, Andrew Thorpe and Laurence Dwyer were prominent. Dwyer was the missing link at the moment, and that made him both a possible suspect and a possible target. Louise glanced up at the image of Dwyer they had from Mountson's social-media account, the blurry outline of the branding mark circled in red, and was wondering what role the man had to play in the incidents when her phone went off, the sound echoing in the empty room.

Louise let her pulse settle before answering the call. 'Yes?' she said, her thoughts always turning to Finch when *unknown caller* appeared on the phone's screen.

'Hi Louise, it's Simon Coulson.'

It seemed like weeks, but hadn't been twenty-four hours since she'd spoken to Coulson. 'Hi Simon, you're up bright and early.'

'Time is a relative concept when you sit behind a screen all your life. Are you able to talk?'

'I'm all yours.'

'Not great news, I'm afraid. I've run full diagnostics on the phones you gave me but I can't find a source for the messages. Whoever sent them is pretty tech savvy, or knows someone who is.'

'OK, I guess that's what we expected.'

'It's not all bad news. If you can find the source, then I think we can prove a link, even if the messages on the other end have been deleted. I know that's not great, but maybe it's something to work on?'

Not great was an understatement. She thanked Simon after arranging to get the phones back. Just thinking about Finch made her think of his sickening citric aftershave. She still couldn't quite believe the lawyer, Natalie, had attended the event with him last night, but one thing she was certain of: Finch would have kept a record of every message and photo he'd sent. He was as predictable as any sociopath she'd tracked before. He clearly got off on the power and would want to keep evidence of his conquests, especially the compromising photos he had of Amira and Terri Marsden, and most likely countless other women.

Now all she had to do was find out where he was storing everything.

The team had all filtered in by 9 a.m., including Thomas, who failed to meet her eye as he joined the briefing. Robertson watched as she gave out the duties, his hangover evident in his hangdog look. Louise reiterated that the main focus was on finding Laurence Dwyer and finding out the names and location of everyone else who might have been part of the group David Mountson, Andrew Thorpe and Poppy Westfield had hung out with.

Thomas waited until everyone had dispersed before approaching Louise. Her pulse quickened as he stopped by her desk, scratching the back of his head like an errant schoolboy. 'Thanks for the lift home last night,' he said.

Louise smiled. She found his awkwardness endearing, but still wanted to hear what he said next. 'You're welcome.'

'I guess I made a bit of a fool of myself?' he said.

'I wouldn't say fool.'

'Well, I'm sorry. I overstepped a boundary. I shouldn't have . . .'

Louise shook her head. 'Don't be silly, it's fine. The way you were knocking back that champagne . . . honestly, let's forget it.'

Thomas nodded. She sensed he wanted to say more, but it was the wrong time and with the incident room and surrounding office filled with colleagues, definitely the wrong place.

Although they had MIT helping, Louise felt frustrated by the lack of progress. Teams were out there searching for Dwyer but still it felt as if they were being reactive, as if waiting for the next incident. Mountson and Carrigan were due to be released that morning and more manpower would be needed to keep track of them. Last night's event had deflected some of the attention that was coming her way, but if results didn't start happening soon it would only be a matter of time before the pressure was heaped on her and the department.

For what felt like the hundredth time, she read through the report on the teenagers at Brean from five years ago. She wasn't sure what was making her so hesitant, but she'd yet to speak to Baker about it. Perhaps she'd been waiting for him to approach her, but she couldn't delay the conversation any more.

She found him in his office on the third floor. His door was open and she knocked before walking in.

'Louise, to what do I owe the pleasure?' asked Baker, getting to his feet as if to display his height. 'Please,' he said, pointing to the chair opposite him.

Louise caught a glimpse of his wife's image in the photo frame to his side as she sat down. She looked even younger in it, and it made her wonder even more about their unlikely relationship. 'I see you shut down another bar last night?'

'My team did, yes. I think we're getting the message out there, slowly but surely. That's why you're here?'

'No, much more interesting than that,' said Louise, placing the Brean file on his desk. 'You remember this?'

Baker took out a pair of spectacles from his top drawer and perched them on the end of his nose. 'Oh, I see. Two of your victims are named on here.' He placed the document on the desk and rubbed his chin, deep in thought. 'I have a vague memory of this. A bit of a waste of time, if I remember correctly. I apologise, though, I should have remembered the names.'

'What can you tell me about it?'

'It was my predecessor's operation,' said Baker, picking up the file again. 'To be fair, it was one of many going on at the time. We were going through a crackdown on teenage gangs. Seemed like we were looking at a new one every week. Nothing out of the ordinary in this one. We'd had reports of drug dealing, but there was nothing like that going on, from what we could tell.'

'Do you remember seeing this man?' said Louise, showing him a picture of Laurence Dwyer.

'He was on the list?'

Louise inched the photo closer to Baker. 'Can you see the mark on his arm?'

Baker adjusted his spectacles and glanced at the image again. 'Oh, yes. That is intriguing. And he was on the list of people we were watching?'

'Yes.'

Baker took off his spectacles and looked at her. 'You know how it is, Louise. That was five years ago. If I'd seen that mark on him, I would probably have remembered. As it is, he's just one of hundreds, if not thousands, of young people I've dealt with in the last few years.'

'Of course, Dan, I get it. Maybe if anything comes to mind you can let me know?'

Baker stood up. 'You'll be the first to know, Louise,' he said.

Louise got to her feet. 'Thanks, Dan. Your wife enjoy the Winter Gardens last night?'

'Most definitely. Couldn't have come at a better time for us, really. Not always easy settling back into a new place, but that was a great event.'

'Send her my best wishes, won't you,' said Louise.

'Will do,' said Baker, standing as if to attention as he waited for Louise to leave.

Louise spoke to both Mountson and Carrigan before they were discharged. She urged Mountson to give her more details on Laurence Dwyer, but he remained evasive. She was convinced he was withholding something from her, but that wasn't enough to keep him in custody. She was about to follow the two men out of the station when a voice distracted her.

'Some night.'

Louise took a deep breath and turned to face Finch. 'Not really my scene, Tim. Too much brown-nosing for my liking.'

Finch smiled, but Louise could tell the comment annoyed him. 'It was a bit sad to see you there alone, Louise. At your age, tick-tock, tick-tock,' he said, moving his finger in time to his words.

'Is that really how you see women, Tim?'

Finch held his hands up in mock surrender. 'I'm just saying, you're no spring chicken. Don't want to be left on the scrapheap.'

'Do you not have anything better to do with your time?'

'Just wanted to pass on some friendly advice.'

Louise bit her lip. A number of responses sprung to mind, but Finch would see any comeback as a victory. 'Thanks, I'll take it into account,' she said, turning away.

'There is one more thing. I had a good chat with the ACC last night.'

Louise couldn't resist. Turning back to face Finch, she said, 'As I said, lots of brown-nosing going on last night.'

Finch gave her his best humourless smirk. 'Hilarious. Unlike your investigation into these branding attacks. Morley is very keen on my idea to allow MIT to have greater control over these cases.'

'I bet he is.'

'I don't like to add any pressure on you. That's why I'm going to offer a couple more bods to help you out.'

'You're all heart, Tim.'

'With your hearing coming up, it's the least I could do.'

Finch was positioning himself perfectly. If things went wrong on the case, she would be to blame. If things went well, he would get kudos for helping out. It was a classic win-win situation for him. 'Is that everything?' she said.

Finch stood his ground. Louise took solace from his frustration. Try as he might, he couldn't quite provoke her in the way he wanted. 'Just don't fuck up,' he said, trying to regain control over the situation.

Louise smiled and walked away.

◆ ◆ ◆

Putting the confrontation behind her, she made the short trip to the Mountson residence in Uphill. It didn't feel like the best use of her time, staking out a victim and a potential victim, but it gave her the opportunity to get out of the station and think.

The heat in the car was stifling. She buzzed down all the windows, but the still air outside was as hot. Opening her laptop, she gazed through her notes, struggling to focus. Trying her best to forget about Finch, her mind kept returning to her meeting with Baker, and the less-than-subtle way he'd ushered her from his room. The officer in charge of the original investigation, an Inspector Adam Royston, was retired now. She could call him and get his feedback, but for the moment it felt like overkill. Baker had given her his side of the story and speaking to Royston risked alienating her colleague.

Later in the afternoon, the retired teacher, Groves, left his house and began tending the front garden. She could imagine his fury that Mountson was currently residing in the house next door but wasn't about to discuss the issue with the man. She called members of the team, getting updates. Tracey and Greg Farrell had made the journey to North Wales to speak to Laurence Dwyer's parents. Tracey told her that his parents' relationship with Dwyer had been acrimonious. They hadn't seen Dwyer since he was a young man and had moved to Bristol.

It appeared that Dwyer had since dropped out of society. The last official record they had for him was a bank withdrawal of £70 three and a half years earlier, the exact amount of money that had been in his account at the time. Since then, they had no bank, utility bills or even phone records for the man. That he was living off-grid wasn't that unusual – in a town like Weston with lots of transient, seasonal workers, often paid in cash, it was quite common – but it made tracking him down that bit harder.

She rubbed her eyes, the pollen in the air making them itch. The more she thought about it, the more she grew convinced something was being kept from them. She would have to speak to Poppy again. Everything pointed to the group of teenagers in Brean, and Louise had to find out what had actually happened; why people from that time were turning up as victims.

But for now, she decided to remain outside the Mountson residence. She wasn't sure what she was waiting for – it felt unlikely that Laurence Dwyer was going to return from the wilderness – but she was content to be there for now.

Why she stayed there for so long she didn't know. Even in Louise's mind, it suggested a certain desperation. By the time the sky darkened she was dehydrated, her limbs stiff from being cooped up in the car seat. She found a chocolate bar in the side pocket of the passenger seat, but the heat had made it inedible. One of the first things she'd been told about stake-outs was to prepare, and she'd failed in that regard. But stubbornly she stayed on, past midnight, as if she could out-wait time itself.

The downstairs lights in the Mountson residence had remained on since earlier that evening and, unless they'd escaped through the woodland to the rear of the house, she was sure the two men were still there.

It was a theory she put to the test after receiving a call at 2 a.m. Leaving the car in a rush, she ran to the house and knocked on Mountson's front door until it was opened. Mountson was clearly high as he opened the door in his bathrobe, Carrigan hiding behind him. 'You two have been here all night?' she asked.

'Yes,' said Mountson.

'Good. Don't answer the door again until you've checked who's there,' she said, rushing to the car.

She called the station back as she made her way to the scene and arranged for a patrol car to stay outside the Mountson house. A man had been found, mercifully still alive, outside the Playhouse on the high street, the swan symbol branded on to his neck.

By the time she arrived at the Playhouse she was informed that a second person had also been attacked.

Chapter Thirty-Seven

By the time Louise reached the Playhouse, the first victim, Terrence Maynard, had been rushed to hospital. Photographs had been taken of the injuries inflicted on the man. Louise scrolled through the images of the swan symbol 2, red raw on the side of Maynard's neck. Maynard appeared to be homeless. He'd been sleeping under the shelter of the Playhouse foyer. His soiled sleeping bag and belongings were still there, untouched, waiting for the SOCOs to arrive.

Louise had already instructed Thomas to head straight for Weston General and to get as much information from Maynard as possible. The first responder had spoken to Maynard before he'd been taken away and he had confirmed there had been two attackers, both wearing masks. Louise left the first responder at the scene to wait for the SOCOs, before taking the short walk to Grove Park, where another team were dealing with the second attack.

Despite the late hour, heat still hung in the air. It wasn't lost on her that only a few days ago she'd watched David Mountson walk along the very same street and cross to the park, where he'd got into an altercation with the dealer, Ben Abbey. It was a different place tonight, everywhere shut, only the illumination of the flashing lights in the car park hinting at any nocturnal life.

The park had been cordoned off. 'There's a pond over to the left, ma'am,' said one of the uniformed officers, pointing to an area on the other side of the park lit by flashing blue lights, where a group of officers and emergency personnel had gathered.

It was impossible to take anything positive from the situation, but at least Terrence Maynard was still alive. After Thorpe's murder, Louise had feared that it would become the attacker's new MO. However, that there had been a second attack, so close by and within a short time frame, was a great concern to Louise. It suggested that at least one of the attacks was random and that the attackers were either getting careless, more confident, or an unhealthy mixture of both.

She cut across the grass, the anguished cries of the second victim reaching her before she'd passed the bandstand in the centre of the green. As she approached the small area of the park next to the pond, the noise intensified. The first responder had done a good job, cordoning off the area where the second victim was receiving treatment from the paramedics and not allowing anyone else to enter. Louise walked up to the tape and spoke to the officer.

'Raymond Oxford. We think he was sleeping here. I've run a check back at the station and up until last week he was staying at a hostel in Ashcombe.'

'He's been branded?' said Louise.

'Yes, ma'am. Right side of his shoulder. Same symbol as the others.'

The light was poor and it appeared that the paramedics had covered the wound with a bandage. The man's shrieks had diminished, but he was still wide-eyed, as if he had no idea what was happening to him.

'It's pretty nasty,' said one of the paramedics. 'Whatever they used, it went partly through his clothing. We need to get the wound treated before it gets infected.'

'Mr Oxford. My name is Detective Inspector Louise Blackwell. Did you see who did this to you?' said Louise, as the paramedics wheeled the victim along the pathway to the waiting ambulance.

The man stared at her, terror still in his eyes. Spittle fell from his lips as he mouthed something that sounded like 'Man, two', and she didn't manage to get any more sense from him by the time he was placed on to the back of the ambulance.

Louise checked in with all the teams as she waited for the SOCOs to arrive. It was late, and she was sore from sitting in the car all day. She couldn't be sure if she was thinking straight, but these latest developments didn't make sense to her.

She found it unlikely that Terrence Maynard and Raymond Oxford had links to the other victims. And that worried her. It seemed the attackers had gone off plan. Where they had seemingly indulged themselves in mock hunting Sam and Poppy, and more than likely Andrew Thorpe, it appeared as if they'd struck their latest two victims where they slept. That there were homeless people on the streets of Weston was a damning indictment on the council. Maybe the fact that they were now subject to these aggravated attacks would make those in authority act more quickly. It made her wonder again about Dan Baker and his closure of the rehab centre in Milton. Everyone moved on from the centre had either returned home or had been rehoused, but she made a note to recheck the list of occupants once she was back at the station, though she couldn't recall reading Maynard's or Oxford's name before.

After watching the SOCOs set up, Louise walked up the hill to the top of the park towards the gated children's playground where she'd stopped the altercation between David Mountson and the drug dealer Abbey. In the darkness, the playground reminded her of some disquieting photographs she'd seen on the internet, of an abandoned theme park covered by the spread of woodland.

Beneath the covering of trees, the leaves gently rippling on the breeze, it was hard to believe that a couple of hundred yards away the SOCOs were examining the sites where Oxford and Maynard had been brutally attacked. As she opened the creaking iron gate into the playground, she took some solace in the fact that the two victims were alive. Again, it was an unusual turn of events. After killing Thorpe, the usual pattern would have been for the attackers to continue killing. That they'd managed to refrain from doing so suggested a sense of control which to Louise's mind was even more troubling.

A scurrying sound towards Upper Church Road interrupted her thoughts. She turned towards the sound, not expecting to see anything, but in the shadows next to a street lamp she thought she could see the outline of two figures. 'Stop!' she shouted, fumbling for her torch.

Jumping over the metal railings, swearing as she clipped her ankle on the top of the metal bar, she scrambled across the foliage to the stone wall perimeter of the park. The dim beam of the torch held out in front of her, she glanced down the street in both directions, but if anyone had ever been there, they had now disappeared.

Chapter Thirty-Eight

D told her it was a pointless risk, and he'd been right. The first mark wasn't enough, and even the second had done little to quench her need. She'd enjoyed the sound and smells as the iron had breached the prey's skin but had been left with an empty feeling when it was all over. Although there was a certain thrill in knowing these men would carry her with them at all times, it wasn't what she really wanted.

D had discovered that Mountson had spent the night in custody, only to lose him once he'd been discharged. She couldn't hide her disappointment and had instructed D that they were going to find a random target that night. But after the two attacks, her need to connect was even greater.

Mountson had to pay for what he'd done, but her need was increasingly focused elsewhere. It hadn't been what she'd planned when she'd returned to Weston. She hadn't come looking for the family she'd never had, but it had presented itself.

D had called it an obsession, and maybe he was right. He'd tried to persuade her to leave the scene quickly. But after the second branding at the foot of Grove Park, she'd insisted they wait.

She not only wanted to see Louise again; she needed to see her.

They had watched from the top of the hill, her heart hammering, Thorpe's mark on her back aflame, as the policewoman arrived.

She imagined the woman's hands on the homeless man's wounds, her fingers trailing the raw and ragged mark; imagined her doing the same to her own marks, a delicious shiver running down her body.

And then, as if she had known she was being watched, Louise had started to walk towards them.

'I told you,' D had said, the impatient whine in his voice a growing irritant.

'She's not superhuman,' she'd replied, leading them out of the park like a disgruntled dog.

Even then she'd lingered. From the street, she'd watched Louise in the playground. She had such poise, such ease at being by herself. She half-wondered if Louise understood that she was being watched, that she wanted her to connect them for ever.

'Come on,' D muttered, but she couldn't stop herself. Louise's skin was cloaked in shadows, but she could taste its milky softness. She shuddered as she imagined the iron breaking that perfect skin, easing down into her soft flesh, at which point Louise had looked up and called out.

In the end, D had all but dragged her away. She'd kept her eyes on Louise's approaching figure until the last second, desperate for another glimpse of her haunting skin; a perverse need to tell her that they would see each other again soon.

Chapter Thirty-Nine

Louise had chased after the figures. She still wasn't sure if she'd imagined them or if they'd been a trick of the light. It was feasible, considering the dark, and her tiredness, that she'd made something out of nothing; that her desire to find some answers had made her see things that weren't there.

By the time she returned to the foot of the hill, she had been notified of a complication with Raymond Oxford. The attack had triggered an underlying condition and Oxford had slipped into a coma. She left one of her team at the site to liaise with the already stretched SOCOs and made the short journey through the deserted town to Weston General.

She'd been here so many times in the middle of the night that the eerie glow of the hospital building and the desolate corridors felt like a second home. The two victims had initially been placed on the same ward, but Oxford had been sent to ICU while Maynard was resting after being sedated.

'It could be a matter of hours, or maybe weeks, months,' said the doctor, explaining the heart issues Mr Oxford suffered with.

'Did Mr Oxford say anything when he was admitted?'

'No, his vitals were very low and by the time he reached A&E he was out of it.'

'Can I see him?'

The doctor shook his head. 'We cleaned the wound and took some images of the branding mark, if that is what you want. Going into ICU would be pointless.'

Louise gave her number to the doctor, who forwarded images of both victims. The mark was the same as on the others, Oxford's wounds the messiest of the bunch, as if the branding iron had been applied in a rush. The curve of the 2 was distorted where the attackers had singed through his clothing.

After thanking the doctor, Louise bought herself a coffee from a vending machine on the ground floor. She took one sip and spat the tasteless sludge back into the cup before throwing it in the bin. Finding the darkest spot in the empty waiting room, she sat down and closed her eyes. After the inactivity of sitting in the car all day, the excitement of recent events had sapped her energy and after some internal struggle she managed to fall asleep.

It was still dark when she was roused by the sound of voices sometime later. She jumped in her seat, momentarily lost in her dream world, seeing herself back in Grove Park, two human figures scuttling away in the undergrowth.

Her back creaked as she sat up, the penalty for being cooped up in the car. 'Could you two keep it down? I was trying to get some sleep,' she said, recognising the figures of Thomas and Tracey standing in the corridor, having also made the mistake of sampling the vending-machine coffee.

Tracey grinned. 'We were wondering where you'd got to?' Despite the hour, she looked alert and well presented, the antithesis to how Louise felt.

Thomas still looked hung-over. His face was covered in stubble, his eyes heavy with small bloodlines. 'We've checked on Poppy and Sam. Both safe,' he said.

Louise declined to tell them what she might have seen at the top of the hill, deciding it served no purpose. 'They're getting reckless, either by choice or complacency,' she said, reiterating her thoughts from earlier. 'You two should go and get some rest.'

'What, that twenty-minute sleep sort you out?' said Tracey.

'I slept last week,' said Louise. 'Seriously, it's fine. We'll need you more in the daytime. We can't speak to either victim yet so there's no use us all hanging about in here.'

The two officers were reluctant to move and Louise had to walk them out of the hospital to their cars. 'We'll do a briefing at ten a.m.,' she said to Thomas.

'Cool, should be able to get a good three hours' sleep in. You going home as well?'

'I'll wait here until morning, see if Mr Oxford's condition improves.'

'I could keep you company, if you like?' said Thomas, as Tracey looked over from the car door.

'Get some rest,' said Louise.

Louise tried heeding her own advice. She managed a couple of ten-minute naps, giving up as soon as the sun began filtering through the foyer windows, the first of the morning shift arriving into the hospital.

Unable to face another machine-dispensed coffee, she drove to the Kalimera for an Americano to go. Walking along the seafront, she allowed the morning breeze to refresh her. The familiar smells of seaweed and salt rushed through her as the sand-inflected air bristled her skin. As it always did, the island of Steep Holm six miles out from shore called to her, her leg aching in remembrance of the injury she'd suffered on the island during her first major case in the seaside town. So much had happened since then. She'd suffered excruciating lows but had always fought back and returned stronger, yet knowing she could turn things around wasn't a comfort at that moment. Maybe it was the early morning, and lack of sleep, but she felt as if they were back at the beginning. They were no closer to identifying the attackers, and the threat of further incidents was more real than it had ever been.

Tired of waiting for things to happen, she retrieved the last-known address they had for Laurence Dwyer and made her way to a smallholding outside the village of Brent Knoll.

Brent Knoll was the name of a large hill that dominated the skyline of the local area. The small village of the same name was ten miles out from Weston. To the south of the village lay farmland, and the abandoned shack where Dwyer had once lived. Officers had visited the property already but Louise wanted to see it for herself. She didn't imagine anything would come of it, but Dwyer was the closest thing they had to a suspect at present and she wanted to get a better understanding of the man.

Peering through the stone walls of the single-floor dwelling, she was surprised anyone had ever lived there. It had probably stood abandoned for the best part of four years but, aside from a couple of months in the summer, it felt too open to the elements for anyone to call it home. The battered wooden front door flapped in the wind, the air inside much cooler than out. In many ways it was an idyllic location, especially if you appreciated solitude. Louise made a note to question Poppy and the others about the place. She could easily imagine a group of teenagers partying in the surrounding fields, and as she drove back to Weston she wondered if this was a location Baker and his colleagues had missed during their surveillance.

◆ ◆ ◆

A shadow swept across the interior of the CID office as Louise pored over the case file on the branding investigation. Raymond Oxford was still unconscious, but before leaving the hospital she'd managed to speak with Mr Maynard. Maynard was thirty. He had been divorced three years ago, his ex-wife taking their son and daughter abroad with her new lover. He'd moved to Weston a couple of months ago, hiking from his old town near Leeds. He'd told Louise as much with something approaching nostalgia, as if any memory was preferable to what had happened to him the previous night.

He'd been asleep when the attack occurred, the smell of gas and fire waking him seconds before he felt the pain on his skin. Both his attackers had worn masks and he hadn't recognised any of the photos of the other victims, nor of Mountson and Dwyer. As he told Louise this, he kept glancing down at his bandages, as if in fear of the mark beneath.

Maynard's photo now had a place on the crime board, alongside that of Mr Oxford. From what they'd uncovered, Oxford was as transient as his fellow victim. The last-known address prior to Weston had been in Plaistow in East London, where he'd been living in a shared house less than eighteen months ago. Louise had spent the last few hours trying in vain to link either man to the other victims. The latest two attacks had triggered more press coverage, and after speaking to Robertson, the only saving grace she could take from the current situation was that Finch was conspicuous by his absence; a note of optimism she regretted feeling when her phone rang, the words *unknown caller* prominent on the screen.

Chiding herself for thinking the worst – Finch had only ever sent messages anonymously – she was still relieved when she heard Amira's voice on the other end of the line.

'Sorry, I should have called you,' said Louise, under her breath, aware of the members of MIT circulating the office.

'I take it there was no luck with your IT guy.'

'No, I'm afraid not.'

Amira sighed, her anguish palpable even over the phone. Louise shared her frustration and wanted to help but she couldn't be sure it was the right time.

'I know you must be really busy with this new case, but I was wondering if we could meet tonight. Maybe catch a drink or something?' said Amira.

Louise couldn't recall the last time she'd had a good night's sleep. She didn't want to disappoint the woman but she could feel her energy drain at the thought of going anywhere else later other than straight to sleep. 'Perhaps we could talk tomorrow?' she said, hating the compromise she heard in her voice.

Amira sighed again, this time with a hint of impatience. 'I didn't want to speak about this over the phone, really.'

'What's it about, Amira?'

'It's about DCI Finch,' said Amira, whispering as if her voice was carrying beyond Louise's headset.

'What about him?' said Louise, matching Amira's hushed tone.

'He's on annual leave. He's gone away with some solicitor woman. This might be our only chance.'

Two hours later, Louise found herself in Amira's car, parked on the street where DCI Finch lived. Amira turned towards her, her large eyes full of hope and, Louise thought, a hint of naivety. She'd agreed to meet her out of a panic that Amira was about to make a large mistake.

'I can do it. I'm sure you can too,' said Amira, eyes still locked on to Louise, as if she held Amira's fate in her hands.

'I'm sure we both have the potential to break into Finch's home, Amira. I don't think that's the question. Putting aside the illegality and the definite ending of our careers, what makes you think he would leave anything incriminating lying around?'

'You know how these people can be. It's all about power and control. He'd want access to a reminder of that. He's also supremely arrogant. He thinks he's too clever to be caught. That could make him sloppy.'

'It could, but it would be foolish to underestimate him. We already know he might be on to us. If he's going away, he's more likely to take precautions.'

'Maybe he's distracted by that pretty solicitor,' said Amira.

'Too many maybes for me,' said Louise. She was worried she'd heard a tone of jealousy in Amira's voice, and was reminded she knew very little about the woman. She'd done a bit of research on her, and had mentioned her to Tracey, who had only positive things to say, but it was difficult not to be circumspect. Louise hadn't even had confirmation that Finch was on annual leave. She hated the paranoia Finch induced in her, but it wasn't a great leap to imagine him setting the whole thing up. He'd tried everything else to get rid of her, so why not this? 'The second we break into his home, we jeopardise everything. Unless we find something, no one would ever take us seriously again.'

'We could argue reasonable suspicion,' said Amira, turning away.

'No, we couldn't, Amira. You know that.'

Louise noted a line of four red spots on the back of Amira's neck. With exhaustion creeping over her, the thoughts in her head began to merge and she had an overwhelming desire to ask Amira to show her any tattoos she might have on her skin, as if somehow the officer would reveal a swan symbol somewhere on her body and things would start to make sense.

'I can't give up,' said Amira.

'I'm not asking you to do that, but this isn't the way,' said Louise.

Amira sighed and started the engine. 'I'll drop you back at your car,' she said.

Chapter Forty

Louise drove home, calling Simon Coulson on the car's hands-free system, seeking confirmation from him, rather than from Tracey or Greg Farrell, that Finch was on annual leave. With that established, she turned her attention back to the investigation at hand. Raymond Oxford was still in a coma, but Terrence Maynard was on the mend. Thomas had arranged for him to stay at a local hostel and had questioned him again about the attack.

She hadn't given much thought to Maynard's situation, but stuck within the slow-moving traffic on the M5 back into Weston she had the opportunity to lament the position the man found himself in. One thing working in the police had taught her was the fragility of a so-called normal life. Ever since her time on the beat, she'd seen so many lives transformed. From road-traffic accidents, through to serious assaults and murder, each crime left behind it a legacy that extended way beyond the victim. Maynard was a case in point. His life already damaged irrevocably by his family split, Louise thought he would struggle even to get past this attack. Maybe his former wife would take some sort of pity on him, but Louise imagined the branding mark would haunt him and exacerbate his addictions. Somewhere there were hundreds of other stories she would never know the end of, other victims like Maynard she'd dealt with over her years on the force. She knew it couldn't become her concern – she would never function successfully if she was always dwelling on the past – but her frustration, both with the case, and with Amira's investigation into Finch, was making her maudlin. She needed to get back, eat, then sleep, but she was stuck in what appeared to be an endless stream of traffic, a mixture of commuters and tourists making their way to Devon and Cornwall, making the most of the continuing good weather.

It was still light by the time she reached home. The family were in the garden, Molly running loops around Emily while Louise's parents sat on garden chairs enjoying the view.

'Hello, stranger,' said her dad, as she collapsed into the soft cushion of a garden chair, Molly bounding over as if she hadn't seen her in weeks.

Louise patted the dog, accepting the glass of cold wine from her dad without objection. The effect of the drink was immediate, the citric, slightly bitter tang of the wine rushing into her system, a glow forming over her as she sank further into the cushions of the chair.

For the next hour, it was like she was in a world out of time. She all but forgot about Finch and the murderous attackers terrorising the town. She was content to live in the bubble of the family garden, the only people in her life her parents and niece, the taste of the sea air, and the second glass of wine, easing all her tension away for the briefest, and most blissful of times.

◆　◆　◆

Drinking coffee in the quiet of her living room the following morning, Louise was amazed by how refreshed she felt. After Emily had gone to bed, she'd heated up the dinner prepared by her parents and had been in bed by ten. She couldn't remember the last time she'd had eight hours of uninterrupted sleep and, with the resulting clarity of thought, she promised herself she would try and make it a regular occurrence, while ignoring the voice of reason in her mind telling her it would be an impossibility.

She made plans for the day as she drove along the seafront and out towards Worle, buoyed by the opportunity the day held for her; and for the consolation that she hadn't been called in during the night to attend another crime scene.

After going through the case book, and briefing the team, she made plans to speak to Poppy Westfield again. The young woman's mother was reluctant and Louise had to be a little firmer than she would have liked on the phone.

She checked in with the hospital before leaving for the Westfields' house, discouraged but not surprised to be informed that Raymond Oxford was still in a coma.

In the station car park she was stopped by Thomas, who also looked like he'd caught up on some sleep. He was freshly shaven, which always took a good few years off him, and his eyes were clear and bright. They exchanged some small talk, but an awkwardness remained. Louise was sure they would get past it at some point, and a part of her was enjoying the way they were tiptoeing around one another. It reminded her of the first few weeks of seeing someone new, the excitement and insecurity interlinked.

'I've been following up on the ownership of that piece of land where Laurence Dwyer used to live,' said Thomas, getting straight to the investigation.

The shack in Brent Knoll felt like a distant memory, though she'd only been there yesterday. She pictured the open spaces of the abode, the coldness of the stone interior, and reminded herself to question Poppy about it. 'It belongs to the attackers and they've confessed and are on their way in for questioning?'

'Not this time. Belongs to the owner of the adjacent farmland. Norris Harding. He remembers Laurence Dwyer. Used to help out on the farm in lieu of rent. Apparently, he up and left without a word. Even left most of his stuff behind.'

'What happened to it?'

'Mr Harding said he disposed of it. Not heard from Dwyer since.'

'Can't blame him for that, I guess. OK, see what you can find out about Mr Harding. See if we can make some connections.'

◆ ◆ ◆

Both Poppy's parents were at home. Their animosity regarding another visit from the police was understandable. Louise was another reminder of how their lives had once again been shifted. They'd obviously worked hard as a family to move on from Poppy's teenage mistakes, and now they had been thrust back into the centre of their lives in the most extreme manner imaginable.

Louise was led to the open-plan kitchen. The area was spotless, the smell of coffee and fresh baking in the air. The Westfields were trying to continue to live their lives in the most normal way possible. Louise accepted the offered cup of coffee, as Mrs Westfield wiped an invisible mark from the work surface.

'Poppy will be down in a minute,' said Mr Westfield, receiving a stern look from his wife, as if somehow he was betraying her.

'How is she?'

'She's still on painkillers,' said Mr Westfield.

'That's not what she means, Greg,' said Mrs Westfield. 'How the hell do you think she is? First the attack, and then to find out her ex has been murdered. We had no time for Andrew, obviously, but she loved him. Or thought she did.'

Poppy appeared just as her mother stopped speaking. She was barefooted, and they hadn't heard her approach.

'Poppy, dear, would you like something to eat?' asked her mother.

Poppy ignored her and poured herself a coffee, filling a third of the cup with milk. She sat down on a high-backed kitchen chair, pulling her legs up on to the seat. Her pink pyjamas and unbrushed hair made her look much younger than her nineteen years.

'Thank you for seeing me,' said Louise.

'Have you found them?'

'Not yet. I'd like to ask you a few questions, if I may?'

Poppy looked at her parents. At first, Louise thought she was asking for their permission, but she was waiting for them to leave. Mr Westfield left the room with his head down, his wife shooting Louise a look laced with accusation as she followed shortly after.

'Are you sure you don't want your parents here?' said Louise, drinking the coffee and feeling guilty for savouring the taste.

'What do you want to know?' said Poppy, holding her cup of coffee as if for warmth.

'This is, in part, about Andrew?'

Poppy sniffed, fighting back tears.

'You used to go with him to the beach over in Brean, is that correct?'

'Sometimes.'

'There was a group of you?'

'Sometimes.'

Louise showed her the picture of Laurence Dwyer and David Mountson. 'Did you ever see these men?'

Poppy pointed to Mountson. 'David.'

'You were friends with him?'

'Not really. He was older than us. Most of us, anyway.'

'The other man?'

'I wasn't friends with him.'

'You know his name?'

'Laurence.'

'Tell me about him, Poppy.'

'I didn't really know him. He was sort of the leader, I guess, of a group of boys who occasionally would turn up. I always felt a bit uneasy around him, to be honest. He was a bit creepy.'

'How did Andrew get on with him?'

'They were friends.'

'When did you last see Laurence?'

'Not since those days. Not since I, you know, had to move out.'

'Did Andrew ever take you to a place in Brent Knoll?' said Louise, showing her a photo of Dwyer's abandoned shack.

Poppy pursed her lips and shook her head. 'I only went to the beach with them a few times. When Andrew and I . . . started seeing each other, we just wanted to be together.'

'Anything else you can tell me about David Mountson and Laurence Dwyer? Anything you may think would help with the investigation?'

Poppy sat stony-faced.

'You're not going to get into trouble, Poppy. I'm just trying to find out who did this to you.'

'I think he used to sell drugs to them. The kids on the beach.'

'Laurence Dwyer?'

'Yes.'

'How about David Mountson?' said Louise, showing her the photo again.

'Not that I'm aware of.'

The beeper on the cooker went off, Mrs Westfield rushing back into the kitchen and retrieving a tray of cookies from the oven.

'I'll just leave these here, but remember, they're hot,' she said, glancing anxiously at Poppy, who ignored her gaze.

Louise smiled, and waited for Mrs Westfield to leave before continuing. 'When you were with the group, you were stopped by the police one time in Brean. Do you remember that?'

'Sort of. We were always getting hassle from them. Because we were drinking, that sort of thing.'

'And drugs?'

'Not me.'

Louise didn't buy the denial, noting the way Poppy looked away before answering. 'Do you remember anything specific about the police from that time? Any officers in particular who seemed to be on your case?' Louise wasn't sure why she'd asked the question, or what she'd hoped to achieve by asking it. The awkward conversation with Inspector Baker was still fresh in her mind. She wanted to know if Poppy remembered him, but the young woman stared back, her face devoid of emotion.

'There was one thing, actually,' said Poppy, after Louise had all but given up hope of getting some answers from her. 'I hadn't thought about it before, until you mentioned the police, but there was this boy in school. Carl Payton.'

Louise remained quiet, not wanting to risk Poppy losing the thread of her story.

'He had a thing for me, you know. But he was only a boy,' said Poppy. 'Anyway, he seemed to know about me and Andrew. It really pissed him off. And once, just before I moved away, he told me that it was him who'd gone to the police about Andrew. I almost tore his eyes out – one of my friends had to stop me – but I didn't really believe him.'

Louise couldn't remember the name in any of the records. 'Does he still live in Weston?'

'I heard he moved Cheddar way,' said Poppy. 'Is that it? I'm feeling very sleepy.'

'Thanks, Poppy. I'm sorry to have put you through this,' said Louise, but Poppy was already out of her seat and walking back towards her bedroom.

Chapter Forty-One

Louise grabbed a sandwich from the Kalimera before heading out to the village of Cheddar where she'd obtained an address for Carl Payton. She ate as she drove, hungrier than she'd realised.

The journey to Cheddar was one she'd made on a frequent basis earlier that year, working on a missing persons case. Cheddar was home to the famous gorge that bisected the area. It was a stunning place, but Louise wasn't in a rush to see it again. As she drove through the picturesque village with its quaint olde-worlde shops, she was struck by the transformation in the place. When she'd been there around the Easter period, the village had been struggling for tourist trade, having been hit by the poor weather and the fallout after the eleven-year-old girl had gone missing. Now, the traffic through the main road was at a standstill as cars battled to find parking spaces, hundreds of holidaymakers crossing the narrow roads to the tourist attractions and walking up the steps towards the cliffs that loomed over the area.

The address she had for Carl Payton was another ten minutes out, in Bradley Cross. Although she'd wished Poppy had mentioned him before, she didn't blame her. Sometimes questioning had to be specific, and if Louise hadn't mentioned the police watching her group in Brean, then chances were high that Payton would never have crossed Poppy's mind again.

Louise was forced to park up halfway on the pavement outside the terraced house where Payton lived. Further down the street a group of teenagers had congregated, smoking and holding energy drinks. They glanced Louise's way, their attention not lasting as she knocked on the door.

A heavyset woman in a dark jumpsuit answered. A cigarette was stuck to the underside of her upper lip, and in her arms was a young child. She looked at Louise with disdain. 'What?' she said.

Louise flashed her identification. 'Is Carl in?'

'What's he done now?'

'Nothing. We just need his help on something.'

The woman frowned, and without looking away from Louise, screamed out, 'Carl, there's someone at the door for you.'

Seconds later, Louise heard the sound of footsteps coming down the stairs, the woman making way for a man in his early twenties. 'Yeah?' said the man, who was at least twice the size of the woman standing behind him.

'Carl Payton?'

'Yeah.'

'I'd like to speak to you about Poppy Westfield.'

Payton's face fell, the tension in his body suggesting he was panicking. 'Can she come in, Mum?'

'Take her through to the back room. I'm busy,' said the woman, stomping off down the narrow corridor, the child in her arms glancing over her shoulder at Louise.

Louise followed Payton through a narrow corridor to a small sitting room. Peeling wallpaper fell from the walls, the deep pile carpet was rough and worn. Payton sat down on a patterned sofa – its dark brown colours like something out of the seventies – somehow out of breath.

'May I?' said Louise, moving a pile of laundry off a lone armchair.

'Be my guest. What's this all about? I'm a busy man,' said Payton.

'What is it you do, Mr Payton?'

'What's that got to with anything?'

Louise dispensed with the small talk. She told Payton her reasons for being there, studying his reactions as she told him about Poppy and the other victims. 'You remember Poppy Westfield, don't you, Mr Payton?'

'Sort of.'

'Sort of? Poppy has some clear memories about you.'

'Is that right?'

'She mentioned that you claimed to have informed the police about her relationship with Mr Thorpe. Is that correct?'

'Of course not.'

'But you told her that's what happened?'

'Who can remember? It was so long ago.'

'It was five years.'

Payton shrugged.

Louise decided to try a different tack. 'What do you remember about the people Poppy was hanging around with at the time? You're not in any trouble. I'm trying to find those responsible, and you could be of great help to me,' she said, playing to Payton's ego.

His mouth still hung open, as if he were trying to catch the stale air in the room. 'They weren't very nice people. I did try and warn Poppy, but she wouldn't listen.'

'In what way weren't they nice, Mr Payton?'

'They used to hang around the school gates, chatting to the girls, you know? They were older, and had cars.'

'That must have been difficult to compete with.'

'It wasn't that. They used to buy the girls gifts, you know? To get them to go with them. I think there were drugs too.'

'Didn't the school do something about it?'

'Not really. Some of the teachers would come out and warn them now and again, but they'd just move off down the road. Anyway, it was too late by then. Poppy fell in with them.'

'Do you recognise any of these men?' said Louise, showing Payton photos of Mountson and Dwyer.

'Him. He was the main one,' said Payton, curling his lip as he pointed to Dwyer. 'He used to call me names. You know, because of my weight and that.'

'You remember his name?'

'Laurence Dwyer. He used to be mates with that other guy, David Mountson. Dwyer was expelled.'

'Poppy knew them both?'

Payton shrugged again, drawing into himself, as if he'd said too much. 'I don't know. Maybe. Probably. It was only Dwyer I used to see. Him and these other men I didn't know. They were the ones hanging around. I heard they sold weed and some other stuff, and they were definitely grooming those girls.'

'Can you remember anything more specific about that time? The names of the other men hanging around with Dwyer, the girls involved?'

'Look, I don't want anything more to do with this,' said Payton, pushing himself off the sofa with considerable effort.

'Sit back down, Mr Payton,' said Louise, unmoving.

He glanced at the door as if considering summoning his mother. His breathing was rapid, his chest expanding and contracting against his clothes.

'I told you, I didn't know the other men Dwyer was hanging out with. As for the girls, they were all in Poppy's year or younger, you should ask her.' Payton wiped away a bead of sweat that was dripping towards his nose. 'Do you think Dwyer has been making these attacks?' he said, collapsing back down into the creaking sofa.

'Do you think he's capable of that?'

The fear was evident on Payton's face, as if he thought he was a potential victim. 'He was off his head, I know that. I heard lots of stories about him. Insane stuff.'

'Such as?'

'This . . . branding stuff that's in the papers. I heard he'd done that to himself and that he was making others do it as well. You know, to be part of the gang. And the stuff with the girls. They used to share them, like sweets. They'd buy them gifts and next thing they were missing from school; some never came back.'

'How long did this go on for?'

'Pretty much until Poppy left school. Didn't use to see them around there any more. I heard that Dwyer had moved on somewhere else. It was a shame it was too late for Poppy.'

Chapter Forty-Two

She grabbed D's hand and moved along the shore, her other hand reaching for the packet in her pocket. She had to all but drag him along the sand, his body limp, his face slack as he gazed down at his sandals. D had told her it was becoming an addiction, as if she didn't already understand that herself.

It was as if she'd known the place all her life, as if she'd made the short walk from the back of the house to the sea a thousand times. She'd only felt this way once before and, although that had not ended well, this could be different.

She opened the packet as the dog got nearer, trying to make contact. The dog bounded over and sniffed her, its owners in no rush to catch up with the Labrador.

She bent and stroked it. 'She's beautiful,' she said, as the little girl approached. 'What's she called?'

'Molly,' said the girl.

'What a lovely name.'

The grandparents caught up after a time. She saw glimpses of Louise in their features, and in those of Louise's niece. 'She seems to like you,' said Louise's father, as the dog snuffled in her pockets.

'I think she can smell something,' she said. 'Have a lovely day,' she added, as the girl skipped ahead and called to the dog.

'I don't know what you're doing,' said D, once they were out of earshot.

'You don't need to know,' she said, pleased both to have met Louise's family face to face, and that the dog now knew her scent.

She envied Louise – how peaceful it must be to have such a loving family – but also felt sorry for her. She didn't even have any ink on her, so couldn't possibly understand the transformative power of the mark. But she could change that. She could give Louise that power, at the same time getting to savour the love of her family.

D would never understand. He was beginning to resent every second they spent watching. He claimed to want more action, that their focus should be on finding Mountson, but she'd noticed the creeping change in him. He needed to be reminded of what the mark could do.

'OK, let's go,' she said.

'Go where?'

She looked directly at him, searching for a hint of weakness. 'To give you your reward.'

Chapter Forty-Three

Louise diverted more resources to finding Laurence Dwyer when she returned to the station. Even with the help from MIT, the department was stretched and focusing more on Dwyer felt like the logical step.

She spent the next few hours searching through reports on the school from the period when Poppy had developed her relationship with Thorpe. As Carl Payton had suggested, there had been issues with older children and young adults hanging around outside the school. The school had liaised a number of times with the police, and officers had been stationed on the streets outside the school, including on occasion the then Constable Dan Baker. According to the reports, no official action had been taken. Baker had gone home for the day so Louise would have to wait until tomorrow for his version of events.

Louise drummed her fingers on her desk. A wanted mark had been placed on the national database for Dwyer. All it would take was one sighting, and possibly all the unanswered questions in the branding case would be revealed. Yet there was a risk that Dwyer would never be found, or that if they did find him, he would turn out to have no bearing or connection to the case.

Unfinished cases plagued every station in the country. The recent attacks had felt careless and unplanned, and although Louise didn't want to see any further attacks, she also feared the attackers had lost confidence in whatever twisted mission they had planned and would now disappear.

Glancing out of the window, Louise was surprised to see it was already dark. She was alone in the incident room but couldn't face going home. So many things were swarming through her head. At another time, she might have gone to the bar and drunk away the tension. Instead, she did something that, even as she did it, felt even more ill advised.

◆ ◆ ◆

The lights were on inside the Mountson house by the time she arrived outside, twenty minutes later. It was 9.45 p.m., and without any real development in the case, it felt like an unsociable time for her to call. If Mountson complained, it could cause her hassle, especially with the misconduct meeting coming up. However, she felt justified in knocking on his door. He was intricately linked to what was going on, and she wasn't going to let fear of a rebuke stop her.

Mountson was holding a glass of clear liquid when he answered the door. By his glazed look, she was sure it wasn't water. 'We were wondering when you were going to show up,' he said, holding his hand out to indicate Louise could enter.

'After you, Mr Mountson,' said Louise, shutting the door behind her as Mountson walked off down the corridor.

'Hey,' said Sam Carrigan, as she entered the living room, raising his own glass of clear liquid, as if they were best friends. He was wearing a vest, the branded mark clearly visible on his arm. 'It's looking good, isn't it?' he said, catching her gaze.

'We've decided to embrace it,' said Mountson. 'Sam is going to make it his own. Take away the power from the monsters who did it. Drink?' he added, moving towards a nearly finished bottle of vodka.

'No, thank you,' said Louise. She was impressed with the idea of Sam reclaiming the mark for himself, but it was obvious that both men had yet to fully come to terms with what had happened.

'I need to speak to you about Laurence Dwyer again,' she said, sensing that the window to get any sense out of either man was closing fast.

'We don't want to talk about him any more,' said Sam.

'It's OK, Sam,' said Mountson, wincing as he drank the neat vodka. 'I've told you all I know,' he said to Louise.

Louise relayed the information she'd received from Carl Payton.

'I don't know anything about that,' said Mountson.

'You knew he was selling drugs to these girls, didn't you?' said Louise.

'I told you, I had nothing to do with that. As you can see, I'm not interested in women. I heard he was messing around with that shit. It wasn't for me.'

'You knew about Poppy and Andrew Thorpe, though?'

'That was different.'

'How?'

'Thorpe was slimy and he should never have been messing around with that girl as she was too young. But I do think it was consensual.'

'You can't consent if you're underage.'

'I know, I know, but you know what I mean. I honestly thought she was seventeen or eighteen. They were genuinely into each other. It wasn't like the other stuff. The thing you're talking about.'

'The grooming?'

'Yeah.'

'So that was going on?'

Mountson turned away, realising he'd been caught in a lie. 'I heard about it. I didn't know if it was going on for sure, but it definitely wasn't happening with the people I was hanging out with. We were just having some fun. I would never have anything to do with that.'

'But you knew Dwyer used to hang out at the schools?'

Mountson shrugged. 'I'd moved on from him by then.'

'Moved on?'

'We fell out about it, OK? We had a massive fight. He didn't like the way I refused to follow him. There were lots of things he didn't like at that point.'

'When was the last time you heard from him, David? Tell me the truth.'

'I told you, the man disappeared, and I wasn't sorry to see him go. He could have a hold on you. With him gone, I managed to get my life back in order. Until recently, of course,' said Mountson, looking around at the wreck of his parents' living room.

Louise stopped short of telling the men it wasn't too late, that they could still get some help. They were too inebriated, and her words would be wasted. Perhaps, when this was all over, Mountson would come to his senses and return to his fight against his addictions and would offer the help he'd initially given to Sam. 'I know you don't want this to happen to someone again,' she said, to both men. 'Please, try to remember. There must be something you're forgetting. Something about that time that would help us find who is doing this.'

Mountson sipped on his vodka, sinking further back into the sofa. It was impossible to tell if he was too far gone or was simply lost in thought. 'It's probably nothing,' he said, slurring as his eyes struggled to focus on her.

Louise couldn't recall how many times she'd heard those words before, so often a prelude to something of significance. So much of her work was determining the minutiae of an investigation. Often what someone thought was of least importance turned out to be pivotal. 'What is it, David?'

Mountson had started shaking. 'It's only a rumour, but I heard he fell in with the wrong people. Some gang from Bristol. He pissed off the wrong person. That's why I don't think he did all this.'

'Why, David?'

'Because I think he's dead.'

Chapter Forty-Four

D begged and whined like a child, but she'd left him there on the massage bed until he calmed down. She'd wanted to see if he truly understood their work together. It was true that she wouldn't be here if it wasn't for him, but sometimes people changed; something she was only too aware of.

In the gloom of the room the branding mark on his back appeared to glow, as hot as the branding iron cooling on the side. She touched the tattoo that crawled up her shoulder, gazing around at the collected artwork on her walls as she waited for his cries to subside. He wouldn't stop going on about the policewoman and how foolish it was to pursue her; it was as if he had a personal stake in the matter.

He'd never been branded before, despite her continued pestering. This time he'd understood it wasn't an option. She needed him to understand, to accept her mark on him, to become part of her family. Reluctantly, he'd agreed, allowing her to bind him to the bed, a rag in his mouth, while he'd sweated and convulsed. She'd even numbed the area for him but still he'd squealed, no different to the others.

Eventually his crying subsided, and she untied him. As he shuffled from the bed, she saw the transformation in his eyes, but it hadn't been what she'd hoped to see. He was like a dog understanding his order in the pack. He wouldn't meet her gaze as he shuffled off to the bathroom to get some painkillers.

'Put your clothes on,' she instructed. 'I want to go back.'

An hour later they were sitting in the woods, her binoculars focused on the house. D hadn't spoken to her since his branding and was sitting on the ground, eyes downcast, looking at the mud beneath his sandals. 'You want to look?' she said, offering him the binoculars.

'I want to go home and rest. I need to put something on it,' said D.

It hadn't felt the same, giving him her mark. Although he'd been restrained and there had been a little coercion on her part, he'd been a willing partner. She'd hoped it would invigorate him, as had happened to her, that they'd become closer, but it was having the opposite effect. 'We're staying here until she returns home,' she said, not giving him the satisfaction of looking at him.

Perhaps it was the tone of her voice, or a final grab of power on his part, but this dismissal sprung him into life. He jumped up and grabbed her by the arm. 'You're hurting me,' she said, his vice-like grip holding her in place, his nails pinching against her skin.

'You can't attack a serving police officer,' he said, for the first time since that afternoon matching her gaze.

The pain from his grip wasn't unpleasant, but that wasn't the point. 'Let me go,' she said.

Maybe he was trying to take some of the power from her, but he was hurting her, and he understood the one rule he couldn't break. She stared at him, issuing him a silent challenge.

He released her and turned away, beaten. 'We'll stay here until she returns,' she said, having already decided what she would need to do to him.

Chapter Forty-Five

Louise was unable to gather any more information from Mountson. He claimed not to know any more about the so-called gang in Bristol, and he started crying, Sam rushing to his side to comfort him. Louise wondered if the tears were for his lost friend or himself. She'd already seen too many people in tears during this investigation. Whether they were linked or not to the brandings, so many events from the past were leaving a trail of destruction. She left her card on the mantelpiece and asked Mountson to call if he remembered anything else, but she doubted that by morning either man would recall her even paying them a visit.

As she drove home, Louise wondered if she was growing too fixated on finding Laurence Dwyer. She wasn't about to take Mountson's suggestion that Dwyer was dead seriously, but Dwyer had been off the grid for the last four years. If he had got in with the wrong crowd and suffered the consequences, then it would be a big hit to the investigation.

As she took the old toll road back towards Sand Bay, she tried to shake the feeling that she was being followed again. Her car was the only vehicle on the dimly lit road, so she would have been aware if she was being tracked. Amira had a lot to answer for, and she was reminded that she hadn't spoken to the woman since she'd sat in the car with her outside Finch's house. Was it possible that the actual

Ghost Squad were following her? After working with Amira, she'd put that possibility to one side. But the disciplinary hearing was coming up, and Finch could easily have called in some favours to get them to investigate her.

It was too late now to return to the station and scour through everything to try and track Dwyer, but she came close to doing so. She stopped at the turning towards her house, deciding whether to continue straight on and take the back route through Worle to the station. Rest wouldn't come easy, but she would find the following day much easier even with a few hours of sleep, so reluctantly she headed for home.

The lights in the house were off and she made a mental note to install floodlights to the drive at the front as she made her way across the gravel. She wondered if she would feel this tightness in her chest every time she returned to the house without seeing Emily before bedtime. It was an excruciating guilt, made all the worse by the lack of progress in the case.

Upstairs, she made a sandwich and headed for the living room, where she had her own crime board, a mini replica of the one at the station. She took a red felt pen and scribbled a circle around the photograph of Dwyer once more. Directly or not, the man was becoming central to the case. She couldn't be sure whether he was one of the attackers, but everything, aside from last night's seemingly random attacks, pointed towards his involvement.

She sat back and gazed at the board, the chicken in her sandwich dry. She often worked this way, staring at the board as if it were a puzzle she could unravel through sheer will power. Sometimes patterns emerged, sometimes things only became more clouded. Unlike the board at the station, her crime wall held a photograph of Inspector Dan Baker. She was still unsure about him and the role he had to play in the past. If anyone from the station could see the board, they would question her thought process; if they knew she was working with Amira, they would possibly question her sanity. She had no evidence of either man's criminality, and whereas she knew Finch was guilty of something, her animosity to Baker was based on feeling and a possible coincidence, both poor starting places. Her hand reached towards his photo, but at the last second she left it where it was, deciding that he'd yet to be fully open with her and so warranted his place.

As she suspected, sleep didn't come easy. Outside, the seagulls were engaged in an operetta that usually took place in the light of the morning. As Louise closed her eyes once more, her head was filled with their shrill cries as imagined visions of the injuries inflicted on the victims played through her mind and made her skin itch.

She was about to give in and watch some mindless television to help guide her to slumber when the squalling of the seagulls stopped. It was most likely her imagination, but she was convinced the area behind her curtains had lit up briefly.

Yawning, Louise scrabbled out of bed and pulled on her dressing gown. Now that she'd been dragged into action, tiredness seeped through her body and instructed her to go back to bed, but she struggled across the floorboards to the window and inched open her curtain.

At first, she conceded she'd been a victim of her overworked imagination. But as she eased open the curtains and adjusted to the darkness outside, she made out the silhouette of an object to the left of the driveway entrance. Squinting, she thought it was the shape of a car, which would explain the ray of light she'd seen, but she couldn't be sure as the landscape was a blur of dark shapes and shadows.

It wasn't something she could let go. Maybe if she'd been alone, still living in the bungalow, she would have gone back to sleep, but she had her family to think of now and even the smallest of risks was too great. She put on the trainers she left by the front door and placed a can of pepper spray inside her dressing-gown pocket as she retrieved her torch and expandable baton from her utility belt.

The sound of the sea carried along the cold breeze as she opened the door, the seagulls still in retreat. She kept the torch off, her eyes adjusting to the darkness, and edged along the side of the house so she had a better view of the driveway entrance, where she saw the outline of a parked car. Usually, she would have returned to the house, but her curiosity had been piqued now. Keeping the torch off, her right hand firmly on the baton, she edged down the driveway.

She stopped five metres from the car as a torch beam shone directly into her face.

Chapter Forty-Six

'Put that down,' said Louise, her baton raised.

The beam fell from her face, lighting the ground between her and the owner of the torch. 'God, I'm so sorry, Louise,' came a voice.

'Amira, is that you?' said Louise, moving towards the sound until she could see her fellow officer.

'I'm sorry. I thought you'd be asleep. I was going to wait here until morning.'

Louise's heightened pulse began to drop. Even in the dim light, she could see Amira was agitated. Her eyes were downcast, as if she'd been caught out doing something she shouldn't. Louise thought back to the day she'd discovered Amira was following her and wondered if this was the first time she'd parked up outside her house. 'What could be so important that you couldn't wait and call me in the morning?' she said.

'I think I've done something a bit foolish.'

'What have you done, Amira?' said Louise, sensing her career spiralling away from her. 'You didn't break into Finch's house?'

'Not quite,' said Amira, holding out a key ring. 'Finch gave me a set of keys once. And I may have got a copy cut. I know, psycho-bunny behaviour, but he hasn't changed the locks.'

It was an oversight, but arrogance was the one thing that could make Finch reckless. Louise would have invited Amira in, but she was annoyed both by her intrusion and her deception. 'You should have told me you had the keys and you definitely shouldn't have used them.'

'You might not say that when you know what I discovered.'

Louise swore under her breath. She'd somehow cornered herself into a problem not of her making. She would have to report Amira, but do that and there would be too many questions to answer. 'What did you find?'

'I found the laptop he was using to send the messages. At least, I think I did.'

'You do all this to tell me that?'

'I found a laptop he'd hidden, and next to it were some print-outs. Photographs. Of me, of Terri, of seven other women,' said Amira, anger distorting her face.

'Unfortunately, that's not a crime, Amira.'

'No, but if we can crack that laptop, I know the messages will be on it.'

Louise was torn. All logic appeared to have fled from the officer, replaced with an unwieldy paranoia that threatened to get them both into trouble. Yet, Louise couldn't deny the potential of the situation. She wouldn't normally condone doing something illegal, but that resolve could be tested if it resulted in Finch being brought to justice. He was playing with Amira's life, and, if Amira was to be believed, at least seven others. And if he was willing to do that to them, what else was he capable of?

Louise realised she already knew the answer to that. 'Where is the laptop now?'

'Everything is still there, like it's never been touched. I have an idea, Louise.'

'You have an idea? I have an idea, and that's to report this straight away so I don't lose my job,' said Louise.

'No one saw me, and if they did, I have a key. Finch never explicitly told me not to return to his house, and I didn't take anything.'

'Fuck me, that's flimsy at best, and you know it.' Louise regretted losing her temper. She scratched the back of her head and laughed at how absurd it was to be standing outside in the middle of the night in her dressing gown and trainers. 'You need to let this go now,' she said.

'That's easy for you to say.'

'No, it isn't. I want him gone as much as you do, but this isn't the way to do it.'

'Think about what he's done, Louise. To you and me, to Terri, to countless others. I can't believe you're going to get squeamish on me now, when we're this close.'

Louise paused. Maybe she was protesting too much. For once, things seemed to be falling in her favour, so why was she presenting Amira with so many obstacles? 'Even if there is something on the laptop, this isn't the way to go about it.'

'What do you suggest, we ask him nicely to hand himself in?'

'Well, what do you suggest, Amira?'

'He's back this weekend.'

'And . . .'

'Hear me out first,' said Amira, desperation in her voice. 'We stage a break-in.'

'Oh, come off it.'

'We stage a break-in and we make sure the right officers attend the scene.'

'This is ludicrous. You're suggesting they just happen to stumble across the photos and laptop?'

'If it's the right people.'

'No one is going to take in the laptop of a serving DCI.'

'I was thinking about that. What if we tip off someone from the Ghost Squad? If they have an idea this is going on, then they would be more likely to investigate the bastard.'

Louise played both scenarios in her head – the ludicrous suggestion of staging a break-in and the possibility of going to the internal investigation team. Neither played out well. Staging a break-in went against everything she believed in. Getting Anti-Corruption involved would be a long and drawn-out process and would probably give Finch enough time to cover his tracks.

But was she simply making excuses not to act? If the videos could be recovered from his house, then hopefully more evidence would be there. All it would take would be proof that he'd been sending the anonymous messages to Amira and the others and Finch's career would be over and he would almost certainly face a custodial sentence. 'Do you have his keys?' she asked.

'Yes, why?' said Amira.

'Give them to me.'

'Why? We have him.'

'I need to think about it.'

'You don't trust me, is that it?'

'You broke into his house – give me the keys. Let me think about our next move.'

Amira tore two keys from the key ring and handed them to Louise. Her eyes were at once pleading and accusatory. Louise understood her frustration but wasn't about to be swayed by it. 'Go home. I've got your number and I'll let you know what we do next. Don't do anything else.'

Amira clenched her jaw but didn't speak.

'Do you understand?' said Louise.

Amira glared at her before returning to her car. 'I understand,' she said, starting the car and driving off.

Chapter Forty-Seven

Louise grabbed a couple of hours' sleep before heading back to work. A light drizzle peppered the sky as she drove through the back roads to Worle, the lack of colour seeping into everything and everyone accentuating her foul mood. She locked away Finch's keys into her glove compartment before heading into the station. She was still coming to terms with Amira's actions. Part of her wanted to drive round to Finch's now, take the laptop and get Coulson to run tests on it. It would be worth jeopardising her career if it meant she could put an end to Finch's tyranny. But despite Amira's understandable impatience, they couldn't rush into it. At the very least, they would need to scope Finch's property. They still had a few days before he was due back, and doing something now in a rush of emotion would only lead to disaster. That was why she'd taken the keys from Amira, and why she was holding them from her for the time being.

As she stood before the assembled team, she realised how isolated she'd become on the case over the last couple of days, busy running the investigation as if it were a personal project. It was an aspect to her way of working that she'd received criticism for in the past. DCI Robertson had picked her up on it during review meetings. He'd subtly suggested that it might be what was holding her back career-wise. 'Learn to delegate,' he'd told her. 'I'm a master of it.'

It wasn't as if she didn't trust her team. With Thomas from Weston and Tracey and Farrell seconded from MIT, she couldn't wish for a better group of officers. It was more her own perfectionism standing in her way, a single-mindedness she couldn't expect anyone else to have. Who else would have sat outside David Mountson's house all evening, waiting for something to happen, she thought as she relayed to her team her recent meeting with Carl Payton and her late-night visit with Mountson and Carrigan.

Louise had invited Inspector Baker along, under the guise that she would need more of his uniformed officers over the coming days, when in truth she wanted to watch his reaction when she said Mountson thought Dwyer was dead. There wasn't a flicker, and Baker's lack of emotion was matched by the rest of the team, who were all too battle-worn to react to unfounded suppositions.

'I might have a lead on that,' said Thomas. 'I interviewed one of Dwyer's old bosses yesterday. A farmer over Brent Knoll way.'

Louise sat down and let Thomas continue, his voice having a comforting effect on her mood.

'It was about the time we believe Dwyer went missing. Surprisingly, he was on PAYE, so it was the last official documentation we have for him. The farmer said that he was a good worker in general. He had a licence to drive the tractors and even worked the combine harvester they had. He mentioned that all was going well until the last couple of months, when Dwyer started hanging around with this girl he hadn't seen before. Apparently, she kept turning up at the farm, and his work suffered. Next thing he knew, Dwyer had upped and left.'

'I don't suppose we have anything as useful as a name for this girl?' asked Louise.

'I'm afraid not. Most of the workers from that time have moved on, but I have some names so will follow up.'

'Description?'

'Petite. Black hair. Pretty. Farmer was sure she had some tattoos,' said Thomas, sounding more hopeful than positive.

'It's a start,' said Louise, regretting her choice of words. With five victims, including one dead, they shouldn't be thinking in terms of starting. 'Tracey, I want you to follow up on this grooming activity,' she added, one eye on Baker, who remained stoic. 'There must be some old reports on this. Try the other schools as well.'

Tracey nodded, and Louise welcomed the hint of expectation and promise in the room – a feeling that was dashed twenty minutes later when DCI Finch arrived, seemingly having returned from his holiday early.

Louise's first thought was of the keys in her car. After having dissuaded Amira from returning to his house, she now faced the absurd reversal where she feared Finch could demand to inspect her car, suspecting someone had been in his house.

'Louise,' he said, walking past her towards Robertson's office, his citric aftershave trailing after him.

She would have asked him why he was back from his holiday so soon if it wouldn't have aroused his suspicion. As it was, she was as curious about why he wanted to see Robertson as soon as he was back. Again, she was struck by how easy it was for him to make her feel on edge and paranoid. If he wanted to see Robertson about her investigation, then she should be present. Robertson not only knew this, but understood how irate she would be if anything went on behind her back. Why then did it trouble her so to see Finch close the office door behind him and for her not to be admitted?

'Ah, Louise, just the person.'

Louise turned to face the ramrod-straight figure of Inspector Baker, who'd crept up on her with the stealth of a cat burglar. She wondered if Baker had caught her minimal exchange with Finch, and if he'd noted her agitation as the DCI walked past her to meet Robertson. 'What can I do for you, Dan?'

'Your briefing got me thinking. I uploaded some of the case files from that time. I remember the CID team were looking into the activity at local schools. I had some names that might be useful,' he said, handing her a file.

Louise had already gone through some old investigations with Thomas after the briefing. Both Thomas and Farrell had been involved in some of the questioning during that period and they already had a list of people to speak to. The cynical side of her thought Baker was trying to garner favour for some unknown reason, but she thanked him as she took the papers.

'Any idea why Tim is here today?' he said.

'No idea. You?'

'I heard some more rumours on Saturday about the restructuring,' he said, speaking freely, as if they were lifelong conspirators.

Louise tended to steer clear of rumours, but as Baker had the ear of the senior officers in the area, she asked him what he'd heard.

'Possible amalgamation with Portishead. Downsizing here.'

'Just CID?' said Louise.

'Who knows? It's all a bit troubling, to be honest, after having just moved back to the area.'

'I can imagine,' said Louise, thinking about Baker's wife and her comments about returning to Weston. 'I wouldn't worry about it too much. Finch is hardly in charge of logistics. Thanks again for this,' she said, waving the file in the air as she returned to her desk.

◆ ◆ ◆

She didn't want Finch to control her actions, but Louise couldn't leave the office until he did. She flicked through the file Baker had left, cross referencing it with the information the team had already collected, while trying not to glance towards Robertson's door. Ignoring the absurd thought of calling the solicitor, Natalie Gurgenstein, to ask why she and Finch were back from their holiday so soon, Louise sent a text to Thomas.

With the new information Thomas had uncovered about Dwyer possibly having vanished with a girlfriend, she wanted to question Mountson and the others again. Only three women appeared on the lists they had so far – one of them being Poppy Westfield – but there must have been many more out there. If Carl Payton was correct, Dwyer and his cronies had been stalking teenage girls at the school. If that was so, then there were many names they were missing. One of which could be that of Dwyer's so-called girlfriend.

Finch left the office five minutes later, lacking his usual poise. One of the things Louise could rely on was Robertson's support. He'd never come out and said it, but she was confident her boss detested Finch in much the same way she did. On more than one occasion he'd refused to let Finch stamp over their investigations just because he headed up MIT, and from the forlorn look on Finch's face she wondered if this was another of those occasions. Louise pretended to study her computer screen as she studied Finch in her peripheral vision. He was talking to members of his team one by one before leaving, without a word to her – an occurrence so unusual that it convinced her he was rattled by something.

'Ready?' said Thomas, dangling a set of car keys in front of her.

Louise sent a quick message to Amira, warning her of Finch's return. 'Let's go.'

'What did Finch want with Robbo?' said Thomas, as he pulled out of the car park.

It was strange how comfortable she felt in Thomas's presence. Despite the awkwardness of Saturday night, she felt relaxed, almost soothed by being alone with him. She told him what Baker had said.

'Not sure I fancy a daily commute to Portishead.'

'It's hardly the other end of the world.'

'You have been there, haven't you?'

'I quite like it there.'

'You could move back to Bristol,' said Thomas.

'Those days are long gone,' said Louise, thinking back to her old flat in Clifton. 'My parents wouldn't let me move out unless I took Emily with me, and she's had enough disruption to last a lifetime.'

'Do you think you ever will, though?'

Louise paused. 'Ever what?'

'Move on your own with Emily?'

'Who knows? Maybe one day,' she said, noting a growing tension in the car that reminded her of the night he'd tried to kiss her. Despite her reservations, part of her wanted him to make some sort of move, to suggest they go out one evening when this was all over. Yes, it was complicated, but was it complicated enough not to be workable? Maybe she should be the one to ask the question, she thought, too late, as they arrived in Uphill, spots of rain decorating the windscreen as they parked up.

Louise had spent so much time in this street recently, but it felt different beneath the covering of grey cloud, the heat she'd experienced the last time she'd been here a distant memory.

It was still morning and Louise wouldn't have been surprised if the two men were asleep, so she was a little taken aback when the front door opened seconds after she'd rung the bell, an elderly man in matching light-green shorts and short-sleeved shirt answering the door. 'Yes?' he said, fiddling with a pair of spectacles that had slid down his nose.

'Mr Mountson?' said Louise.

'That is correct,' said the man, stiffening.

'DI Blackwell, and DS Ireland. Is your son in?'

'No, he isn't,' said Mr Mountson, his friendly demeanour changing in an instant to a look of hostility and rage. 'I kicked him and his buddy out this morning.'

Chapter Forty-Eight

Thomas drove Louise to Sam's new rehab centre. They were shown to his room, where they discovered that all his belongings were gone. 'When did you last see Mr Carrigan?' she asked the centre assistant, who looked nonplussed.

'I haven't been in for a few days, so the last time I saw him was Friday.'

'You have some sort of log, though?'

The man shrugged. 'If they use it.'

Although she despaired of the man's attitude, Louise understood he wasn't directly to blame. Like David Mountson, he would be on a minimum wage, part of an underfunded machinery trying to do its best.

'It looks to me as if he's packed up and walked out of here,' said Thomas.

'It happens. The rooms are cleaned over the weekend so I'm surprised someone didn't draw that conclusion. Then again, the cleaners are contract so they don't always know which rooms are supposed to be empty.'

They drove to the last address they had for Mountson, Louise arranging for her team to check the local train and bus stations in Weston and Bristol. 'Where would they go?' said Thomas, after they'd found Mountson's old flat as desolate as Sam's room.

Both Carrigan's and Mountson's phones were going straight to answerphone, and so far no family members or friends had heard from either man – aside from the Mountsons, who had made it clear to the police they wanted nothing more to do with their son unless he cleaned up his act. Although still unclear as to Mountson's and Carrigan's role in the events, Louise's main concern was for their safety. 'Your guess is as good as mine,' she said, part of her hoping that they were both a safe distance away.

At the station, she broke the news about Mountson and Carrigan to Robertson, who gave the typical deadpan response of 'Great work.' The words were as cutting as if he'd bawled her out in front of everyone. It would have been easy to argue it wasn't her fault, but she accepted the blame. She'd been watching them for the last few days and had been to their house last night. Maybe she'd taken things a little bit too lightly, believing the two men would be holed up in the house indefinitely, when it seemed they had been planning to leave.

'Anything else?' said Robertson, accentuating the growl of his accent, as happened when he was agitated.

'I don't know. Is there?' said Louise, immune to his show of emotion.

Robertson frowned, though Louise was sure he understood. She had so much to do that she didn't want to bring Finch into the conversation, but with Amira's unpredictable behaviour of late, she felt she had no option.

'What are you getting at?' asked Robertson, half-heartedly.

'Let's not do this, shall we, sir?'

Robertson smiled, a gesture his face always struggled with. It was impossible to tell if it was forced or genuine. 'This is about DCI Finch? I was wondering why you hadn't battered down my door about this already.'

'What's going on?'

'Usual bullshit politics, that's all.'

'He wanted to take the case from us.'

'Sort of.'

'Sort of?'

'You have the case, don't you?' said Robertson, his agitation even clearer to read.

Louise placed her hands in front of her. She wanted to share everything about Finch, up to the information about Amira breaking into his house. Since moving to Weston, Robertson had always been a trustworthy ally, even during the difficult period at the beginning. He'd sided with her on the fallouts with Finch and understood it went much deeper than simple animosity.

If she shared the information now, it would become official, yet she remained sitting, considering it. It was what was needed. Louise owed it to Amira, and the countless other people Finch had screwed with, to push for his dismissal.

But try as she might, the words wouldn't leave her mouth. The second she gave Robertson the details, her current investigation into the branding attacks would be thrown into disarray. Instead, she asked about the restructuring.

'It's a possibility, but nothing to concern yourself with for now,' said Robertson.

Louise stood. It seemed, for now, both of them had things they weren't yet willing to share.

Louise thought about what was being hidden from her as she returned to the crowded incident room. The investigation was also clouded with secrets, as they so often were. This felt particularly frustrating, as she sensed an answer was waiting to present itself. Mountson and Poppy were hiding something from her, either purposely or because they didn't think it was relevant, and that was down to her. She went back over every meeting she'd had with Poppy, Mountson and Sam Carrigan. Had her questions been direct and probing enough? What had she missed? She considered Andrew Thorpe, Steven Boyne from the nightclub, Poppy's parents, the retired head teacher Mr Groves, Terrence Maynard and Raymond Oxford, who was still in a coma. She read report after report, searching and hoping to uncover that one vital piece of information she might have missed.

In the end, the office felt too claustrophobic. Tracey had been due to interview one of Poppy's old schoolfriends later that day, so Louise took the role for herself, keen to get out of the cloying atmosphere.

Forty minutes later, she was waiting for the woman in the cafeteria in the local Sainsbury's. As she nursed a coffee, she was approached by one of the shopworkers, who introduced herself as Claire Aveyard. 'Are you the police officer?' she said.

'Is it that obvious?' said Louise, standing as she showed her ID. 'Tracey couldn't make it. My name is DI Louise Blackwell.'

'Hello,' said Claire, taking a seat. 'I'm afraid I only have fifteen minutes.'

'I'll get straight to it, then. You used to go to school with Poppy Westfield?'

The woman blushed, as if embarrassed by the revelation. 'I heard about the attack on her. Poor thing. I haven't seen her since school.'

'Were you in the same class?'

'Some of them. We weren't friends-friends, if you know what I mean, but we always got on quite well.'

'I will come clean with you, Claire. You're not in any trouble,' said Louise, causing Claire to move back as if she'd been struck. 'Your name appears on a report we have from the period when you were at school. There was a small investigation into a gang of youths who were hanging around the school. They were suspected of selling drugs, among other things.'

'I never did drugs,' said Claire, her forearm tensing.

'No, that's fine, Claire. As I said, you're not in trouble in any way. We're trying to track a man. Laurence Dwyer, you may remember him,' said Louise, showing her the photo on her phone.

Claire nodded. 'I knew him.'

'Did you have anything to do with him?'

'No. Some of those boys . . . I got the impression they were up to no good. Some of my friends started hanging out with them. I know Poppy started seeing Andrew Thorpe. He was quite a bit older than her. And I know that he . . .' Claire stopped speaking, as if she'd lost her train of thought.

'Did you ever see Andrew and Laurence together?'

Claire shook her head. 'I don't think I can help you, really. I think Andrew was one of those boys who used to hang around outside, but I don't know if he was friends with Laurence or not. They were all a few years older than us, and I heard some things.'

'Things?'

Claire sighed, as if the memory was a millstone around her neck. 'They used to take the girls to remote places. Do things, you know. Some of the girls thought it was exciting. To begin with, anyway.'

'Were they made to do things against their will?'

'I'm not sure. I know a couple of girls left the school.'

'Do you remember their names?'

Claire shook her head. 'Sorry.'

'Did you ever notice if Laurence was interested in any girl in particular? Anyone who might have been considered his girlfriend.'

'No, sorry. I did my best to steer clear of the whole situation. The other girls talked about it, but I tried not to take any notice. I have to get back,' said Claire.

Louise handed her a card. 'Thank you, you have been helpful.'

Claire stood and smiled. 'Actually, it's probably nothing,' she said, laughing.

'Go on.'

'Well, there was this girl in the year below. Francesca Regan. A bit of a wild card, if you know what I mean. She used to be adamant that she was going with Laurence. It was ludicrous. She was too young, even for them.'

'Did you ever see them hanging out together?'

'No. Well . . . I did see her out there by the cars sometimes, but everyone ignored her. I felt a bit sorry for her.'

'Do you happen to know where she lives?'

'Sorry, no. I heard she moved to Cornwall after we finished school. Haven't seen her since then.'

By the time Louise reached Poppy's house, she had an address for Francesca Regan in Redruth. It was probably nothing, but she wanted to run the name by Poppy to gauge the woman's reaction. She ignored the niggling sense of panic she felt when no one answered the door. The Westfields hadn't been put under house arrest, but with David Mountson and Sam Carrigan still unaccounted for, it was hard not to worry about Poppy's safety.

She checked on the neighbours, who hadn't seen them leave, before calling each of the Westfields in turn. All three numbers went straight to answerphone and Louise felt compelled to call Thomas to update him and the team. 'Probably nothing,' she said, echoing her earlier thought about Francesca Regan.

'I'm sure they've turned their phones off to get some peace, but I'll make sure everyone is on the lookout,' said Thomas.

Louise left her car parked outside the Westfield residence, walked up two streets and across the main road to the seafront. She checked in the café at the Tropicana, the former open-air swimming pool where she used to go with her family on special days out. The place was an empty space now, occasionally used for music events, and as she peered in for a sight of the Westfields she felt a stab of nostalgia for those lost days. The smells of chlorine and sun cream, the giant fibreglass pineapples and the dizzy excitement of the admittedly tame water slides she'd raced down with Paul.

Walking back along the promenade towards the Grand Pier, she scanned the large crowds on the beach for Poppy and her parents, but it was a pointless task. There were too many faces scattered along the stretch of sand, some risking the extended walk through the mud to reach the murky sea lapping at the fringes of the pier. If Poppy was out there, only good luck would find her now. Instead, she turned back through the amusement arcades on Regent Street, doing a lap through Walliscote Road and back on to Clevedon Road towards the Westfields' house, deciding the sensible thing was to wait for them to return.

From the car, she called Amira, who, like everyone else, at that moment was seemingly unreachable. Louise wasn't happy with the way she'd left things with the woman. 'He's back,' she said, on Amira's answerphone, worried the officer would do something stupid, despite the fact that Finch's house keys were in Louise's glove compartment.

The relief was palpable, thirty minutes later, when Poppy and her parents appeared at the end of the road. Louise sent a message to Thomas before leaving the car and greeting the family by the entrance to their house.

'What now?' said Mrs Westfield.

Louise understood her dismay. This was probably Poppy's first time out of the house since the incident, and the last thing her parents would want for their daughter was to see Louise waiting for them, bringing back the bad memories they'd been trying to evade for the last few hours. 'I'm sorry, I just need a quick word with Poppy and I'll be gone. I promise.'

'It's fine, Mum,' said Poppy, who seemed invigorated by her walk. Her hair was loose against her shoulders and she appeared more relaxed than at any point since Louise had met her.

Mrs Westfield scowled at her husband, as if he should be doing something, before allowing Louise into the house.

'I won't stay long, Poppy. I spoke to one of your former school-mates today, Claire Aveyard,' said Louise.

'Oh, Claire, how is she? That seems like a lifetime ago.'

'Yes, she seems well,' said Louise, remembering how time had a different value in your teens and early twenties. 'She mentioned a girl by the name of Francesca Regan.'

The acknowledgement in Poppy's eyes was unmistakable. 'I remember Francesca,' she said, looking away as if picturing the girl had brought back a painful memory.

'Were you friends?'

'No,' said Poppy, with a laugh that suggested a different, unkind side to her. 'She was a year below. That made a lot of difference back then, if you know what I mean?'

Louise nodded but didn't answer.

Poppy frowned. 'She was a bit weird, to be honest.'

'In what way?'

'She lived in a care home. Not that that made her weird, but she was always trying to hang around with us.'

'With you?'

Poppy looked over at her mother, who was pretending to dry dishes. 'You know, when we were talking to the boys. Andrew and the others.'

'And Laurence Dwyer?'

'I guess so. When he was there. They wanted nothing to do with her. She was still a girl at the time, you know?'

'You were all girls,' said Louise.

'I guess. But she was young in more ways than one. She was small, not developed. And she did strange things.'

'Like what?'

'She showed me her arm once. She'd cut herself. You could see the blood. It was a deep incision. She told me she did it with the sharp end of a compass in a maths lesson.'

'She self-harmed?'

'I guess that's what you'd call it.'

'Did you try and help her in any way?'

'I told her to stop doing it,' said Poppy, raising her voice. 'She wasn't my friend. I didn't ask to see her wounds, and it wasn't my responsibility.'

Louise caught the disapproving look from Mrs Westfield. She wasn't sure if it was aimed at her or at Poppy. 'When you joined the gang, Poppy—'

'It wasn't a gang,' said Poppy, interrupting.

'OK, when you started hanging around with Andrew and the others, did Francesca ever join you?'

Poppy hesitated. 'I told you, she never used to hang around with us.'

'I think something happened. The sooner you tell me, the sooner I get out of your hair.'

'Why are you asking these questions? Francesca wasn't the one who attacked me.'

'No one is saying that. But would you know if Francesca was one of your attackers? When did you last see her? And wasn't she wearing a mask?'

Poppy exchanged looks with her mother. 'I guess I haven't seen her for years, but I can't—'

'For God's sake, Poppy, just tell her,' said Mrs Westfield, screaming at her daughter with surprising force.

Poppy appeared as surprised as Louise, as if her mother had slapped her. 'I never thought of it,' she said, trying to defend herself. Rolling her eyes, she continued, 'She did show up sometimes. It was at the beginning. I wasn't seeing Andrew then. There was a big group of us used to go to the beach in the summer.'

'In Brean?'

'No, this was in Weston. We used to go over by the dunes.'

'By the dunes, where Sam Carrigan was attacked?'

Poppy's face reddened. 'And sometimes to the park, where I was attacked.'

'Why didn't you tell us this before, Poppy?'

'It didn't occur to me.'

'What happened with Francesca? Did she become friends with Laurence Dwyer?'

'I doubt that very much.'

'Why?'

'She used to turn up. There were no rules – anyone could turn up – but she was so much younger and, I hate to say it, but she *was* weird. Very strange. She used to hang out on the fringes, you know, watching. Then you would find her in the middle of things, drinking White Lightning and making an idiot of herself. Anyway, I don't know what happened, but Laurence got angry with her and told her to go away. She did, but she turned up next time and they . . .'

'They what, Poppy?'

'They drove off with her.'

Mrs Westfield gasped, as if it were the first time she'd heard the story.

'Who exactly drove off with her?'

'Laurence Dwyer and two of his friends.'

'David Mountson?'

'No, no, David wasn't like that. I think one of them was Scott, the other was maybe Kevin?'

'What happened, Poppy?'

'I don't know. They said they were going to drive her to a field and dump her there to stop her coming back. It sounds horrible, I know, but we were only kids, it was a bit of a laugh.'

Louise wanted Poppy to keep talking so didn't argue with her brittle defence of only being kids. 'And what actually happened?'

Poppy frowned. Through gritted teeth, her mother told her to continue. 'She didn't turn up to school for a week. I felt a bit guilty, but there was no report of her going missing or anything. When she did return, she was different. Withdrawn. She wouldn't speak to us and stopped trying to hang out all the time.'

'You think Laurence and the other boys attacked her?'

'Look, maybe I should have said something about this before, but I didn't think. There was a rumour going around the school at the time that she was besotted with Laurence. Apparently, some of the girls had seen her getting changed in PE and had seen something on her.'

Louise closed her eyes. 'A mark?'

'I didn't pay it much attention at the time. But it was a tattoo of sorts. Definitely not done properly.'

'What was it a tattoo of?'

'No one could tell for sure, but they thought it was a letter *L*.'

Chapter Forty-Nine

Louise recognised Finch's car as she left the station and tried to ignore his silhouetted form behind the steering wheel. It was the day after Poppy's revelation about Francesca Regan, and Louise had spent every waking hour since trying to track the woman. Like Dwyer, Francesca had been off grid for years. The last record they had of her was studying at a technical college while working part-time at a fast-food restaurant in Cornwall. Somehow, she'd managed to be able to rent at an address in Redruth and had left the care system, only to leave her job and flat sometime after her sixteenth birthday, since which there were no public records for her.

Louise was struggling to think straight and needed some rest. Her mind was constantly trying to piece together the evidence, which she conceded was mostly anecdotal. However, in addition to Dwyer, Poppy had given them the names of Scott Turnbull and Kevin Westley. Like Dwyer, both men were off-grid and had been for the last four years and, while that could be a coincidence – thousands of people nationwide were currently missing long term, or unaccounted for – it was definitely a coincidence that had to be fully investigated.

Why Poppy Westfield hadn't mentioned Francesca Regan earlier was still a mystery. Poppy claimed that the connection hadn't occurred to her until Louise had mentioned Francesca's name. Louise half-believed her. The trauma of a violent attack could do staggering things to a person, and Louise had witnessed first-hand the fallout Poppy had endured.

She took a deep breath and walked across the car park to her car. She wasn't scared of Finch, and certainly wouldn't give him any indication to that effect, but it was difficult to ignore him. She still had his keys in her glove compartment, knew that potentially damaging evidence was waiting in his house. She was halfway to the car when he opened his door and called out to her.

'Not now, Timothy,' she said, trying to keep her pace steady as she continued moving forward.

'Yes, now,' he said.

Instinctively, Louise's hand moved close to the pepper-spray canister she'd been keeping on her person at all times recently. Even Finch wouldn't be stupid enough to do something in the station car park, but she liked the security of knowing the canister was there as she turned to face him. 'I've had a long day. What do you want?'

The artificial glow of the car-park lighting made Finch look as tired as she felt. He'd been in and out of the office all day, but his contribution to the case had been minimal. As he stopped, a step too close for her liking, he didn't even bother with his usual pretence. For a second, she wondered if he was reeling from Natalie leaving him – it would explain why his holiday had been cut short – but that would mean crediting him with deeper feelings than he was capable of. She'd suspected, but not quite realised, the extent of his sociopathic tendencies when they'd worked together. Finch was incapable of thinking beyond his own concerns and a failed relationship wouldn't even register with him.

'What have you been up to?' he said, close enough for her to smell his aftershave.

That she had ever been attracted to the man was a mystery she would never unravel. 'What the hell are you going on about, Timothy?'

'Don't call me that,' he said, not even trying to look composed. 'You've been talking to someone, haven't you?'

Did he mean Amira? Louise had put his recent behaviour down to the talk of amalgamation, thinking that maybe he was worried for his job, or more likely concerned what his way of working would become under closer scrutiny. But there was genuine anger in his features, and something she hadn't seen in Finch for a long time: fear. 'You've lost me.'

Finch sucked in a breath. 'Remember what I told you before, Louise.'

'You've told me a lot of things before. I'm not scared of you. Never have been and never will be. I hope you get over whatever is troubling you,' she said, opening her car door.

Finch went to place his arm on her but stopped. He knew as well as she did that cameras covered every angle of the car park. If he so much as touched her, he could be done for. 'It's not just you, though, is it?'

Louise stopped, one hand on her car door, the other around the pepper spray in her pocket. It was taking all her strength not to use it. Finch was a master of understatement, but she knew he was talking about Emily. He'd made assertions about her before. His threats were always vague, meant to antagonise her while keeping himself free of blame, and this time it was working. She wanted nothing more than to empty the pepper spray into his face, to blind him where he stood. 'I'd think carefully before you say anything else to me.'

Finch took a step back, as if he knew the wild thoughts going through her mind. 'Whatever you're doing, you need to stop. I can make life very difficult for you, but I can also make it easy if I want. There could be an opening. I'd be happy to recommend you. I'll promise not to interfere with any of your work. Draw a line under everything.'

Louise tried to hide her surprise. He was trying to bargain with her, but beyond Amira's involvement, she didn't know what threat she was to him. 'You'll need to clarify that a bit more,' she said.

'You've heard the talk of restructuring? There may be an opportunity for promotion for you, here in Weston. I can make it happen, if you play ball. Better the devil you know and all that.'

If there was going to be a promotion spot available in Weston, that meant Robertson would be moving on. Maybe that was what the clandestine discussions between him and Finch had been about. Not that it made a difference to Louise. She didn't need or want Finch's support, but she wasn't going to let him know just yet.

'I'll think about it,' she said, closing the car door, pleased but confused by Finch's troubled look as she drove away.

Chapter Fifty

She touched the tender skin where D had grabbed her. He'd broken the one rule, and would have to pay.

They'd stayed late outside Louise's house, almost caught out by the woman who'd arrived in her car during the night. She could still feel the hammer of her heart, the voyeuristic thrill, as she watched Louise leave her house still dressed in her night clothes. The woman knew no fear. She looked radiant walking through the shadows. She'd wanted to strike then, so overcome had she been by the need to touch that flawless skin, but it hadn't been the right time.

By morning light, a bruise had formed on her arm. She looked at it now, the speckles of blue offending her almost as much as the mark above it given to her all those years ago. She touched it, the skin sensitive. D probably considered it a minor thing, and she'd rectified his disobedience, but she'd made a promise to herself before that no man would ever do that to her again.

D was busy working in the other room, continuing the pretence of his other life, when all she wanted to do was finish what they had started.

'You can't attack a serving police officer,' he'd said to her, his pincer-like grip tight on her arm, as if that were the final word.

She couldn't see what difference it made then, and she couldn't see the difference it made now. He thought he'd been showing her his strength, but in reality he was displaying the weakness she'd seen in him from the beginning.

Together they'd decided on Sam Carrigan as their first target. After watching Mountson's secret relationship with the man, it felt like a fitting opening gambit. But when she'd insisted that they attack Mountson next, D had argued against it. He'd told her there would be too much focus on him, and although she thought he was right, now she was worried that Mountson had got away with it.

With Poppy and Andrew, D had understood, had even started to enjoy himself as much as she did. But the thing with Louise had started to come between them in an irrevocable way. She wanted to place her mark on Louise, and not just for the simple joy of feeling the metal on her skin. The mark would link them for ever. Louise and her family would become the family she never had.

And of course, there was the added bonus that with Louise as victim, the police's attention would be diverted and she could refocus on Mountson. He was the last one. He'd been there that day and was as complicit in the crime as Poppy and Andrew; as the three men who'd given her the mark.

'Again,' she said, opening the door to his room, the place now empty.

'Why?'

'You only have the one mark. I don't want you to miss out,' she said.

Maybe if he'd been more willing, she would have changed her mind, but he was crying by the time he'd stripped down to his waist and laid down on the bed. Aside from the ruptured flesh of the mark she'd placed on him, his back was a beautiful smooth canvas waiting for her touch. She caressed the soft area where she would make the next mark. 'You want me to restrain you?' she asked, softening her voice.

He nodded, and she took out the strip of leather and fed it into his mouth, a satisfying groan coming from him as she pulled back tight on the leather and locked it in place so his complaints would be muffled. She strapped him to the table as he writhed in anticipation. He was face down on the bed so she lifted his head and turned it to the side so she could see his reaction.

His eyes were wide – half adoring, half fearful – as she fired up the blowtorch. It was a pity. Despite the things they'd done together, he was still naive. When they met, she'd been reeling from what had happened to her, and he'd been a surprising comforter.

But he'd broken the rules. He'd known what those men had done to her and should have known she wouldn't accept any man doing that to her again. It might have only been a bruise, but that was how it started. If he was capable of hurting her in that small way, he was capable of anything.

She lit the metal, and he closed his eyes, drooling with expectation.

She touched the skin on his back, a final, soft caress. 'You need to open your eyes for this,' she said, the white-hot metal the last thing he would ever see.

Chapter Fifty-One

Another evening, another distraction. Where she should have been focused solely on the branding case, locating Francesca Regan and Laurence Dwyer, Louise found herself thinking about Tim Finch – an occurrence that had plagued her these last few years.

Only, instead of threatening her this time, he had been willing to bargain. She'd never seen him so ruffled. It made her wonder if Amira had actually taken something from his place, or if she was the only one on to him. Where she should have been pleased, she was concerned. When Finch was in trouble, he was also at his most dangerous. As she'd discovered that night on the Walton farm, he was capable of anything. And although he'd pleaded with her for her help, he would betray her in a heartbeat.

She called Amira as she drove home, cursing as the phone went straight to answerphone. Yes, she wanted Finch out of her life, but her focus had to be on the investigation. What she needed to do was grab a few hours' sleep and get back to it. Regan and Dwyer wouldn't find themselves, and whoever the attackers were, they were bound to attack again soon.

She left the car in darkness, all the lights in the house switched off – another regular occurrence of late. Over the last few weeks, she'd felt more guilty than she'd ever done when she'd lived away from Emily. Somehow, living in the same house was making things worse. It was another distraction, but as she opened the front door and walked up the stairs, it preoccupied her. It was as if, every day, Emily changed in some subtle way; and on the few occasions she'd seen the girl over the last few weeks, Louise had felt the loss of those missed days more than ever. As she slumped down in front of the television – above which the only photo they had of Francesca Regan, a grainy bus-pass photo of her as a fourteen-year-old, took centre stage on the crime board – she tried to convince herself that one day soon that would all change, knowing, even as she thought it, she was lying to herself.

◆ ◆ ◆

Her phone rang as she was changing for bed, Amira returning her call. As soon as Amira spoke Louise could tell she'd been drinking. 'I missed your call,' she said, slurring.

'Where are you? Is everything OK?'

'Everything is dandy, no thanks to you.'

'Where are you, Amira?'

'At my bed and breakfast. Why?'

'Nothing, I just wanted to check in with you,' said Louise, worried that any mention of Finch in Amira's current state could provoke an unwanted response.

'That's good of you, Louise. Seen DCI Finch today?' said Amira.

'As a matter of fact, I have.'

'And how was he?'

Louise rubbed her forehead, pleased she had Finch's keys in her car. 'Have you done something?'

'I've done what you should have done, and I'm about to finish off the job.'

'Amira, you need to stop and think. Tell me what has happened.'

'I'm not stupid, you know,' said Amira, sounding drunker by the second.

'No one thinks that.'

'I have another key. You must have known that.'

Louise wondered if Amira was telling the truth, and that she'd been fooling herself; waiting for Amira to take action where she couldn't or wouldn't. 'You didn't go back?'

'I did. As soon as you told me he was back off holiday, I went back and took his hard drive.'

'Why didn't you tell me that, Amira?' said Louise, raising her voice.

'It doesn't matter. Everyone will know soon.'

'What do you mean?'

'I mean, as soon as Finch gets home, I'm going to confront him directly.'

'Don't be ridiculous. You'll put yourself in danger.'

'No need to worry, everyone will know where I am.'

Louise went to reply but the line had already gone dead.

Louise wasted no time, grabbing a coat and heading straight for the car. A number of conflicting emotions ran through her as she drove the narrow lanes out of Sand Bay towards Worle and the motorway. She was angry with Amira for acting so impetuously – she risked jeopardising everything, including both their careers – but she also feared for the woman. Finch wouldn't take kindly to being accosted at his own house. Louise had already witnessed his unstable behaviour earlier that evening, and there was no telling what he would do if Amira turned up unannounced.

Despite those concerns, she couldn't deny the sense of hope the call had given her. Amira had alluded to the fact that she'd uncovered some evidence about Finch on the hard drive she'd taken. It was the wrong way to go about it, and could endanger any future prosecution, but it could be enough to bring Finch's misdemeanours to light.

She tried calling as she headed on to the deserted M5, the sky a blanket of stars above her, but Amira had switched her phone off. Louise refrained from turning on her police lights as she moved into the fast lane. Amira's phone calls to her would be logged, but she didn't want to make anything official yet. She needed to get to Finch's house before Amira. Hope was fine, but the reality was she couldn't let the woman go through with it.

She left the motorway at the Portway, rushing through the streets as safely as she could, desperate not to draw the attention of any patrol cars in the area. As she passed the ground of an amateur football club, the sight of the Clifton Suspension Bridge a blurry light off to her left, she called Amira again, but it went straight to answerphone.

Chapter Fifty-Two

Louise sped through the back streets. Amira was brave, but bravery alone wouldn't protect her. Finch was more than a sociopath. He hadn't made a mistake that night at the Walton farmhouse. He'd told Louise that Walton was armed because he wanted to see what would happen. She was convinced he'd taken a perverse joy in her shooting the man. If he was capable of that, he was a threat to Amira.

Her hand kept going to her radio as she drove, but calling it in now would risk everything. Although she hadn't let herself into Finch's house, she knew Amira had done so. Amira's argument that she had a key was flimsy at best. Yes, Finch had given her a key, but she'd made copies and their relationship had ended some time ago. It would be argued that as soon as Louise knew about Amira's actions she should have reported her. It was almost inconceivable that it wouldn't come to light. She could hope Amira kept quiet about it, and that the focus would be centred on Finch's criminality, but chances were she would be implicated at some point.

Her heart was racing by the time she parked up around the corner from Finch's road. She secured the utility harness over her shoulders, making sure the pepper spray and baton were in place, and leaned over to retrieve Finch's house keys from the glove compartment. She considered calling Thomas and Tracey, but again she didn't want to implicate anyone. She conceded she might have handled Amira the wrong way. She'd seen an opportunity to bring Finch down and had jumped at it, and here she was, walking unannounced to his house, blind as to what was waiting for her.

Amira's car was parked two doors down. The vehicle was locked, and Louise tried the officer's phone once more before edging towards Finch's house.

The lights were switched off downstairs. Through the frosted glass of the front door, Louise could see a light in the distance. Finch had an open-plan kitchen-dining area at the rear of the property. The house was terraced and she had no way of approaching from the rear without getting the neighbours involved.

She hesitated by the front door, trying to convince herself that Amira could be trusted. She wouldn't put it beyond Finch to have manufactured all this, but there was a real possibility that Amira was in danger and that wasn't something Louise was prepared to risk.

Through the front door she could hear the distant sound of loud music. Hoping that would be enough to drown out the sound of her opening the door, she took the set of keys from her pocket and slid the key into the lock. As she eased open the door, the music increased in volume. She slipped inside and shut the door. As she'd thought, the music was coming from the kitchen area, where the lights were on.

Louise took out her expandable baton and edged down the hallway. She couldn't hear any voices, but if Finch and Amira were speaking softly, they would easily be drowned out by the music.

A sliding door, halfway open, separated the hallway from the kitchen. Louise moved forwards so she was behind the door. Her breathing sounded conspicuously loud and she tried to control it as she peered through the opening to see Amira sitting on the kitchen chair. She was gagged, her hands tied behind her back.

Amira's eyes darted to her, and it was then that Finch came into view.

'Well don't just stand there, Louise, we've been waiting for you,' he said.

Chapter Fifty-Three

Louise acted on instinct. She could tell from Finch's intonation that he'd been drinking and hoped his inebriation would work to her advantage. She stepped through the opening, baton in hand. 'Are you OK, Amira?' she asked.

'Amira is fine,' said Finch, slurring. 'But she won't be for long,' he added, lifting a kitchen knife from the counter.

Finch was too far away to reach with the pepper spray and, with the knife in his hand, Louise didn't want to make any sudden movements. 'Tim, I'm not sure what your end plan is here. Do yourself a major favour and put the knife down. This has gone too far, but if you hurt her, you'll never see daylight again.'

'You mean like you hurt Walton?' said Finch.

'Backup is on its way, Tim. Just put that down.'

'Remember that, don't you?' said Finch, ignoring her. 'The man you killed in cold blood.'

Louise clenched the baton tighter. Her fear now was that Finch was so far gone he had nothing to lose. 'I remember,' she said, trying her best to humour the man when all she wanted to do was use his face as practice for her baton-swinging.

'I remember it too,' said Finch with a smile. 'But I could never quite get rid of you, could I, Louise? I should have shot you there and then. Fitted up Walton for it and come out a hero. Really you should be thanking me for letting you live.'

Louise glanced at the bottle of whisky on the sideboard and wondered how much Finch had taken. 'Just put the knife down. This has nothing to do with Amira.'

Finch's bottom lip jutted out and, nodding, he approached her from the kitchen countertop. 'You're right on that count. This has always been about you and me, hasn't it, Louise?' Finch waved the knife in the air. 'You were the only one. The only one I couldn't beat. You should be proud of that.'

'Please put the knife down, Tim.'

Finch kept inching closer. 'One thing you could never get over though, wasn't there, Louise?'

Louise ground her teeth. 'What's that?'

'Your lack of trust,' said Finch, taking a further step forward.

'Don't,' said Louise.

Finch held his hands up in the air, the knife almost close enough for Louise to reach out and touch it. 'I take the blame for some of that, of course. After I made you kill Walton, I guess it must have been very difficult for you to trust anyone. Unfortunately for you, that has now backfired, hasn't it?'

'I don't know what you're talking about.'

'Oh, but you do. There's no backup coming, is there, Louise? That would mean putting your trust in someone other than yourself. You weren't very good at that before, and now it's something you're unable to do.'

Louise glanced at Amira, who was trying to say something through her gag. 'I've pressed the emergency button on my phone, Tim. You're just incriminating yourself.'

'Bullshit,' said Finch, taking another step towards her.

Much of what he'd said was true. It had been much harder for her to trust her colleagues since the Walton farm incident, but

Finch hadn't been as successful as he imagined in changing her personality. She'd pressed the emergency button on her phone as soon as she'd seen Amira tied to the chair. It wasn't really a choice for her to make. Finch had incriminated himself. Everything he'd said had been recorded by her phone, and seconds from now the door would be crashing down as backup arrived. For now, all she had to do was manage the situation so Finch didn't hurt anyone.

'It's over,' she said, lifting up the phone.

Finch's eyes narrowed as it dawned on him that he'd been wrong. He began glancing around the kitchen, as if looking for something or someone to attack. 'You just had to, didn't you?' he said, his voice a higher pitch than she'd ever heard from him.

'Put the knife down, Tim,' she said, but he was beyond reasoning with.

He gripped the handle, pointing the blade towards her. 'Let's take you out of the equation once and for all.'

Finch looked at her baton as he moved towards her. The hand holding the knife was close enough to grab and Finch began stabbing at the air, the blade making a whooshing noise.

Louise transferred the baton to her left hand and was about to make a grab for the pepper spray when Finch lunged towards her. There wasn't time to activate the spray as Finch swung the knife at her, missing by centimetres.

As he lunged, he planted his right leg with his knee bent. On instinct, Louise used a former self-defence technique she'd learnt. She lifted her foot and aimed a kick at Finch's knee.

The response was instant. A cracking noise filled the room as Finch's leg snapped back on itself and he collapsed on the ground. Louise cracked down hard on his wrist with the heel of her shoe, Finch's grip loosening enough that she was able to kick the knife away.

She stood over Finch, who was convulsing. She felt the weight of the baton in her hand and stared at the back of Finch's skull as all the years of torment played through her mind. She swung the baton through the air, thinking how easy it would be to rain blows on to the man for what he'd done to her and so many others. Who would blame her? She would plead self-defence and, once they'd seen the photos on his hard drive and heard the testimony of the other women, no one would look too much into it. Only Amira would know for sure what had really happened.

Louise blinked, forcing herself out of her fugue-like state. Amira, she thought, rushing to the woman's side and pulling the gag from her mouth. 'I'm so sorry, Amira,' she said. 'Are you OK? Did he hurt you?'

'I'm fine. Did you really call it in?' asked Amira, just as the front door crashed open and the backup finally arrived.

Chapter Fifty-Four

Louise watched a team of officers she'd never seen before take Finch away, then she was questioned by a detective from Anti-Corruption, who told her they'd been investigating Finch for a number of months. She stopped short of telling the officer they'd left it a bit late, happy for now that Finch was in custody.

Amira hadn't stopped shaking since being untied. Louise hugged her and told her it was all over. 'Now go with the paramedics and rest,' she said.

'You need to come in too,' said one of the paramedics. 'Procedure after something like this.'

'I'm fine,' said Louise, giving Amira a final hug before walking outside and almost straight into DCI Robertson.

'Sorry, sir,' said Louise.

Robertson stood there, his face blank, as if dumbstruck. 'What are you sorry for?' he said. Hesitantly, he placed his hand on her shoulder, the gesture at once paternal and awkward. 'You're OK?'

'I'm fine, Iain, thanks.'

'Come, sit.'

They sat on the wall outside Finch's house, the street filled with emergency vehicles, blue lights flashing in the night sky. 'I need to put you on leave,' said Robertson.

'Like hell,' said Louise.

'It's procedure,' said Robertson, echoing the paramedic's earlier words.

Louise dropped her head, the earlier burst of adrenaline leaving her burnt out. 'At any other time, I'd agree with you, but I can't drop everything.'

'Louise, I mean this in a nice way, but you're a wreck,' said Robertson.

Louise chuckled at his deadpan delivery. 'You're all charm, Iain.'

'Seriously, I'm worried about you. You shouldn't have kept all this to yourself.'

Louise went to protest but lacked the strength.

'That's beside the point, I know,' said Robertson. 'You've caught that thug, and that's what's important. But what's important to me, is you. You must realise the mental toll of what just happened to you in there.'

'It's not as if I haven't been here before, Iain.'

'No, that's true, but you've needed to rest.'

Robertson was alluding to one particularly harrowing case when Louise had taken enforced leave for a number of months. 'Don't throw that back at me,' said Louise.

'I'm not, I'm not. You needed the break then, and I think you need the break now. Even if it's for a few days. They'll want to speak to you again anyway,' said Robertson, gesturing to two Anti-Corruption officers standing outside Finch's property.

'How about I take the rest of the night off?' said Louise.

'Very funny.'

'Seriously, Iain. Let me get some rest and we can reassess it in the morning.'

Robertson puffed out his cheeks. 'I don't know whether to be proud of you, or annoyed that you don't ever listen to my orders.'

'Perhaps a bit of both then, sir,' said Louise, pins and needles filling her legs as she stood up.

If Robertson saw her momentary loss of balance, he ignored it. 'Right, get out of here before I change my mind. I'll speak to the AC guys on your behalf. But please, get some rest.'

'Will do, sir.'

Louise made her way back to the car and sat for a few minutes in silence behind the steering wheel. She held her head in her hands and allowed herself a brief cry, before wiping away her tears and heading back to Weston.

She was heading off the Portway when Tracey called. Louise almost didn't answer, not ready to face the inevitable questions about Finch, but in the end, curiosity got the best of her.

'Hello, boss,' said Tracey, using the term even though she was the same rank as Louise.

'Everything OK?'

'Yes, some news for you,' said Tracey.

It appeared that news of Finch's arrest had yet to reach Tracey, for which Louise was grateful. 'Don't leave me in suspense, then,' said Louise.

'I know you're trying to get some rest, but we just heard from the hospital. Raymond Oxford has regained consciousness.'

Chapter Fifty-Five

Louise called Simon Coulson as she drove to Weston General. She wanted to warn him about what was happening with Finch, especially after the covert work he'd completed for her on the phones.

Coulson sounded surprised to hear from her. 'Are you OK?' he said, before she had the chance to say anything.

'You've heard then?'

'It's gone crazy here. Are you sure you're OK?'

'I'm fine. He didn't hurt me. What do you know?' said Louise, an uneasy mixture of excitement and alarm causing adrenaline to flood her system.

'Hang on,' said Coulson, the line going dead for a few seconds before he returned. 'From what I understand, the Ghost Squad were already on to him, seems to have been some kind of long-term operation.'

Louise eased back on the accelerator, her speed having reached 100 mph. 'I know you would, but just make sure to be upfront on any questioning. It's fine to tell them I approached you about the phones. Don't feel you have to protect me in any way.'

'Thanks for letting me know, Louise. How is Amira holding up?'

'She's safe. She's going to be shaken up by what happened to her, but she'll get through.'

'That's a relief. I'm glad you're OK,' said Simon, the concern obvious in his voice.

'Thanks, Simon. For everything. I'll catch up with you soon, and remember what I said. We need to be one hundred per cent upfront,' said Louise, ending the call as she pulled the car across the motorway just in time to reach the turning to Weston.

Tracey was waiting for her in the hospital car park. 'The doctor's agreed to give us five minutes,' she said, by way of greeting, her stilted tone evidence enough for Louise that she'd heard about Finch.

'I'm fine, Tracey.'

Tracey reached forward and hugged her. 'He pulled a knife on you?'

'I can't think about it for now,' said Louise. 'Let's get this done, shall we?'

Tracey still had hold of her, and Louise grew concerned she would never let go. 'Come on,' she said, prying her friend away and leading her through the main doors into the dimly lit and deserted reception area.

Tracey appeared to be more in shock than Louise. Louise had never questioned where her loyalty lay. She'd always been supportive, but Finch was her direct boss and that had made things awkward for them both. That Tracey had survived Finch's purge of the section had always surprised them. Out of everyone at MIT, Tracey had been given something approaching a free rein. In her more self-obsessed moments, Louise had believed Finch had kept Tracey on as a means to keep tracks on her, though the fact that Tracey was an exceptional detective was probably closer to the truth. 'Honestly, I'm fine,' said Louise, as Tracey stumbled after her. 'I'm sure this will hit me more when I've had a chance to think about it. So, for now, let's not think about it. Let's focus on Mr Oxford,' she said, putting an end to the conversation for now.

Dr Bainbridge met them in the corridor outside ICU. His sunken grey eyes made him look as tired as Louise felt. 'Only one of you, please,' he said, opening the door to Oxford's room.

Oxford was slightly elevated on his bed, his eyes wide and staring. Dr Bainbridge frowned as he introduced Louise.

'Mr Oxford,' said Louise. 'I'll only take a few minutes of your time. Can you remember anything about your attack?'

'I remember you,' said Oxford, his voice a dry rasp.

'That's right. I was there before you were taken to hospital.'

'Manitou,' said Oxford.

'Manitou? That's what you said before?' said Louise.

'The attacker,' said Oxford, every word clearly painful.

'I don't understand, Mr Oxford,' said Louise, stepping closer as his heart-rate monitor began to rise.

Mr Oxford's hands twitched, his right hand reaching for his collarbone. 'There. I saw it,' he said, his eyes closing.

'We'll have to leave it there,' said Dr Bainbridge.

'What did you see?' said Louise, as Dr Bainbridge guided her out of the room.

Mr Oxford kept his eyes closed, his voice just about carrying to Louise as he repeated the word 'manitou', before the door was shut.

Back in the foyer, Louise relayed the conversation to Tracey.

'It's some kind of monster, isn't it?' said Tracey, typing 'manitou' into her phone. 'Here we go, a spiritual and fundamental life force in Native American theology. A Native American God. That doesn't help much.'

'He was pointing to his collarbone. I wonder,' said Louise, taking the phone from Tracey and clicking on images.

The image results for 'manitou' were varied. From what she could see, there didn't seem to be a definitive idea of what a mani-tou looked like. She scrolled through images of dragons, bear-like monsters and crude images of Native Americans elevated to super-natural proportions. 'What are you thinking?' said Tracey.

'Long shot, but the area where Oxford was found was very well lit. He said "manitou" to me when I arrived at the scene. I thought in his bewilderment he was saying "man, two". Maybe he managed to get hold of one of them and saw the image of a manitou on their collarbone.'

'A tattoo, you think?'

'Exactly,' said Louise. She typed 'manitou tattoo' into the phone and felt the heat rise on her face as on the fourth page of results she saw an image she'd seen before.

Chapter Fifty-Six

Too often, cases could come down to a small piece of evidence, or even blind luck. Louise knew she shouldn't blame herself – since the investigation, she'd seen more tattoos than she'd cared for in a very small amount of time – but with Oxford's revelation it was hard not to take some of the blame. She should have been more methodical about his words when she'd first heard them. The only positive for now was the fact that Mr Oxford was hopefully going to be the attacker's last victim.

Tracey wasted no time, switching on the lights and the siren as they raced out of the hospital towards Meadow Street. Time moved at a different speed as the car meandered through the quiet back roads of the centre. So much had happened since Louise had last been here that it was hard to believe that less than two weeks ago she'd walked along Meadow Street from the Boulevard to this very same tattoo parlour. That she'd met the possible attacker then – the young woman who'd called herself Frankie but who in all likelihood was Francesca Regan – would be something Louise would find harder to forgive herself for. She'd thought nothing of the manitou tattoo she'd seen on the woman that day, hadn't even known that the image was of a manitou. She'd been too preoccupied with the branding attack on Sam Carrigan, and the small cartoon-like figure on the woman's collarbone had been one of a number of ink marks that had covered almost every inch of her visible flesh.

Louise replayed the conversation in her head as Tracey drove unblinking, her hands tight on the steering wheel. The woman had come across as young and naive. At one point she'd suggested getting in one of her colleagues – Bill, if she remembered correctly – before she'd relaxed into the questioning. Her answers had been no different to the workers at the other tattoo parlours. If anything, she'd been more accommodating and had even let her leave the premises by the back door.

'Everything OK?' said Tracey, as they pulled up outside the tattoo parlour.

'I'm trying to think if I missed anything when I spoke to her,' said Louise, getting out of the car and peering through the painted shop windows into the darkness within. 'Frankie, Francesca.'

'Come on, boss, even you can't blame yourself for this. Even if she is the attacker, you would have had no way of knowing.'

A preliminary report came back from the station on the name Francesca Regan. Of the three hits locally, none of them matched the person Louise had previously met.

It was 4 a.m. but Tracey knocked on the door anyway. 'We have reasonable suspicion,' she said, testing the strength of the doorframe.

'Let's try the back first,' said Louise, running towards the side street.

As they reached the narrow alleyway, the sound of sirens from the backup cars reached her ears. The alley smelled of garbage and urine, a shadowy object scurrying along the ground as she approached the back door. 'It's open,' said Louise, withdrawing her expandable baton from her utility belt.

Tracey brushed up to her side, her breathing audible in the narrow confines of the hallway. As Tracey called their position in,

Louise was taken back to the Walton farm. Although she now had only the baton as a weapon, the same sense of dread overcame her as she creaked open the door and stepped into the darkness at the rear of the tattoo parlour.

With her left hand, Louise found a light switch, the neon strip light flickering on and bringing the room into a harsh focus. Louise nodded to Tracey as she stepped through the hallway, where a second door was ajar. The last time she'd been there, the sound of a whirring tattoo gun had vibrated through the walls. Now the only sound was their breathing as Louise opened the door.

She didn't need to turn on the lights to know there was a body. She could see its limp form in the shadows, head slumped to the side as it lay back on the reclining chair. 'Stay back,' she said to Tracey, holding her position as she searched for a light switch, not wanting to contaminate the crime scene.

Tracey found the switch, images of the corpse flickering in front of Louise's eyes as the light came to life, leaving Louise in no doubt that they were looking at a murder scene.

Chapter Fifty-Seven

Three of them had taken her, and three of them had watched.

Francesca had been in love with Laurence Dwyer, or at least as in love as a naive thirteen-year-old girl could be. She knew no one really liked her in the group. At best, she was a tolerated nuisance. Despite being less than a year younger than Poppy, the others considered her a child. Sometimes they would send her on errands – to the newsagent's or the coffee shop – and would be gone by the time she came back. She was used to being shunned. She'd been spurned by her parents and was little more than an inconvenience at the care home. The sad fact was that Laurence's group was the closest she had to a family, and she'd lived for the occasional moments of kindness he would show to her – letting her sip on his alcohol, supplying her first cigarette, the time when he'd asked what she thought about what they should do that evening. She'd since come to understand that the way he'd treated her had been wrong, and she wished the lesson had been learnt much earlier.

An edge had already developed within the group before that day. That was why there were so few of them there. Damon – who was the only one who ever showed her continuous kindness – wasn't there. He was far from being the leader, but he had a level head which often stopped the group from going too far. David and

Laurence weren't speaking to each other, and Francesca sensed a tension long before Laurence began giving out the pills.

David, Poppy and Andrew all refused, and she wasn't offered one. Laurence swallowed his pill with a manic intensity matched by his friends, Scott and Kevin.

It didn't start immediately. The seven of them sat in the dunes, two groups of three with her in the middle, as the sea muddled its way towards them. Foolishly, she'd tried to lighten the mood, which had only resulted in her alienating both sides. When Laurence and his two goons had picked her up, she'd seen a look of hesitancy from David, Poppy and Andrew, but none of them had moved from the spot. Laurence liked to play these little games and maybe they'd told themselves that he wouldn't do anything beyond dunking her in the water or leaving her somewhere along the beach.

But she'd known different and so should they have.

He must have planned it beforehand; otherwise, why had he brought the blowtorch and the metal? Laurence was proud of the branding on his arm, and she'd been fascinated by it. Now and then he would let her run her fingers over the ridges of the letter, and she didn't think she'd ever seen anything more glorious in her life.

Why he had to let them do what they did she would never understand. She'd pleaded with him to make them stop as he lit the iron bar, said she would willingly take his mark, but he'd been either too out of it or had simply refused to listen.

Everything changed after that night. The group disbanded, the family she thought she'd had disappeared. The only person who ever came to see her was Damon. She'd shown him what Laurence and the others had done and together they'd hatched a plan.

She thought about him now as she watched Louise and one of her colleagues break into the parlour. It was a shame she'd had to do that to Damon, but he'd known more than anyone what she couldn't accept. Her only regret was that they hadn't been able to get to David Mountson together; she would have liked to share Mountson's marking with Damon.

If nothing else, to claim the full set.

Mountson's time would come, but it was Louise she wanted to see next. She'd lost Damon, her only family, and now she needed to start creating her next. It wouldn't take long for Louise to work out her address, and that gave her some extra time.

Chapter Fifty-Eight

Louise took photos of the victim before waiting outside for the SOCOs to arrive. There had been no need to check for a pulse, as a metal instrument like a knitting needle was protruding from one of the dead body's eyes. Like the other victims, the man had been marked with the *2* symbol. Only this time it had been placed on his forehead. Louise showed the photographs to Tracey, both of them noting the mottled skin covering half of the victim's face. 'Acid-attack victim?' asked Louise.

'Could be. I don't recognise him. Do you think it's Laurence Dwyer?'

Louise had been tempted to check the body for the branding mark on Dwyer's arm but had decided it was better to wait until the SOCOs arrived. The photographs of Dwyer were dated and indistinct. Her gut feeling was this was someone else, and they would know soon enough.

By the time Janice Sutton arrived and confirmed there was no branding mark on the victim's arm, though there were two fresh branding marks on his back, they had discovered the parlour was leased to someone by the name of Damon Kessler. Kessler had signed a lease deal three months ago, and after a little digging it became apparent that Kessler was the latest victim.

'I've got an address for him,' said Tracey, hanging up her phone.

Louise was loath to leave the crime scene, but there was little she could do while the SOCOs documented everything. 'Where?'

'Five minutes out from Hutton.'

'Let's go,' said Louise, placing a ruffled-looking Thomas in charge of the scene as she left through the front door with Tracey.

They took the back roads – via Marchfields Way, past the out-of-town superstores – towards Hutton Moor Lane. Louise was trying to focus on the potential challenges ahead, trying her best to ignore the nagging accusation at the back of her mind that this was her fault. That it would have been all but impossible to have known from a simple meeting that the woman who'd called herself Frankie was the attacker felt irrelevant. Louise replayed their encounter in her head over and over again, searching for an indication she might have missed something. The young woman had come across as being a bit shy though obviously passionate about her work. She'd been helpful when Louise had quizzed her about branding, while remaining wary of the questioning, as if fearing she could implicate herself.

Try as she might, Louise couldn't recall anything that suggested *Frankie* had been a potential suspect. Even now, they had no actual proof it was her. That Damon Kessler's body had been found at the parlour was an indication she had played a part, but it was impossible to rule out Laurence Dwyer.

As Tracey pulled up along a quaint terraced street off the main road, Louise thought that in a perfect world Laurence Dwyer and Francesca Regan would be waiting behind the door of the house, ideally asleep; a fantasy she dismissed after knocking on the front door for two minutes with no response or indication of life within.

'Shall we call for backup?' said Tracey.

Louise didn't want to wait for backup, but with no sign of life within they didn't have reasonable suspicion and thus a legal justification to enter without a warrant. 'I thought I heard someone moving within, didn't you?' she said. 'Let's go in,' she added, once confirmation for backup had been granted. 'Sooner we find out what's going on behind that door, the better.'

'Sure thing,' said Tracey, without hesitation.

As she waited for Tracey to reach the back of the property, Louise was again struck by the similarities to the night at the Walton farm. That night, they hadn't waited for backup either, but she wasn't going to be deterred by that.

'Ready!' called Tracey, her voice carrying from the back.

Louise swung the weighted ram, the contact enough to smash the lock. Dropping it, she checked for her pepper spray before taking out her baton. Images of Finch's exposed skull filled her mind and she made herself forget how close she'd come to repeatedly using the baton on him.

The interior was filled with a dank, musky odour, and as Louise reached the back door and let Tracey in she noticed a number of black bags on the kitchen countertop.

'Heads?' said Tracey, with gallows humour as Louise pushed her baton into the bags.

'Squishy, if they are,' said Louise, tearing open one of the bags, to be rewarded with a pile of rubbish spilling over her hands and down her arms. 'Must be bin day tomorrow,' she said, dropping the bag as a sour liquid spilled from it on to her clothes. 'Fantastic,' she said, the smell of rancid soup on her sleeves making her gag.

Together they searched the house, the dank smell now accompanied by the stench of the foul liquid that had spilled on to Louise's clothes. In the living room, a dim single light bulb revealed walls covered in numerous paintings and photographs. Above a mock fireplace, an unsettling painting of a creature, half woman, half fantastical monster, took centre stage. The image was surrounded by flames, the colours dark and rich, the woman's body covered in illustrations akin to tattoos, as well as scars and wounds.

In the main bedroom they found a reclining chair, a smaller replica of the one in the tattoo parlour. 'Look here,' said Louise, placing on gloves before lifting a blowtorch. The top of the canister appeared to be the same as the plastic top they'd found at Clarence Park.

A photograph of Damon Kessler with the woman Louise had met in the tattoo parlour sat on the bedside table. The pair were at the seaside, smiling, with their arms around one another, as behind them a crashing wave froze in perpetuity. Louise loaded the only photo they had of Francesca Regan on to her phone, the image too blurry to be confirmed as a match to the woman in the photograph. The domestic bliss of the shot was in stark contrast to the artwork on the walls. More images of fantasised humans – the skin of a young woman stretched to breaking point as she was held between two points, a man metamorphosing into a many-horned beast, a pair of lovers with text scrolled over inches of their naked skin – covered the walls.

Louise pointed to the space above the bed. 'Look,' she said, mesmerised by the print on the wall. It was a black-and-white image of a creature. The top half was a swan, wings raised as if in flight; the bottom half was human legs, emerging from the water.

'Cycnus,' said Tracey.

Louise had come across the image before when making a cursory search on the swan image. Cycnus was from Greek mythology, a name given to a number of characters who could transform their shape into swans. 'I think we have an explanation for the marks,' she said.

'Here,' said Tracey, a few minutes later, handing Louise a small box holding two passports.

Louise flicked through the identification. The first passport confirmed the deceased man in the parlour was Damon Kessler; the second that the woman Louise had met at the parlour – Frankie – was in fact Francesca Regan.

Chapter Fifty-Nine

Louise waited outside with Tracey as a more thorough search of the house was conducted. 'You stink,' said Tracey, lighting a cigarette.

'Tell me about it,' said Louise, taking a sniff of her top, which was still wet from the spilled liquid. 'I'm not even sure what this is,' she added, wincing.

Thomas called. The SOCOs were still working the scene at the tattoo parlour. A wanted notice had been placed nationwide for Francesca Regan. With Damon Kessler's death, Louise feared that the woman had left the town. Why she'd wanted Kessler dead, she didn't know, but it had the feel of finished business to it. Despite what she'd learnt about Francesca Regan, Louise was convinced Laurence Dwyer still had a role to play. She imagined the pair of them together, leaving Weston behind as they moved on to another town.

'I can't take this any longer. I need to get changed,' said Louise.

'OK, I'll hold up things here,' said Tracey.

Louise glanced at her watch. 'I'll go home now, and then back to the parlour. Shouldn't be any longer than thirty minutes,' she said.

Tracey nodded, stubbing out her cigarette on the pavement.

◆ ◆ ◆

The temperature had dropped further by the time Louise left the car outside her house. It was the second half of August and Emily would be back at school soon, she thought, as she walked along the gravel. The summer had slipped by unnoticed and, although she'd spent nearly every waking hour at work, Louise felt a sense of loss for the time wasted – for the hours she could have spent with her family.

Every step was an effort. The confrontation with Finch was weighing on her. She had yet to speak to Amira since she'd been taken to hospital, and Louise wondered if she would be able to continue working without some rest.

Molly barked as Louise opened the door. She pictured the excited dog on the other side of the wall. She wanted to open the dividing door to see her, to seek out the dog's comforting effect, but her sodden clothes couldn't wait.

She tried to run upstairs, but tiredness overcame her. It felt like days since she'd been asleep and she had to drag herself upwards, wondering how feasible it would be to try and take a power nap before returning. Opening the door, she reached out into the darkness of her apartment and switched on the light.

Yawning as she stepped through into the open living area, she immediately sensed something was wrong. She put it down to her always questioning, analytical mind. Although she couldn't pinpoint it, there was something about the way the place was arranged that was different to the last time she'd been there the previous morning. It was the same sense she got when someone had cleaned up in her absence, and she thought that maybe her mother had decided to do some home cleaning, before remembering that her parents had planned to take Emily out for the day.

She barely had time to register the thought, when a dull pain reached her head, sending first a wave of nausea through her before leading her to unconsciousness.

◆ ◆ ◆

Louise couldn't tell if the image of the woman was her or not. Her pale skin appeared to be merging with the flesh of something mythical. As she looked down at her arms and legs, every inch of her appeared to be desecrated with tiny lines of ink, with bumps and abrasions that felt like extensions of her body.

'I see you're back with us.'

For a second, Louise thought the voice belonged to her. She blinked open her eyes, her mind playing tricks with her, as if she were waking to the worst hangover of her life. Her head and back ached. She looked down to find she was lying on the wooden slats of her bed, ropes binding her in place. She cleared her mind, refusing to succumb to panic. She gave herself a few seconds before deciding what to do next. Her main priority was keeping her family safe. Two obvious options presented themselves to her: one, to keep her captor talking for as long as possible to give time for a rescue; two, to work on the binds so she could escape.

'I am going to take this off you now,' said the woman, reaching for the gag in Louise's mouth. 'If you scream, or call for help, this will not end well for you or your family. Do you understand?'

Louise fought the anger triggered by the mention of her family. She moved her head as much as she was able, her words muffled through the gag.

'Good,' said the woman, undoing the gag and propping Louise's head up behind a pillow with a surprising tenderness.

'How long have I been out, Francesca? It is Francesca, isn't it? Or Frankie?'

'You've got me. A few minutes. Apologies for the crudeness of my attack. I've checked the wound on your head. You're fine.'

'Thank you,' said Louise, trying to keep the woman on her side. A glance at her demonstrated how foolish first impressions could sometimes be. She was a petite woman, smaller in height than Louise remembered from the tattoo parlour. Thin arms poked out from a black T-shirt, and her skin was covered in tattoos, including the monster-like figure Louise now knew as the manitou. 'We've found Damon.'

'I know. I saw you. I left him for you.'

'What's this all about, Francesca? Why are you in my home?'

'Is this where I'm supposed to spill my guts? Tell you why I've done these horrible things?' said Francesca, pronouncing 'horrible' with a sarcastic flourish. 'No one wanted to listen to me before. When I was a girl.'

'I know some terrible things have happened to you, Francesca. I can help with that.'

Goosebumps rushed over Louise as Francesca lightly touched the skin of her forearm.

'You are helping, Louise,' said Francesca.

'Tell me what happened,' said Louise, not sure if she wanted to know what Francesca meant by her last comment. 'It was Laurence Dwyer, yes? He did something to you?'

Francesca's face changed at the mention of Dwyer. 'You know about him?' she said, through gritted teeth.

'He hurt you?'

Francesca took off her T-shirt and turned her back on Louise. Louise lifted her neck to look closer as Francesca sat on the bed next to her. The young woman's back was a canvas, a replica of the cycnus print inked on to her skin. Beneath the ink, her flesh was a mishmash of scar tissue, as if she'd undergone a number of random operations. 'My right shoulder,' she said, her voice a whisper.

Merged into the wings of the metamorphosing swan, Louise made out the branding, the *L* mark all but hidden by the skilled tattoo. Lower down her back, Louise caught sight of another set of branding marks arranged neatly to the right of the scar she'd displayed. Six mini swan symbols, three of which looked raw and fresh.

'He didn't just hurt me, he changed me. Do you understand that?'

'I do,' said Louise.

'You don't, but you will,' said Francesca, putting her T-shirt back on and placing the gag on Louise again with the same strange tenderness. 'I'll just be a minute.'

Louise struggled against the binds. Her arms were tied down with rope, with looser plastic binds securing her body. She was trying not to think about Francesca's purpose, but it was clear what she intended to do. Whether she would stop after she'd branded her was another question, and, with her family downstairs, it was what she would do next that most troubled Louise.

She screamed against the gag, writhing her body against the ropes, the binding against her wrist loosening slightly as Francesca returned carrying a blowtorch and a long, thick branding iron.

It was hard not to panic. Police training could only take you so far, and the immediacy of threat, the thought of the white-hot metal on her skin and the memory of seeing the bodies of both Andrew Thorpe and Damon Kessler was enough to provoke a visceral response. Louise found herself hyperventilating, the gag being sucked into her mouth with each desperate breath.

'Now, now,' said Francesca, removing the gag and rubbing Louise's brow like a nurse.

Louise closed her eyes and tried to control her breathing. She thought about Emily and her parents and concentrated on her breathing, sucking air in through her nose and out of her mouth.

'Better?' said Francesca, as if they were best friends.

'I've been hurt by men before,' said Louise, her breathing still strained but returning to normal.

'Haven't we all, honey?'

'You probably wouldn't believe this, but I was attacked at knife point tonight by a man I used to work with. I truly can help you. My colleagues are searching for Laurence Dwyer as we speak. We'll find him, and the others, and bring them to justice.'

Louise saw a flicker of compassion in Francesca's eyes, before her expression quickly changed. She smiled, and Louise didn't much care for the gesture. It transformed the woman, the hints of warmth and kindness vanishing, her eyes morphing into glassy voids. 'Their justice has already been served.'

'Then why are you doing this? What did the others do to deserve what you did? Why are you doing this to me?'

'You told me you didn't have any ink?' asked Francesca.

'No.'

'It can change people. Not always, probably not even very often, but it can change you. Inside and out, do you understand?'

'I can understand that. I imagine people get tattoos for numerous different reasons,' said Louise, wondering if she'd been missed by her colleagues yet. If Francesca had switched off Louise's police-issued phone, that would hopefully raise suspicions, if anyone had tried to phone her, that was. She needed to keep the woman talking. 'Why did you get your first tattoo?'

'That's a good question,' said Francesca, taking her hands off the large blowtorch. 'You see, I wanted to change. It sounds crass, but that's just the facts. I didn't like who I was at the time, and I thought a tattoo would change the way I viewed myself, and I was right.' She rolled up her black jeans and pulled down a colourful, striped sock to reveal a crude depiction of a star in blue-green ink. 'Did it myself, as you might have guessed.'

'Must have been painful.'

'I was lucky not to get an infection, but things changed after that. I did feel like a different person. I had this secret, you see?

This little part of me that had been transformed. And of course, I didn't want to stop there.'

'I'm sure it can become very addictive.'

Francesca shook her head. She looked disappointed and Louise feared she was going to reach for the blowtorch again. 'It's not an addiction. Yes, I added more ink, but it had nothing to do with addiction. I was doing it for me, you understand?'

'Of course,' said Louise. 'I wasn't trying to imply . . .'

'And that's why, when he did this to me,' said Francesca, pointing to her shoulder, 'it was the worst thing he could have done. *He* changed me, do you understand? He made me into something else, and I had no choice over the matter.'

'I can't begin to imagine what that must have been like. And you blamed them? Poppy, Andrew and the others?'

Francesca shook her head once more and reached for the blowtorch again. 'They watched while Dwyer and the others dragged me away. They didn't do anything to help. Poppy and Thorpe were pretending to be in love, and I knew David wanted to help but was too scared to speak up.'

'Why did you kill Andrew Thorpe?'

'Thorpe was like the ones who did this to me. He was a predator, a creep who deserved to die. Poppy was almost as much a victim as I was. Now we'll be forever connected.'

'Connected by the markings.'

'You're starting to get it, Louise.'

Louise shuddered. 'But why Sam Carrigan? He wasn't involved.' She was breathless and it was taking all her will to keep the woman talking.

'I knew he was with David. There was a certain symmetry to attacking his lover. But David will get what's coming to him.'

'And the others? Mr Maynard and Mr Oxford?'

'Don't you see, they're part of my family now? They all are. I'm helping them, transforming them.' The vacancy returned to her eyes as she turned the knob on the canister and lit the flame. 'And you're going to be part of my family now as well, Louise. As is that pretty little niece of yours,' she added, replacing the gag before Louise had time to scream her objection.

Chapter Sixty

Louise wasn't sure what was more terrifying – the heat of the flame or the thunderous sound of the gas fuelling it. She fought with all her might, her hands tearing at the ropes. She felt the wetness of her blood where the rope had burned through the skin, but she continued fighting, the binds cutting deeper into her flesh as Francesca Regan placed the flame to the branding iron.

'It will only make it worse if you fight,' said the woman, the manic emptiness in her eyes as terrifying as the white heat of the metal. With her spare hand, she pulled up the sleeve of Louise's shirt. 'Such pretty skin,' she said.

Louise continued to struggle, the heat from the iron prickling her skin, her body covered in sweat.

'It will look much better if you lie still,' said Francesca, as if that could ever truly be an option.

'You don't need to do this,' said Louise, her words muffled by the gag. She could face the pain, but she needed to stay conscious, had to do everything in her power to stop the woman going for Emily and her parents.

Louise's eyes watered as Francesca elbowed her in the face, the blow hitting her right eye. 'Stay still,' said the woman, as Louise tried to recover from the blow. 'That's better,' said Francesca, about to place the metal on to Louise's arm when there was a knock on the door.

'Louise, are you in there?'

It was her father. Louise was torn between the simple relief of hearing his voice and the fear of what Francesca would do. Her father was still strong and fit, but Francesca had both the element of surprise and the willingness to do anything to achieve her goals. When it came to contests of physical strength and strength of will, those with no compunction were more often than not the victors.

Francesca switched off the flame, the metal still glowing in her hand as she put her left index finger up to her mouth.

Louise screamed behind her gag, telling her father to go, to get Emily and her mother to safety, and Francesca elbowed her once again. The pain was stunning. It was as if time had stopped and she was stuck in her head. She wondered if she'd been knocked unconscious again, only for the sound of the door crashing in bringing her back to the present.

Among the screams and shouts, she heard Francesca whisper, 'I guess it will have to be now.'

Louise felt the heat hover over her flesh, her skin blistering. She screamed out in pain as she managed to free her hand, turning away from the branding iron a split second too late. The edge of it caught the flesh of her upper arm, as she managed to wriggle away before Francesca could apply any pressure.

Francesca stumbled back, the branding iron still in her hand. She lunged at Louise, the iron aimed at Louise's face. Louise watched the attack as if in slow motion and managed to grasp hold of Francesca's wrist, the branding iron – still glowing – inches from her face. 'It's over,' she said, sweat dripping from her face as she used every ounce of strength to keep Francesca at bay.

But Francesca wasn't finished. She pulled back, tearing her arm free of Louise at the same instant she was tackled by Thomas, who'd appeared through the broken door. Louise heard the scream and looked down from the bed to see that Francesca had managed to bring the branding iron back towards her own face, a large welt forming on her neck as Thomas secured the branding iron and, despite her protestations, cuffed Francesca's hands behind her back.

'Took your time,' said Louise, as Thomas helped loose her from the remaining ties.

'Are you OK?' said Thomas, who appeared more in shock than she felt at that moment.

'I'm fine, just a little nick,' said Louise, pointing to the raised inflamed skin that hurt so much she was close to passing out. 'Emily and my parents?' she said, with a desperation more painful than the small mark on her arm.

'They're fine,' said Thomas, as Louise's dad barged past the uniformed officer, a look of sheer panic on his face, and did the same to Thomas, before embracing her.

'I'm OK, Dad. Mum and Emily OK?'

'They're OK, both downstairs. I think Emily has slept through it all. We had no idea. I thought you had a guest over, then I heard the noise. I'm so sorry, Louise, we would never have . . .' he said, his words faltering as he began to cry.

Louise grabbed him. 'It's not you who needs to apologise,' she said, wondering if she would ever be able to forgive herself for bringing such danger into the house.

Epilogue

Louise gripped the steering wheel as she drove over what must have been a patch of black ice. Steadying the car, she glanced in the rear-view mirror at Francesca Regan, who caught her looking and smiled back. Francesca was cuffed and was sitting next to Tracey. Louise could see the scarring on the woman's neck from where she'd branded herself.

It had been three and a half months since Francesca Regan had tied Louise up and tried to brand her. At the memory, Louise felt the piece of damaged skin on her arm tingle. She would never give Francesca the satisfaction of rubbing the mark – which was barely bigger than a pin prick – but it was a constant reminder of that night and the atrocities Francesca had committed.

Since her arrest, Francesca had been more than happy to confess to all her actions, and that was why they were driving to Brent Knoll in the cold snap of December, the top of the knoll visible in the distance, topped with a smothering of snow.

Much of what Francesca had confessed to during interview had been a repeat of what she'd told Louise that night. After her trial, she'd been sent for psychiatric evaluation before sentencing for the attacks on Sam Carrigan, Poppy Westfield, Terrence Maynard and Raymond Oxford and the murders of Andrew Thorpe and Damon Kessler, as well as the attack on Louise. While under evaluation, she'd also confessed to the murders of three men – Laurence Dwyer, and the two men, Scott Turnbull and Kevin Westley – who'd taken her that day at the beach, when Poppy, Andrew and David had failed to intervene. And that was why Louise was returning to the farmland where Laurence Dwyer had once lived.

The ground was rock hard beneath their feet as they left the car, Louise's slipping on the icy covering. Three cars pulled up behind them with other members from Louise's team, including DCI Robertson and Thomas.

Francesca was led from the car. In the king-size coat she was wearing she looked like a child. Her face was childlike too, grinning as if the frosty outside was a new, exciting experience for her. She dispelled the notion by stumbling towards Louise, her hands cuffed behind her, and asking in a manic hush, 'Do you feel different?'

Tracey caught up with her and gave the woman a gentle shove. 'You're not wasting our time, Francesca, are you?' she said.

Francesca shrugged, the same manic smile on her face. 'Follow me,' she said, heading across the frozen farmland.

'They took you here?' asked Louise, who remained in step with the woman as the rest of the team followed behind.

'They raped me over there,' said Francesca, pointing to the shack Louise had visited before. 'Then they held me down, and Laurence gave me that lovely memento on my shoulder.'

'I'm sorry that happened to you, Francesca,' said Louise.

Francesca's smile faded. 'We thought it was fitting to bring them back here,' she said, leading Louise through to a woodland area, frozen leaves crunching beneath their feet.

'You and Damon?'

'I wouldn't have been able to do it without him.'

Louise already knew the story – at least, Francesca's version of it. In the interviews, she'd asked why she'd decided to kill Damon. Francesca had told her that Damon had made the mistake of hurting her, and for that he'd paid the ultimate price. 'He never really understood,' she'd said, with a chilling finality.

Neither Laurence Dwyer, Scott Turnbull nor Kevin Westley had ever been reported missing. No public records had been recovered for any of the men since that time, and Louise was convinced Francesca was telling the truth.

'I have a vague idea where we're going. It would be easier if you uncuffed me,' said Francesca.

'What are we looking for?' asked Louise, her fellow officers grouped up behind her, each apprehensive, as if waiting for the prisoner to make a run for it.

'We marked the spot, naturally,' said Francesca. 'We're looking for three oak trees with their own special mark.'

The SOCO, Janice Sutton, had accompanied them to the forest. As they all made their way through the dense, frozen undergrowth, Louise grew increasingly concerned that she was wasting everyone's time. She sensed the tension from the other officers, who, Thomas and Tracey included, all appeared on edge, ready to tackle Francesca, should she try anything.

Louise kept close to her. It was hard to believe that three months ago she'd been at the mercy of this woman. Francesca looked half elated, half bewildered, as she stumbled through the white-coated woodland, lost beneath the oversized coat they'd provided for her. When she began running moments later, it was like she was the leader of a pack of dogs. She'd only taken five or six steps before one of Louise's team had caught up with her.

'It's here,' said Francesca, leading them to a copse of three oak trees that leaned towards one another, as if in conversation. 'Look,' she said, pointing to the thick inscriptions on the first of the trees. The 2 symbol carved into the wood, still prominent high up the trunk. 'This is it. This is where we buried them,' she added, stomping her feet on the hard ground beneath them.

Louise arrived back at the site early the following afternoon. She'd spent the morning with members of the Ghost Squad and the CPS working on the case against Finch.

After Finch's arrest, he'd been denied bail, and was currently on remand in isolation at Ashfield Prison. The overwhelming evidence secured from his house and Louise's phone and the testimonies of the women who'd come forward after his arrest had proved enough for Finch to offer a confession. Not that it had been an act of altruism. Like all of Finch's actions, his admission was a means to help himself rather than his victims. With the confession and evidence, the prosecution had assured Louise that they would push for the longest sentence possible, but no doubt Finch's legal advisers would use the offered confession as a means of mitigation.

Finch's arrest had meant that her misconduct meeting had become a procession that was over within an hour, but others hadn't fared so well. Following the stresses of bringing Finch to justice, Amira had left the force, as had four other former colleagues of Finch who would be testifying at the trial. Louise considered herself fortunate that Finch's betrayals had led only to her moving to Weston. Yes, her career had been derailed, but it still existed and she would get to continue it in Finch's absence. The other victims, some of whom they would never know about, weren't so lucky. And despite the assurances she'd received to the contrary, Louise felt she was in part to blame. However much she told herself there was nothing she could have done, her conscience told her that she had failed those women by not putting a stop to Finch earlier.

The least she could do was make sure that he was brought to justice. A number of encrypted files had been discovered on Finch's computer, containing the anonymous messages that had been sent to Louise's phone. Her evidence would only provide support to the prosecution case. It had been concluded that nothing in the messages themselves was a criminal offence, despite the numerous hints of threat. Louise understood that taking the witness stand would mean her relationship with Finch would be revealed, but it wasn't a secret within the force.

Yes, she owed it to Amira and all the other women whose lives had been affected by Finch to testify against him. But more than that, she owed it to herself. It would have been so easy to have walked away following her effective demotion to Weston, but she'd stuck at it, and as a result had faced the constant strain of knowing Finch was there on the sidelines, scheming against her and waiting for her to fail. It had taken three years, but she'd been proven right. Whether or not she'd ever receive an apology from the police, and in particular ACC Morley, was another matter, but for now she would be satisfied with seeing Finch in the dock early next year, and hopefully being sentenced not much longer after.

She bought a takeaway sandwich and made her way over to Brent Knoll, where the digging process had begun.

Although still bitterly cold, the ground was softer than the day before as she crossed the field to the woodland, where Janice Sutton was coordinating with the special teams.

'How did it go?' asked Thomas, who, like everyone else in the area, looked as if the cold was getting to him, a hint of blue in his lips.

'All good. Everyone seems confident that he'll be going away for a long time. What about Madam here?'

'She's been playing silly buggers all morning,' said Thomas, pointing to the cuffed figure of Francesca Regan. 'Nothing yet, but it took us about two hours to decide the best place to start digging.'

'Go and get yourself something hot to drink. I can take over for now,' said Louise, smiling as Thomas jogged up and down on the spot.

'Life-saver,' he said, sprinting off towards his car.

Louise stepped under the cordon and walked over to Francesca. As she approached, she felt the scar on her arm begin to itch. 'You're not going to mess us about now,' she said, once again taken by how young the woman looked.

'They'll find them, don't you worry about that,' said Francesca, smiling as if they were searching for gifts under the trees.

Louise had been quizzed by a local reporter as to how three men could seemingly vanish without anyone noticing. She'd tried to explain as best she could without causing alarm that such things happened all the time. Not everyone had close friends and family who would miss them if they left an area. People were reported missing on a regular basis and were never found; and so many more went missing unreported. It was an unpalatable fact, and Louise noted that the journalist did not pursue it in her article.

Thomas returned later, carrying two coffees. It was already getting dark and, although portable generators were keeping lights on the area, the digging would have to stop soon. 'Thanks for that,' he said, handing her one of the cups.

Louise was about to reply when one of the investigating officers shouted for everyone to stop. Moving away from the hole where he'd been working, he looked around before speaking. 'I think I've found something,' he said.

Louise locked the door behind her, her family waiting outside as she ended her call. Molly bounded over, seemingly oblivious to the freezing temperature. Louise turned away from the dog as she tried to jump on her; she was wearing her best suit beneath her coat and didn't want to get dirt on it before her meeting that afternoon.

'Come on, Molly!' shouted Emily, who, like the rest of the family, was wrapped in layers of clothing.

Louise was thankful for the lack of breeze as they made their way to the beach, the cold air stinging her skin. Above her, seagulls floated in the air, as if controlled by the swirling currents.

'When do you need to go?' asked her dad, as they took the long way round to the beach.

'Thirty minutes or so,' said Louise.

'I'm sure there's nothing to be worried about.'

'I'm not worried. I just wish I could spend the day with you guys,' said Louise, grimacing as Molly galloped towards the glacial sea.

The day was supposed to be one of celebration. It was the station party that evening and, as a group, they had a lot to celebrate. Francesca Regan had been true to her word. The bodies of Laurence Dwyer, Scott Turnbull and Kevin Westley had eventually been discovered in the woodland near Brent Knoll, and Regan had subsequently been charged with three further counts of murder.

The discoveries of the bodies had finally drawn a line under the case. David Mountson and Sam Carrigan had been located trailing the Highlands of Scotland, and both Oxford and Maynard had recovered from their injuries and were receiving help getting their lives back on track. As was Poppy Westfield, who was back at work and trying to get on with her life.

A date had been set for Finch's trial in the new year. Although he'd offered a confession, he was pleading not guilty to the charge of attempted murder the CPS had put forward for his attack on Amira and Louise. A prison sentence was a formality, but Louise wouldn't truly rest until she knew for sure that he was out of her life for good.

As for Weston, an uneasiness remained about the future of the department. Finch's departure had brought further changes in the constabulary. His ally, ACC Morley, had surprised everyone by retiring early, though the feeling was it had been all but forced on him after Finch's prosecution. Today, Louise, along with DCI Robertson, was to meet his successor, Alan Brightman. Talk about restructuring had intensified in the department, and chances were high that Louise's situation would be different this time tomorrow.

For now, she was content to watch Emily run from the dog, whose lower half was now covered in wet mud. She couldn't remember when she'd last felt so contented, and when the time came for her to leave it was difficult to drag herself away.

'It's been five days now,' said her mother, taking her to the side. 'Five days of being sober. I know it's not much, but it's a start.'

'Mum, that's great,' said Louise, giving her mother a hug. Since the night Francesca had attacked her, Louise had eased back on complaining about her mother's drinking. She'd been carrying too much guilt from putting everyone in peril. In the end it had been her father who'd snapped, insisting that her mother resume her counselling.

'It won't be easy, but I want to do this. Not just for you and the family, though that is of course so important to me, but for me as well. I hate being like this, Louise. Hate it.'

'I know you do, Mum. You know I'll always be here for you. We all will. We'll get through this together, yes?'

They hugged again, both smiling as Molly caught up with Emily and dragged her down to the sand, Emily screaming in delight when Molly shook the water from her coat all over her.

◆ ◆ ◆

Weston-super-Mare was in full Christmas mode. As if delaying the inevitable, Louise drove into town along the seafront. The lights and decorations plastered the town, waiting for night to come to life. As was so often the case, she was reminded of her childhood and late-night visits to Weston to see the carnival and the thrill of walking down the high street with its bustling crowds and Christmas lights. She'd never imagined then, or any time since, that Weston would one day be where she lived, but she now felt more at home than anywhere she'd ever lived before.

◆ ◆ ◆

DCI Robertson had shaved for the occasion and was wearing a three-piece suit. 'And you are?' said Louise, entering his office.

'Hilarious,' said Robertson. 'You can shut the door before sitting down.'

Louise did as she was asked. 'I hope you intend buying me a Christmas drink tonight,' she said.

'You've just about earned it, I suppose. Listen, I wanted to speak to you before Brightman arrives.'

'Sounds ominous.'

Robertson was always impossible to read, and now was no exception. He drummed his fingers on his desk, holding her eye contact. 'I've been offered a new job.'

Louise nodded. She wasn't sure what she'd expected to hear, but it hadn't occurred to her that Robertson would be on the move. To her, he was an immovable part of the station. She wasn't sure if she would have survived the first few months in Weston without him, let alone the last three years. 'Back to Glasgow?'

'Christ, no. They wouldn't have me back. MIT in Portishead.'

Louise let out a breath. 'I hear your predecessor was a bit of a wanker,' she said.

Robertson cracked a smile. 'That he was. Anyway, I wanted to let you know.'

'I appreciate it, Iain. And congratulations.'

'Don't congratulate me,' said Robertson, standing as the new ACC arrived in the office. 'You're coming too.'

◆ ◆ ◆

By late afternoon, a melancholy had swept over the department. During her meeting with Robertson and ACC Brightman, Louise had been offered the role of lead detective in what was to be the newly formed Major Crimes division. Weston CID would be amalgamating with the existing MIT department, with Robertson leading the group. Everyone in Weston CID had been offered a new position. The ACC had told her that she should see it as a positive thing, a reward for the successes the small station had achieved since her move.

In many ways, nothing much would change. Louise's section would still be in control of Weston and the surrounding areas. Headquarters was only twenty miles away, and much of the work could still be carried out in the area. The location of the main office didn't really bother her, and Louise accepted the positives. She'd achieved what she'd set out to do. Finch was behind bars and she would soon be back where she belonged. She could choose to dwell on the injustice of being sent to Weston in the first place, but for the first time since the Walton farm incident she was positive about her future, and that of the department. Change was change, and the uncertainty would affect everyone in different ways, but in six months' time the transition would be forgotten and Major Crimes in Portishead would be the new normal.

At six, Robertson cracked open a bottle of champagne and toasted the team and the new move. It was the night of the Christmas party. The members of MIT who'd helped during the branding case had arrived, and soon the melancholy atmosphere dispersed as taxis were arranged to take them to the dinner in Weston.

Louise decided to drive, wanting a way to escape the party if necessary. She took Tracey with her, the combination of perfume and hairspray filling the car by the time she'd parked up on a side street near the seafront.

'It will be good to have you back,' said Tracey, as they walked headlong into the fresh, biting wind on the promenade. The sea was at high tide and bristled against the sea wall as the Christmas lights made reflective patterns along the water. Tracey had been offered a permanent role in Serious Crimes and would work alongside her at headquarters. 'Dream team back together,' said Louise.

'I'll toast to that,' said Tracey.

The night went much as Louise had expected. Now that she rarely drank alcohol, she found it difficult to enjoy such occasions as she once had. In part, she struggled to relax, but, being sober, she could fully appreciate the effect alcohol had on everyone else. And now that her mother was trying to give up, the least she could do was abstain for the time being.

'Not drinking?' asked Thomas, joining her at the bar.

'Driving. Got to be up in the morning,' said Louise. 'Christmas shopping with Emily.'

'I estimate we're about thirty minutes from anarchy,' said Thomas, both of them laughing at the increasingly elaborate dance moves of some of their colleagues.

'I can always give you a lift home. If you're ready to leave?'

'Definitely. There's only so much Christmas music I can take.'

Louise sensed the awkwardness as she drove Thomas home along the all but deserted Locking Road. He was much more sober than the last time they'd been alone in a car together like this. She felt as if he wanted to say something, and her pulse quickened at the thought. 'So how do you feel about the move?' she asked, the silence growing uncomfortable.

'I think it's great. You must be very pleased.'

'How do you feel, Thomas?'

Thomas sighed. 'I was going to wait to tell you, but I've been offered a role elsewhere.'

'Elsewhere?'

'A firm in Bristol is looking for a head of security.'

'I see. Elsewhere-elsewhere, you mean?'

'Yes.'

Louise pulled up outside his house. She was a bit surprised by her visceral reaction to the surprising news. 'Are you going to accept it?'

'I've been thinking about it for some time. It's much better money. Good hours. I need to think about Noah, and the future, you know?'

'Of course,' said Louise. 'It's a bit of a surprise. We'll really miss you.'

'We'll miss you?' said Thomas, with a grin.

Louise matched the grin. 'OK, I suppose I'll miss you a bit too.'

The grin on Thomas's face faded, and Louise felt as if she could hear his heart hammering against his ribcage. 'Maybe you don't have to,' he said.

The silence seemed to last an age. The last time they'd been in this situation, she'd turned her cheek to him and, even now, she didn't know how she would respond if he tried to kiss her. 'I thought maybe, now that we won't be working together . . .' he said, his eyes wide and vulnerable.

'You thought what?' said Louise, softly.

Thomas moved towards her, and this time she didn't turn away.

ACKNOWLEDGMENTS

Huge thanks to my editor Hannah Bond and all the team at Amazon Publishing for giving Louise Blackwell the perfect home and for continually ensuring the books reach as wide an audience as possible; Joanna Swainson and all the team at Hardman & Swainson for their continued support; my development editor, Russel McLean, who always helps me take the story to the next level; and my wonderful and supportive family for giving me a reason to write.

And, as always, many thanks to the lovely people of Weston-super-Mare for putting up with me writing scary stories about their beautiful town.